THE MUSE

LAUREN BLAKELY

LITTLE DOG PRESS

ALSO BY LAUREN BLAKELY

Big Rock Series

Big Rock

Mister O

Well Hung

Full Package

Joy Ride

Hard Wood

The Guys Who Got Away Series

Dear Sexy Ex-Boyfriend

The What If Guy

Thanks for Last Night

The Gift Series

The Engagement Gift

The Virgin Gift

The Decadent Gift

The Extravagant Duet

One Night Only

One Exquisite Touch

MM Standalone Novels

A Guy Walks Into My Bar

ABOUT

The first time a woman stepped out of a painting, I thought I was seeing things.

The second time, I thought I was going mad.

The night *she* emerged from a Renoir, I felt something else entirely — a deep stirring of desire, and the wish to get to know the brilliant beauty who's been trapped inside a painted garden for years.

She can only come out at night in the Musée d'Orsay, where I work. There, after hours, we wander through galleries and step inside the Van Goghs, the Monets, the Toulouse Lautrecs, visiting the Moulin Rouge, kissing under a starry painted sky, and tangling up together on the bridge across the waterlilies.

She opens her heart to me, and I learn her story.

But she keeps secrets too, ones I hope to unravel. Why she was trapped. Why Renoir is hunting her. And why artwork in famous museums across the world is starting to disintegrate.

Why I too seem to be the only person who can repair the masterpieces.

As I fall deeper for the woman who's trapped between two worlds, I'm caught up in another side of Paris after dark, one inhabited by forgers, ghosts of famous artists and, impossibly, by Muses.

But someone is after the woman I'm falling in love with, and it's up to me to save her...even if it means losing everything I've found with her.

THE MUSE

By Lauren Blakely

Want to be the first to learn of sales, new releases, preorders and special freebies? Sign up for my VIP mailing list here!

PROLOGUE

One month ago . . .

Some ex-girlfriends are like too-dark pencil lines on a sketch. Erasing them is impossible—they leave smudges or impressions on the paper that will show through anything you try to put over it. There's nothing for it but to rip out the page and start a fresh one.

It's time to tear out Jenny.

That's the plan as Simon and I head out from my flat on a Friday night in June to catch the Metro to Oberkampf. Rip out the Jenny page and see what, if anything, takes shape on the next.

Maybe that's melodramatic, but this is Paris after all. The French half of me overrules the stiff upper lip issued with my British passport. I grew up with Mum in London but spent summers in France with my dad. Now I'm experiencing everything Paris has to offer—

the food, the dance clubs, the galleries, and the joy of being dumped for Christophe the sculptor.

Would I be nearly so upset if she hadn't left to be with another artist? Simon and I slide onto the semi-crowded train, which feels like a bit of a party already, and I decide introspection can wait.

"All right, Julien," Simon says. "On with part two of the purge of Jenny from Pittsburgh."

"Jenny who?" I feign bewilderment. "Where is Pittsburgh? Is that near Leeds?"

He laughs and punches my shoulder. "That's what I'm talking about." More subtly, he lowers his voice and tips his head to indicate a pair of pretty women sitting not far from us. They're dressed for a night out, with low-cut shirts and lots of leg showing. "We should invite them to come along," he says.

"It's as if you can read my mind."

"Or I just know what's good for you."

"Convenient that it coincides with what you want to do."

"The universe is telling us something, mate. And it sounds like 'Forget what's-her-face and do some high-quality socialization.'"

He offers a hand and we knock fists then head over to chat up the blonde and the brunette. When we find out they're headed to the same stop as we are, Simon flashes a big smile. "What are the chances?"

That's my cue. "We're meeting up with friends at this club. You should come along." I'm getting back out there.

We exchange names as the train rattles into the next

stop, and when the doors open, the four of us walk down the cobbled street in search of a neon-lit door leading to an underground club. Inside, the music is so loud that I can't hear anyone—not the women we just met, not my friends from university, not any of the people that Simon corrals into the dimly lit corner. The dancing and the music drown me in a riot of sound and motion that leaves no room for what's-her-name from Pittsburgh.

Which is all I'm looking for from the evening. I'm not looking to hook up or get wasted or high, and I dance late into the night, surrounded by friends and strangers.

I leave by myself, well after the trains have stopped running, but I'm not ready to go home to my flat. Without really planning it, I find myself at the service entrance of the Musée d'Orsay, where I'm an intern.

I use my key card to get in and greet the security guard. "*Bonsoir*, Charles."

"Working late again?" he asks, looking up from his desk.

"It's the only time it's quiet enough to focus," I tell him, heading for the public galleries.

He shakes his head and shrugs as if baffled by my hours, the faculty's demands, and why I'd put up with it.

Two reasons: my sister is the head of the museum—she didn't help me get the internship, but she definitely makes sure I earn it—and I'm not actually here to work tonight. Tonight and a lot of nights.

Charles lays down the magazine he's reading. "Does

it ever spook you, walking through the galleries at night?"

I pause and glance back, curious what he means. "No. Why would it?"

He gives the kind of "Who can say?" shrug I've never seen anyone give as well as the French. "The lights are low, the portraits watch you go by . . . Some people find it eerie."

"Maybe I just know it too well," I tell him with a grin. He returns it as I get on my way.

I make for the stairs to visit my favorite Van Gogh. But I don't even reach the second floor, because I catch a swish of pale fabric as someone in a skirt rushes into a nearby gallery.

What the . . .?

The skirt rules out another guard patrolling through the galleries. I debate with myself for only a moment—the chances of another nighttime rambler versus the power of suggestion—then I quicken my steps toward the doorway where that bit of floaty material disappeared.

When I turn at the junction between galleries, I have to catch myself against the doorframe so I don't fall over in shock. My heart skids into my ribs with a hard *thump*. It's thunderous to me, but it doesn't interrupt the scene playing out in the ornate room.

If I were going to imagine something, why would it be a young girl in a tulle skirt pirouetting from one soft pool of light to another across the shiny parquet floor in a flurry of white?

I cast a look around for the patrolling night guard, but there's no one aside from me and the dancer.

How much did I drink at the club? One cocktail and then water? If I were seeing pink elephants, or genies riding on magic carpets while huffing on hookahs, or something *truly* outlandish—those would be easy to identify as fantasy. But the ballerina is both real and realistic, from the tips of her dancing shoes to the wisps of hair that have slipped from her bun to frame her delicate face.

My senses ignite, my brain buzzing. I'm too alert to be drunk. It feels more like dreaming while wide awake, because I recognize this girl. I've seen her before, but not like this.

This ballerina has danced her way right out of a Degas painting and into this museum.

1

July—Present Day

A peach falls out of a Cézanne.

I grab the fruit before it rolls down the steps and out to the lion sculptures, near where the security guards make their nightly patrols. This peach looks tasty, rosy, and ripe, begging to be eaten, and I imagine the way it would drip juice down my chin, leaving my face and hands sticky but worth it. When I run my thumb over it, the skin is fuzzy and tender. It feels the same against my lips when I bring it close enough to bite.

But I don't. The peach is a puzzle I view from all angles. One part of me says go ahead and bite. See what happens. At least I will know whether it's real or a figment of my imagination. The rest of me doesn't want to chuck out my understanding of reality after twenty-one years.

Instead, I do what Cézanne did—capture its likeness.

I set the peach down and rustle in my messenger bag for my notebook and pencils. Taking a knee, I balance my sketchbook on the other and sketch quickly. When I'm done, I hold up the drawing so I can compare it to the subject, and I see . . . an accurate rendering of a peach.

That's all. It's a how-to-draw-a-peach tutorial, not something delicious you want to wrap your lips around. Not the kind of peach that evokes a summer day and a sweet, sultry smell that makes you feel something about fruit and the nature of the universe.

This sketch is not something you can have feelings about.

With a bone-deep sigh, I stuff my sketchbook into my bag.

I stand and carry the peach back to its home on the wall and tuck it into its frame. The canvas stretches itself around the piece of fruit with a slurping sound, then goes quiet. The peach is two-dimensional again. It still feels odd, no matter how many times I do it.

Something rubs against my ankles, and I look down to see a black cat winding around my boots.

"Meow," she murmurs. I hadn't noticed her approach. But then I wouldn't—dark cat, shadowed gallery, pussyfooting from where she belongs to swish back and forth against my jeans.

Her chest rumbles against my calf as she purrs, alluring and enticing. No wonder this cat keeps company with Manet's *Olympia*—she's the feline version of the naked woman. Curiosity—at least, that's a safe bet—makes the cat seek me out, but sometimes I think Olympia watches me too. I swear I have seen her eyes following me as I walk from one end of the gallery to the other. She always stays put though, stretched out seductively on the white silken sheets of her painted bed.

"Now, how did you make it all the way over here?" I scoop up the cat and return her to her home. With the fifth floor closed for a summer-long renovation, nearly all of the museum's pieces are here on the main level. "They say black cats are trouble," I tell her, stroking her silky, luxurious fur as I bring her to the edge of her canvas. "Is that true?" She meows one more time—maybe an answer, maybe not—but the sound is cut in half when she folds herself back into her regular pose—arched back, fierce yellow eyes, completely still.

Almost as if she'd never leaped out of the frame.

This is how my nights go now.

It's not why I started coming to the Musée d'Orsay after hours, but it's why I can't stay away.

I hear soft footfalls from another gallery, and I smile. If I was a little surly before—all right, I was definitely surly—my mood lifts at the delicate sound of toes tucked into slippers twirling on the hardwood floor. I head across the hallway, not wanting to miss the dancers. They're beautiful, graceful, and watching them is both breathtaking and relaxing at the same time.

When I turn into the gallery, two dancers in white dresses, including the girl from that first night, have jetéd out of a Degas to spin in dizzying circles. They make regular nighttime appearances now, but not in any set routine. Last week, all of Degas's dancers here in the Musée d'Orsay, plus a few musicians from an orchestra scene too, peeled away from their paint to stage an impromptu midnight performance of *Swan Lake* in the main gallery. What will tonight's show be?

The dark-haired one from the first night dances past me on the way back to her frame but stops before she goes, turns back to grin at me wildly, then launches into a set of pirouettes. She spins en pointe, around and around, a bravura encore to tonight's performance.

She's stunning, and as she whips through the turns, she takes my breath away.

Not from desire though. From appreciation for the way she moves.

Then, at the last moment, she wobbles, and just like a top, she goes over, crashing to the floor.

My heart spikes in alarm, and I rush over to her, kneeling beside her, tense with worry. "Are you okay?"

She nods bravely as she cradles her foot.

"Let me help you," I say gently. She seems too delicate for full volume.

She nods and leans against me, small and lithe. I loop my arm underneath her, and through my concern, I'm curious how she'll feel. I've never touched one of the dancers. I've never touched any of the painted people.

She feels real. Warm skin, beating heart. Like me. Like life. Why that should surprise me, considering I'm surrounded by paintings that leave their frames to traipse through the gallery, nice as you please, I don't know.

I support her as she rises and gets her feet under her. She's a bit unsteady at first, then sturdy again.

A loose tendril of her hair brushes my arm. It's the

unexpected evidence that shakes me, knocks home the realization of how lifelike she is.

Beautiful, talented, and fully alive.

But only at night.

The dancer tucks the stray hair into its proper place and murmurs, "Merci." Then, I help her into her frame, the canvas wrapping gently around her as if being careful of her injury.

The museum is still again.

I'm amazed I don't have more doubts than I do. After all, the dancers don't twirl for the visitors during the day or for my sister when she works well into the evening. And once the dancers take their figurative bow, the galleries will stay quiet for the rest of the night. That's just how it goes.

Whatever the reason, my life has become a Dalí landscape. This has become my version of normal.

On my way out, I stop at the spot where we will hang a new painting soon. *Woman Wandering in the Irises.* I concentrate for a moment, picturing it there, knowing how stunning it will look. The coveted Renoir would look magnificent anywhere.

Displaying *Woman Wandering in the Irises* is a major achievement, and it would be even if it was hideous— which it definitely is not. Lost for more than one hundred years, it's the stuff that art collectors and historians around the world dream about. Now and then, people would claim to have seen it—spotted it in an antique shop, glimpsed it at a flea market. Finally, just weeks ago, the piece was found and authenticated. Now, *Woman Wandering in the Irises* is coming here.

When I give my tours, it'll be one of the final paintings I show. The best for last.

There.

Right there.

That's where it'll be.

My blood rushes faster when I imagine that beauty on the walls.

All the times I've gazed at a copy of that beautiful woman in the irises, and now to think of her here, becoming flesh at night . . .

I can only imagine what that would be like.

How much *more* I might feel.

How much more intense it would be than the moments with the dancers.

I catch myself getting uncomfortably lost in my imagination, and I grimace and give myself a good, hard mental slap.

Pull yourself together, Julien.

I'm a guy with a crush on a painting.

There it is, in all its embarrassing honesty.

I shake it off, laughing a little at myself. I've just built a little bit of a fantasy to fill the gap left by the breakup with Jenny. Transference or something. It's not vastly different than an image of a model or movie star.

Except . . . it's a painting.

And I have to face facts—it's not the strangest thing these days. Or nights, rather.

I head out, saying goodbye to the security guards. Charles isn't at the desk tonight. The gray-haired one, Gustave, is there and gives me a curt nod. He's fiddling with a piece of copper wire and teardrop crystals that he bends and twists into a miniature sculpture. He's an artist too.

Aspiring, I should say. Just like me.

"That piece is coming together," I say, giving him a smile.

"Thanks."

"See you tomorrow, Gustave."

As the door closes behind me, I bring my palm to my nose. My hand smells like a peach. I'm sure of it.

I'm not sure, though, if it means I've gone mad, or the world has.

2

After an evening lecture the next day, I walk home along the inky quiet of the Seine, earbuds in, streaming pop music on Spotify. It works to disrupt the loop of my thoughts about girls and paintings, but in its place is an obnoxiously catchy refrain about infatuation and longing. I'm searching for something to replace that as I turn away from the water and wind through the streets back to my neighborhood.

Running feet pound the uneven pavement behind me.

"Julien! Wait up, mate!"

I pull out one earbud and whirl around. Simon slows to a jog, coming closer. Smart man, because when he gets close enough, I can tell he's had a few drinks. Simon came to Paris four years ago for university and he's stuck to a rigorous training regimen of living life to the fullest all four years.

"Congratulate me, my friend, because I return triumphant from the battlefield of love—also known as the bar around the corner—with the spoils of war." He claps a hand on my shoulder and grins maniacally. I raise a doubtful eyebrow, and my Scottish friend admits, "Okay, right. I have to ask a favor." Then, with a frown, he adds, "And also, it's not the spoils of war. Spoils of the bar? That sounds naff."

I manage to get two things out of that ramble—it must be a big favor, and there is likely a female involved. "I'm going to take a wild guess and say your amorous efforts were well rewarded."

"Reward. Yes, that's good." He waggles his phone at me, grinning again. "Nothing less than the digits of one long-haired, long-legged beauty who may have been custom-made for me."

"Do tell."

"Her name is Lucy, and she is tall, hot, and totally witty. She's from London. She was there with a friend, who's French. Her friend I'll save for you."

"Don't let anyone tell you you're not generous," I say dryly. The nationalities have little to do with his choices – both Simon and I speak English, of course, and French.

Simon waves his hand as if to erase any negative impression. "No, no. The other one, Emilie, she's just kind of shy. But she's a dancer. Very limber, you know. So if you're not game, I'm sure I can manage them both," he says with an exaggerated leer.

"Have fun with that," I tell him, taking it as seriously as he meant it, which is not at all. "I'm headed home. I have catching up to do on this term's independent study."

"Wait," Simon says, and I stop because he looks a bit green with . . . are those nerves? "I have a date with her Thursday night. With Lucy. I need something interesting to do. Not the same old thing."

I keep a stern face. "What am I? Your social director? Date planner?"

"It's because you're the creative one, idiot," Simon says.

"That's no way to talk to someone you want to plan your date," I say, drawing out the torture. "I could give you a list of lame ideas to choose from, but with your taste, how would you know which were good?"

"Come on, Julien," he wheedles. "Be a pal. We can make it a foursome. I'll see if her friend can come along. The dancer, remember?"

"I remember." But the only dancers I'm interested in roam the halls of a museum at night.

God, what am I thinking? I can't be honestly comparing some kind of hallucination with reality.

And yet . . .

"Please?" Simon asks, and I don't want to let my friend down. Not when he's done so much for me.

Besides, maybe this is a stroke of serendipity. His friend is a dancer. The first painting that shimmied out of its frame was Degas's dark-haired dancer. And last night, we talked. Or at least, I imagined we talked. Maybe it's best I zero in on reality. "I think I can suffer through a date with two attractive people plus you."

"And you'll come up with a plan? A fun plan?" He sounds excited but like he's trying not to show it. He must really like this Lucy.

"I will."

"You're a champ." He moves as if he aims to give my shoulder an oafish punch then pulls it back at the last moment, laughing. We part ways with plans to make plans—Simon off to catch the Metro and me headed down the quiet, lamplit street leading to my flat.

The one I share with my sister. She has a doctorate in art history, and at age thirty-five, she's young to run someplace like the Musée d'Orsay, but she's built a reputation as a curator working in New York and London. I'm proud of her, and lucky too. Intern or not, I wouldn't have as much free run of the museum as I do if I wasn't Adaline's brother.

"Julien!"

That's her voice. When I turn, she's seated at a café, enjoying the evening with a glass of red wine and reading an article on her tablet.

"We need to stop meeting like this, sis," I say as I park myself at her table, pulling my messenger bag over my head and setting it down. "First, you follow me to Paris . . ."

She rolls her eyes. "Right, of course. That's why I invited you to share a flat in one of the nicest areas of the city. Because it takes so much work out of stalking you."

The flat belongs to the family, and it's a nicer place in a better neighborhood than I could ever afford on my own. But there's also the fact that I like my sister. Convenient.

"Anything interesting?" I ask, nodding to the article

from *The Guardian* on her tablet, pretending I don't see the words "art forger" in headline-size type.

"Oh, it's just background on that father and daughter with the fake Gauguin last year. Kind of a 'Where Are They Now' piece."

"So . . . where *are* they now?"

She grins. "Still under the radar. Maybe coming so close to being convicted made them rethink their life choices."

I snort. "Maybe they made enough money to buy a small island."

"Somewhere without an extradition arrangement with the UK."

The waiter swings by and asks if I want a glass of wine too.

"Just coffee," I say, and when he leaves, my sister grins at me like she's got a big secret. It's not that different than Simon's grin, actually.

She closes her tablet and sets her laced hands on top of it, eyes dancing. "Do you want to know why I was so excited to see you?"

"Because I'm an utter delight?"

She rolls her eyes, waves a hand dismissively. "Yes, yes, and because we have a meeting." She leans in and lowers her voice to a hushed whisper. "It's about the Renoir."

I go absolutely still, afraid some motion, some expression will give away how much those words thrill me.

She looks vibrant, almost aglow. Art has never been simply her field of study. She lives and breathes it. It's her passion. I recognize it because I feel the same way. "Do you want to see *Woman Wandering in the Irises*? Like, say, tomorrow?"

I'm wary this is too good to be true, that she's putting me on. "I thought it wasn't coming to the museum for a few weeks."

"It won't move yet," Adaline answers. "But I need to meet with the owners to review some final documents, and I thought you might like to come. I want to be able to talk about it with you." She places her palm against her chest, as if the memory of the painting is too much. "It's the most beautiful Renoir I've ever seen. You will be in love. I know you. You're just like me. You fall hard."

Her choice of words is a coincidence, but I can't stop a grimace. Fortunately, she's rooting around in her purse and misses it. But it's not a bad way to describe how it feels to be smitten with a piece of art.

Adaline finds what she's looking for and pulls it out. "This is for you. I almost forgot." She slides a small white ceramic creature with brown spots across the table. It's a calf, but it has an extra leg growing from its back. Renoir once said the idea of women painters was as ridiculous as five-legged calves. I sort of wish I didn't know that about him. Such an amazing artist but not, apparently, what you'd call an equal opportunist. "From the couple who are giving us the painting. It's a gift for you."

I frown at the calf in confusion as I pick it up from the table. "For me? Why? Do they know me from somewhere?"

My sister shrugs as she takes out her wallet. "No

clue. But when I asked them if I could bring you to see the painting, they agreed and asked me to give this to you first. But I need to get to bed. It's nearly ten, and my first meeting is painfully early. The restoration people are coming to look at that sun-damaged portrait. I need to get it fixed before it goes to the joint exhibit at the Louvre," she says.

That painting is another Renoir, a picture of two young girls playing a piano. It had started to fade a few weeks ago, and I'd alerted her when I noticed the damage, and catching the damage before it spread went a long way toward proving I was at the museum on my own merit and not because of my sister.

Adaline pays for her wine and my coffee. "I'll see you tomorrow—I'll probably have turned in when you get home."

I say good night and thank her for the coffee, enjoying a leisurely sip as I examine the calf curiously. The fifth leg—a shrunken baby leg hanging from its back—has a small cap for a hoof. When I take the cap off, a bit of silvery powder with the consistency of confectionary sugar sprinkles loose.

Huh. I shake the calf more, but it's empty now.

Strange. As far as I know, I've never met these people. Why would they want me to have a ceramic five-legged calf? It would be more logical to give it to Adaline, as she's the curator of the museum, as well as the one working on the transfer.

I replace the cap and tuck the calf into my bag, nestled in the sweater I've been carrying around since yesterday. Then I take out my notebook, laying it on the table.

As I finish my coffee, I flick through my sketches, stopping at the one of *Olympia*'s cat from a few nights ago. I'd hoped my drawing of the peach was an anomaly, but seeing the cat, I know it's not. My sketch is technical and precise, like an illustration for a guidebook. Veterinarians might appreciate its lifelike contours and shapes. But it still leaves me feeling . . . flat.

I study it to see if I could maybe have drawn it a different way, a subtler way, to make the cat seem more . . . I don't know . . . enchanting. I run my index finger across the cat's head, but no ideas come to me.

With a sigh, I close the notebook, slide it into my messenger bag, and head to the flat.

But as I unlock the door, strands of black hair shine on my hand, and I raise it to the light filtering in from the street. Sleek hair from a sleek cat.

3

There's a distinct aroma at the top of the stairs. I look around for the source, and my best guess begs the question: "Is there a petting zoo on that balcony?"

Adaline shushes me, then whispers, "Yes, there is. Well, a sheep."

"Who keeps a sheep on their balcony?"

"Some people are eccentric," she says as we arrive at the door of the couple who is donating the Renoir to the museum. They live on the curving corner of a twisting, hilly street in Montmartre. Many artists have walked the cobblestone streets of this neighborhood over the last hundred or more years. Notre Dame might be point zero in Paris, but Montmartre is the epicenter for painters.

"They sent me a five-legged cow," I say under my breath. "Their eccentricity is not in question."

My sister chuckles. "Touché."

As she smooths her hands over her suit, I realize she's . . . not nervous exactly. More like she's feeling the weight of this career-making achievement. I know she's pinned so many hopes on the deal going smoothly. Art may be her personal passion, but she still has to prove the museum made the right decision in trusting her with its greatest pieces.

She presses the buzzer.

"I truly appreciate this, Adaline. The timing is perfect," I say. "Did I tell you that my professor approved my proposal to do my independent study on this painting?"

I get a sharp sisterly elbow in the side. "You did not tell me that. But I can't imagine he would disapprove, considering the piece has such a history, plus there's your personal connection to it."

The words startle me. Have my thoughts become audible? Or am I just that transparent? Hoping she doesn't notice my flush, I ask casually, "What do you mean?"

Adaline gives me a curious glance. "You work for the museum that's going to display it. What did you think I meant?"

I tell an almost truth, shrugging with my hands in my pockets. "Oh, you know. I've gotten really interested in the story behind it."

She glances at the door and smooths her suit jacket again. "Don't bring up the painting's background unless they do, all right?"

I nod. I've pored over every fact and rumor I could find about *Woman Wandering in the Irises*. The garden in question was Monet's—Renoir had painted the portrait during a visit—and the work was exhibited only once, at a gallery show in 1885, then it went missing. The subject of the painting was and is a complete mystery. The rest is hearsay—that there was a whiff of scandal about the woman and the two married artists, and after the single showing, her family hid the painting away to protect her reputation.

"The current owners . . ." I nod to the door. "Are they related to the woman in the painting?"

Adaline shakes her head.

I lower my voice in case the door opens suddenly. "Do you think it's true that both artists were in love with her?"

She shakes her head again. "That story arose well after the portrait disappeared. No contemporary sources mention it at all, let alone confirm it. And the newspapers of the day would have been all over a scandalous love triangle."

I don't consider it a scandal. That's just life and passion, the things that make art. Whether it's this story or something else entirely, I know the woman in the painted garden has one, and I've found myself wondering about it ever since the portrait came to light. Who was she? Did she live in Montmartre? Was the portrait a commission, or did she model for other artists?

"Hello." The voice comes through the buzzer. "Come in, come in."

I push open the heavy green gate etched with curling ironwork panels and hold it for Adaline, then let the door fall behind us. A stone path funnels us into a courtyard ringed with yellow tulips. A young man comes from the other direction to meet us. He looks to be between Adaline and me in years—that's a big spread, but if I had to guess, I'd say late twenties. His hair is super short, and his wardrobe is straight out of *GQ*—tailored trousers that I bet cost a month's tuition, and a crisp maroon shirt that looks like it belongs on a runway.

"Remy Bonheur," he says, and holds out his hand to shake.

"Such a pleasure to see you again," Adaline says. "This is my brother, Julien."

I shake Remy's offered hand. "Good to meet you."

He grins. "*Enchanté.*" He has a firm grip, and he doesn't let go right away. Still smiling, he looks me over, as if comparing me to his expectations. "I've heard so much about you."

I'm not sure what my sister would have said. But this doesn't seem the time to push.

"Thanks for the calf." My gratitude is genuine, despite the strangeness of the gift. "I'll definitely be the only person I know who has one."

I say it with straight-faced earnestness, and Remy laughs. "That is undoubtedly true. But do come inside." We enter by an orange door at the end of the courtyard. The home is massive by Montmartre standards, and except for an elaborate security control screen on the wall in the foyer, the interior is like a trip back in time. Framed posters from the Moulin Rouge and a kaleido-scope of popular stage shows from the last century fill the walls. Old-fashioned carnival music plays on a phonograph in the living room, and in one corner is a two-animal vintage carousel with a tiger and a zebra to ride.

It's an astounding mélange of bohemian and beaux arts, and when Adaline catches my wide-eyed look, she grins at my reaction and mouths, *Eccentric. See?*

Another male voice calls from the kitchen. "Ms. Garnier, I've just finished up the most divine clafoutis to share with you."

"Thank you, Monsieur Clemenceau. And please, I hope you'll call me Adaline."

"In that case, you can hardly call me Monsieur Clemenceau." The owner of the voice pops in from around the door, smiling in a playful way. "Won't you join me in the kitchen?"

"I would be delighted, but first, let me introduce Julien," she says.

"Raphael sometimes forgets there is a world beyond the kitchen," says Remy, then gestures from me to his partner and vice versa. "Julien, my more domestic half. Rafe, Julien Garnier."

His partner grins. "Yes, Remy and Rafe. Nauseatingly precious, isn't it?" He rolls his eyes. "So matchy-matchy, I can hardly stand us sometimes."

I look again from one to the other, at the way they don't touch, aren't even on the same side of the room, but are tangibly connected on some level. "I don't know," I venture. "The names fit together, but I think maybe you both do too."

Remy gives a sharp burst of laughter, and Rafe and Adaline follow, though mostly Rafe. "I like this one." To Adaline, he says, "Your brother has permanent entrée into Chez Clemenceau-Bonheur whenever he wishes to visit."

The tips of my ears burn with embarrassment, and I worry I've been too personal. I don't look at Adaline but try to mitigate any damage I might have done. "That wasn't meant to flatter you. I spoke without thinking."

"I know," Remy says, still grinning widely. "That's why I like you—both honest and extremely insightful." Humor glints in his eyes at that last bit, and I exhale my tension.

Adaline goes with Rafe into the kitchen, and as I look around again—the place is too big and amazing to take it all in at once—I notice a large oak table that's home to dozens of miniature ceramic calves. Moving closer, I see that, like the one Remy gave me, each of these calves has a fifth leg. A brown calf has a meaty extra back leg jutting out of its shoulder. On a black-and-white calf, a skinny front leg hangs from its rear haunches. A trio of black calves have fifth legs that descend from their bellies. "You work in ceramics?"

"I do." Remy gives a "What can I say?" shrug. "I've never been terribly good with a paintbrush, but I do what I can."

"Don't sell yourself short. I like them." I don't touch without invitation, but bend for a closer look. "I dig the irony."

"How else would one make a five-legged calf but with irony?" Remy says, and I chuckle.

"Good point."

He reaches across the table for a black calf with pink polka dots and a fifth leg where its tail should be. "This is my prize calf." He glances toward the kitchen and lowers his voice to confide, "I'm giving it away at my surprise birthday party Thursday night."

I raise a brow. "How is it a surprise if you know about it?"

"Because I'm throwing it." He shushes me when I laugh, then explains, "I hate surprises. I'm that person who reads the last page of a book first. I want to know the movie spoilers, and I've never made it to Christmas morning with unopened gifts. Especially ones I order for myself," he adds with a grin. "So, Rafe and I are throwing an un-surprise party for my twenty-ninth birthday. We all have to act surprised by anything anyone says, and whoever has the best look of shock or awe gets the prize calf."

"That does sound like fun." It's certainly more clever than the usual party games.

Remy sets down the ceramic calf. "You should come. Bring friends if you want. The only requirement is to act surprised."

I gasp in melodramatic astonishment.

"Brilliant." He nods his approval. "A convincing look of surprise will serve you well in life."

"I can see where it would."

"So you'll be here?"

Before I can commit, Rafe and Adaline emerge from the kitchen with dessert and coffee, and we take seats around the table with the calves to enjoy them while talking shop.

"I have the final paperwork," Rafe says, opening a folder of paper documents.

Remy gestures affectionately to his partner. "I've never enjoyed paperwork. Rafe is so much better at the details. *Merci, mon chou!*" he calls out.

Rafe winks. "Someone must manage the humdrum things in life, like dinner and priceless pieces of art."

"And someone must be entertaining."

Rafe laughs. "And indeed you are."

Remy blows a kiss, and Rafe and Adaline begin to go over Remy's family's ownership of the Renoir through the years, the certification by independent authenticators, and reports on the tests of the canvas and pigment and all the other details that prove the painting is not fake.

It would be much more interesting if I were involved instead of watching the tops of their heads as they skim the documents. After a bit, I ask the way to the restroom, and Remy directs me down the hallway to the second door on the left.

"Be sure to have a look around at the art," he says in his cheerfully hospitable way. "We have a Jasper Johns, a Monet, and a Valadon you might like to see."

"Will do," I say as I slip out into the hallway.

Since the trip to the loo is chiefly an excuse to get away from the table, I linger on the paintings Remy mentioned. I particularly admire the way Monet captured the cobalt-blue morning light on the pond near his home, his Japanese bridge arching over the dreamscape of water beneath it. What must it be like to craft such beauty with your own hands? To evoke so much wonder with a brush and pigment? I'm best at technical drawings—accurate, but nothing awe-inspiring. Want a map drawn? I'm your guy. But something this beautiful, this transcendent . . .? I wouldn't know where to start.

I wander a bit, looking for the Valadon Remy mentioned, but I don't see one, so I finally make my way to the second door in the hallway. I open it, and then blink in surprise—genuine, not at all fake bewilderment —because it's not the bathroom. It almost doesn't look like it belongs in the same house at all.

The room is uncluttered, with bright-white walls, a long black leather couch, and a plasma TV screen hanging on the opposite wall. Nothing strange there, other than the jarring modernity and perhaps the latched door in the middle of the floor.

A trapdoor to a basement, maybe? But how can there be a cellar or basement when they live on a steep hill?

But the part that rates a second look is the chalk drawing that covers half the door.

Only half.

I glance furtively over my shoulder, feeling as if I'm snooping but unable to resist. Going in, I circle the door to view the design right side up.

A woman in a pale-pink dress, pale as the inside of a seashell, dances with a partner, her face turned away from him. I know the original of this—Renoir's *Dance at Bougival*—but here, the man hasn't been included in this chalk rendering.

Will someone add him later? It seems like such a deliberate exclusion, as if the woman is what matters. Since I've been studying up on Renoir for my independent study project, I know that the woman in the painting is Suzanne Valadon, an artist herself—the first woman, in fact, to be admitted into art school in France. When Remy suggested I would want to see the Valadon, I'd assumed he'd meant something she'd painted, not a drawing *of* her.

This is just weird.

The voices in the living room are still droning on about the detailed provenance of the painting. Adaline is good at this. History and authenticity—those are her bailiwicks.

My strength is curiosity. I have a passion for exploring, for uncovering answers.

And damn, if it isn't going into overdrive.

I crouch beside the door and unhook the latch, then I pull it open, expecting a creak or a moan of hinges.

I obviously watch too many horror movies.

The door opens without a sound. Below, a circular staircase winds down into darkness. Could it be a cellar far below, deep inside the hill the house sits atop? I imagine Rafe's relatives hiding their art there to keep it safe during the Nazi occupation of Paris. Many families did the same.

No chance to confirm it now, so I close the door and shut the latch, curiosity unsatisfied. Something is going on beneath the surface here, and I don't just mean in the cellar.

A chair scratches across the floor, likely coming from the table in the living room. Time to get out of here.

I close the door behind me as I leave, then I take a

wild guess and open the second door on the right to find, sure enough, it's the bathroom. I duck in, do my business, then leave and close the door again just as Remy comes down the hall.

"Did you lose your way?" he asks, teasing.

I hook my thumb toward Monet's painting of the Japanese bridge in his garden. "You said to take a look at the art."

He smiles with something like approval. "Good, good. And did you get a chance to look at all of it?"

All of it? Including the chalk drawing?

He wanted me to see the trapdoor. I'm certain of it. Was I supposed to find the stairs beneath it too? And why the hell not just say, "*Mon ami*, you should see the stairs in the media room. I promise they don't lead to a dungeon or anything."

I suspect Remy would love a dungeon simply for the irony of there being one in bohemian Montmartre.

The moment passes as Remy tilts his head toward the living room and rolls his eyes. "They're still talking pigment and chemistry and blah, blah, blah. So I figured I'd leave them to it and just show you the painting."

Yes, the painting.

I forget everything else. Adaline and basements and trapdoors and mysteries. All I can think is, *Show me.*

Show me now.

Nerves thrumming with anticipation, I follow Remy to the white door at the end of the hall. He removes a key from his pocket, unlocks the door, turns the brass handle, and it all takes forever. At last, he pushes open the door, and once inside, he gestures to the painting hanging behind an imposing oak desk.

Time stops.

The house goes silent.

Forget trapdoors and five-legged calves. Forget black cats and painted peaches.

Nothing in the world moves outside of my tingling skin, while inside I'm a riot of thoughts and feelings. It's Christmas morning presents and a winning bet at Monte Carlo and free run of the Louvre and love at first sight all rolled into one.

I'm all goosebumps and hammering pulse. Photo reproductions are to this painting what a music box is to a symphony.

The woman stands in the garden.

Her back is mostly to the painter, but she's twisting around, looking over her shoulder with a fierce stare, sharp longing in her eyes. Her gaze is defiant, and her eyes are etched in pools of radiant blue. Long brown hair cascades down her back, and one hand is raised as if she's reaching for something or someone. And all around her, there are flowers hemming her in—irises in shades of violet, royal purple, and a plum so dark it's nearly the color of chocolate.

A chocolate-plum iris.

And the woman. She is the most beautiful woman I have ever seen.

"Shall we return to the others?" Remy asks, jerking me out of the moment.

Maybe I need to be yanked away. I'm not sure I'd leave this room otherwise.

Because I'm enrapt. More than I expected.

"Yes, of course," I say, catching another glimpse of her as I go.

I can't wait a few weeks to see her again at the Musée d'Orsay.

But, I don't have to wait that long.

Without planning it at all, I turn to Remy. "About that invitation. I'll definitely be at your party."

4

Simon and I have zero classes together, as studies in history and studies in art history share only a word and not a department. But my last lecture on Thursday afternoon coincides with his in the same building, so it's our routine to grab a coffee after.

Coffee will be the perfect time to tell him my plan. My mind is still fixated on the painting, but also the staircase, the sounds that came from below. Which means the party is a perfect solution for everyone. As I emerge into the sunshine, he's waiting on the front steps, scrolling through his phone. He looks up at my "Hey," and pockets his cell.

"Hey. My lecture was a snoozefest. I think I'm going to ask for my espresso intravenously."

"That's one way to do it."

The café is hardly a walk at all, and we order our usual and luck into a table.

"So, you asked for my most excellent date planning services for tonight," I remark.

He sits up straighter. "I did indeed. Lay it on me. Lucy's bringing Emilie along, so the answer to this question may determine the future of our friendship."

"As it happens, I'm invited to a party tonight, but I can bring friends. Which I suppose you are. *Technically.*" I tell Simon about Remy's un-surprise party and his house full of oddities, and he rubs his head thoughtfully, leaving his hair sticking up in all directions.

"Well," he says, "Lucy is kind of arty, and it's something no one else could take her to."

I shrug, casually. "You wanted something unique, didn't you?"

That's why he asked me—he didn't need my help to plan a date to a café and a movie. And he really seems to like this woman.

Plus, I quite like the idea of the party. The idea of being in Remy's home again.

For two very powerful reasons.

"All right, I'm in," he says, taking out his phone. "Since *technically* I suppose you're a mate."

I roll my eyes. "Thanks."

He laughs deeply. "I'll text Lucy to meet us in Montmartre."

And I count down the hours.

* * *

Lucy is indeed arty, with enough personality to hold her own with Simon. Her friend Emilie is unmistakably a dancer, from her posture to the way she walks with her toes pointed out. She's also sweet and sort of shy.

We sit outside a crowded café near Remy's home, a place with sleek metal tables and creaky wooden chairs, the perfect mix of old Paris and new Paris. Nearby in the square, an a cappella group performs, upbeat tunes directed by a pristinely put-together older woman, as passersby drop coins into a hat. Lucy and Simon are down the street, checking out Lucy's favorite American retro shop.

"Do you ever go to the ballet?" Emilie asks me, leaning closer as Lucy and Simon laugh loudly at a mime artist performing nearby.

"Sometimes," I say. "My parents were total fanatics— still are. Season tickets, the whole works."

"That's marvelous," she says. "What was the last ballet you saw?"

I answer without thinking. "*Swan Lake*, just the other night."

She tilts her head, her frown puzzled. "Here in Paris? I didn't know it was being staged anywhere nearby."

Of course she doesn't, because I'm an idiot. The impromptu *Swan Lake* hadn't been staged anywhere but at the museum for an audience of one.

"It was just a little indie company," I improvise.

"Oh, how fantastic." She sounds genuinely interested. "What was it like? Good production?"

This time, I consider before I speak, and when I do, I smile at a joke as private as the performance had been. "It looked just like a Degas painting."

She nods pseudo-seriously. "You can never go

wrong with a Degas vibe." Then she breaks into a grin that suddenly makes it easy to picture her onstage.

We talk more about dance, then segue to music, downloading each other's recommendations, and after that, she feels less like a stranger and more like a friend.

The reverse must be true too, because she leans closer and whispers, "Can you keep a secret?"

"Of course."

"I'm auditioning for the ballet next week." Emilie pushes a hand through her black hair, which is straight as a blade.

"The Paris Opera Ballet?"

"The one and only."

I am beyond impressed. "Emilie, that's amazing! Why are you keeping that a secret?"

"Because there's no way I'm getting in." She waves a hand, dismissing the very idea. "Which is fine, but I don't want anyone feeling sorry for me."

I catch a strain of music—not the techno-pop we exchanged earlier, and not the a cappella group. It's familiar and orchestral.

Funny, because it sounds like a ballet I've seen, and here we are talking about ballet.

"I seriously doubt the Paris Opera Ballet gives auditions to dancers who are anything less than outstanding," I tell her.

"I know! I'm sure it was totally a mistake." Her laugh is self-deprecating, and the music crescendos, and I finally recognize it as the ballet *Giselle*. "Hopefully I'll have an early slot, before they realize I'm not supposed to be there."

The notes swirl around Emilie, wrapping her in a cocoon of sweet sound. I don't let it distract me, since it doesn't seem to distract her.

"I'm pretty sure the Paris Opera Ballet double-checks stuff like that. I'm also pretty sure that means you're fantastic." She has to be. I'm surprised at how certain I am.

The violins from *Giselle* keep playing, and I have to ask, "Is your phone still streaming?"

She frowns and shows me her screen. "See? Off. Why?"

Terrific. Now I'm hearing things.

Art comes alive, music plays of its own accord – welcome to your new reality, Julien Garnier.

"I hear music," I say. After all, I might not be imagining it entirely. "Funny thing is, it's ballet music. *Giselle*."

Her eyes widen. "You heard *Giselle*?"

I nod, unsure how to interpret her reaction. It seems less about how I'm hearing music and more about what I'm hearing.

She blinks up at me with those wide eyes and whispers, "That's my audition piece."

As she says that, I picture Emilie on the stage of the Palais Garnier in front of thousands of people in their red upholstered chairs underneath the six-ton candelabra. The rising sounds of the ballet build toward a gorgeous finale as Emilie pirouettes, her head tipped back, giving in to the dance, giving in with abandon.

"You're going to blow them away." I feel compelled

to tell her. "I have no doubt you will be the newest member of the Paris Opera Ballet next week."

Emilie beams, the warmest smile I've ever seen.

And the music stops.

So . . .

What the hell just happened?

Simon and Lucy join us, and she models a skirt with cheeseburger drawings on it.

"Just bought it. Isn't this the best?" Lucy gives a flamboyant twirl, then settles into a chair. Funny that the nondancer is the one bold enough to execute a 360 in a public square. Lucy seems to possess a natural showmanship, from the twirl to the skirt to the emerald streaks in her long brown hair.

"I think I should get a shirt with French fries to go with it," Simon says as the waiter brings our espressos.

"So, what's with the cheeseburgers, Lucy?" I ask.

"I lived in Chicago for a year and decided to make it my mission to try one in every diner in the city."

"Did you complete your mission?"

"No, but it only whetted my appetite for the United States."

"And where else would you want to go in the U.S?" Simon asks.

The conversation turns to which American cities we most want to visit, from New York to Miami to Seattle to Austin, and while we finish our drinks, I notice Emilie watching the singing group in the square. Her foot taps in time to the music, and her eyes are keen and intense, her shoulders tight, as if she's ready to leap after something she's spotted.

Leaning over to her, I say with a smile, "You're thinking about how much you want to be dancing right now."

She smiles ruefully, speaks quietly. "Is it that obvious? I just feel like I should be better prepared for next week."

"So go dance," I tell her, keeping my voice down too.

"Really?" The suggestion surprises her, but her shoulders relax. "I could still squeeze in a class tonight. Practice some more."

"Do it," I urge. I don't want to be rid of her, but she should go where her heart is, and that's not here. I think we'll be friends, but I can tell she's already in love. She's in love with dancing.

"I need to go," Emilie says to the table. "Sorry, Lucy. But I want to take a class."

"Emilie," Lucy says. "C'mon. You're always taking ballet classes. Let's go to a party."

"Sometimes inspiration strikes. And I'm inspired to go dance." Before she leaves, she kisses me on the cheek and whispers in my ear, "Thank you."

Before I can ask what for, she's walking away.

And I'm one step closer to the party. To the painting, and to the staircase and wherever it leads.

5

A sheep grazes above on Remy's spacious balcony, nibbling on a patch of grass.

The sheep keeps company with a goat. The sheep baas and the goat bleats and Simon gleefully rubs his hands together. "A party with farm animals. This is exactly what I needed for my Thursday night."

We ring the buzzer on the green door with the iron gate. Remy opens it and ushers us in grandly. He wears a plain black polo shirt and jeans. A contrast for the fashionable man.

"What a surprising outfit," I remark, and Remy grins in delight that I remembered the theme of his party. *Surprise*. "I'm shocked how much you look like...*not you*."

"Sometimes I feel like...*not me*," he says with a grin.

There's a girl with him, and her perky brown pony-tail swishes as she eyes the three of us with interest. She looks like the underclassmen at university—no, that's not right. She looks like an underclassman at an American school, because I'm not sure a French girl would wear jeans and a faded orange T-shirt with a unicorn leaping over a rainbow.

"This is my little sister, Sophie," Remy says. "She's supposed to be upstairs working on a term paper."

Sophie doesn't look bothered by the comment. "My surprise was escaping the campus to come to his birthday party."

"I'm pretending to be surprised she would flee the dormitory on the least excuse," he says.

"Nice to meet you, Sophie," I tell her. She shares her brother's insouciance, the kind that makes her likable straight away.

"Happy birthday," Lucy says to Remy after I make the introductions, and then to Sophie, "I'm loving the shirt."

"*Merci.*" They exchange grins. "Your skirt is magnificent."

Remy guides us through the courtyard, and Simon comes right out and asks, "What's the story with the goat and sheep?"

"They ward away bad spirits," Remy answers, entirely serious.

Lucy asks with an intrigued hum, "What sort of bad spirits?"

Remy throws open the door from the courtyard to the house, and I'm glad to be heading closer to my goals for the party. "Anything that threatens to ruin a good party," he says.

Sophie slips inside first, walking backward toward the stairs leading to the balcony. "In fact, it's my job to tend to the flock," she says as she excuses herself. "But I wanted to meet you first. I didn't believe Remy when he said there would be guests younger than middle-aged."

He moves like he was going to poke her in the ribs if she didn't dodge. "I will make you eat those words when you turn twenty-nine."

She dances away with a laugh. "I'm not worried. You'll be nearly forty then and too old and decrepit to catch me."

Remy shakes his head as she disappears. "I don't know where she gets such cheek."

I turn a laugh into a cough.

He grins then waves the whole matter away as he closes the door. "Enough of that. Come and enjoy the party."

He escorts us farther in, and Simon and Lucy marvel at the decor. I find my gaze drawn to the end of the hallway and force my focus onto the living room, a vivid swirl of party guests honoring Remy's dress code of bright colors, save himself. His friends are decked out in swirling pinks and deep scarlets and swaths of blues and greens that mirror the sea. There's no phonograph playing carnival music tonight; instead, a high-tech sound system plays upbeat songs from pop superstars in America and England.

As Simon goes to grab drinks for us, Lucy takes the chance to pull me aside and ask, "What happened with Emilie? Did you not like her?"

Talk about straightforward. My eyebrows climb. For as long as I've lived in Paris, I'm still rather English sometimes. "She's lovely. I liked her just fine."

Lucy narrows her eyes, obviously unsatisfied with my answer. "From Simon's description of you, I thought you and she would be perfect for each other. You're very cultured, he said. You know—ballet, art, and such."

"Right." I draw out the word as I imagine how Simon might have said that.

"So maybe we can all go out again?"

"Of course. But you know, Emilie's pretty focused on that whole ballet thing." I'd like to go out again as a group—a friend group—but I don't want to lead anyone on. I lighten it up with a teasing. "In case you hadn't noticed."

Lucy rolls her eyes, but with affection. "That's where you come in. I want her to have a life too. Get out of the studio sometimes. Have fun!"

"Sure. But maybe dancing *is* her life." Immediately, I want to take that back or amend it to something less cliched and . . . cheesy. But it's the truth—and I can understand it. Art requires sacrifice, whether it's comfort or riches or a social life.

Simon rejoins us at the same time as a woman in dark eyeliner and slinky jeans brings around a tray of what look like pillowy pastel shish kebabs. I look from the candy to the woman and raise a brow. "Rafe has been busy in the kitchen, I take it?"

"Who else would he allow in there?" she asks with a smile.

I take a soft raspberry-colored cube and pop it into my mouth, and as it melts, each individual sugar crystal seems to sparkle on my tongue.

Rafe appears from the kitchen and greets me

warmly, as he and Remy make the rounds, pointing out the spread of confections laid out on the table. I spot Sophie by the beverages, making sure everyone has a drink. The hosts are busy, the party is getting lively, and I may not get a better chance to satisfy my twin curiosities.

I tug Simon and Lucy around the corner into the hallway. "I need your help," I whisper as I make my way to the room with the painting, but as I suspected the door doesn't budge when I turn the handle.

"Breaking and entering? You are an excellent social coordinator," Simon says approvingly.

"Indeed. And now can you two coordinate lookout for me?"

Lucy's smile takes on epic proportions. "Yes. What do you need?"

Quietly I pad back to the door to the media room. I turn that handle, and breathe a sigh of relief when it gives.

"I have some recon to do. Keep watch, OK?"

Simon shrugs a yes. "Should we have a secret knock in case someone comes this way?"

"If they do, they're probably looking for the loo." I point across the hall. "Just send them that way."

Lucy tries to get a glimpse into the room as I open the door the rest of the way. "What is it you'll be doing in there? Can't you tell us?"

"Research. *Art* research," I say, quietly closing the door. "Tell Simon about your favorite cheeseburgers."

She laughs, pointing at me. "I like him."

Through the door, I hear Simon say, "Me too. Which is why I put up with his crazy."

I don't waste the window of opportunity, and take a quick look around the room. Nothing has changed since the day I was here, including the drawing on the trapdoor. I slide back the latch and pull it open as soundlessly as before. Below, the stairs corkscrew down into the bedrock of the hill where the house perches. In the dark, there's no telling how far down they go.

I take out my phone and use the flashlight as I descend the spiraling steps. After six or seven rounds, the air feels mustier, heavier. Even with the light, I can only see one stair below, and I seem to circle forever.

I'm dizzy by the time I finally reach the bottom. I step away from the security of the stairs, and my footfalls on the stone echo back to me, giving me a sense of the enclosed space. I point the light on the floor until I reach a wall, then sweep it up over the featureless stone. The other walls are bare too.

Cellars are always a bit creepy somehow, but the emptiness of this one, added to the long trek down and the mystery of its existence, makes it almost unnerving. "Cellar" might not even be the right word, since the space doesn't seem to have any purpose that I can see. It's impractical for storing anything, except perhaps a vampire or maybe the man in the iron mask.

I regret the thought immediately, but it's too late. Now I'm remembering that the door latches from the outside and that all this stone makes the place utterly soundproof. Even with the trapdoor open, I can hear nothing from the world upstairs.

At least, I don't think I do.

I stand still and listen again.

There it is—the faint sound of voices. The quality is too soft and the cadence too melodic to be noise from the party. And it's not coming from above.

The sound rises from below.

From where there's nothing but stone and earth and bedrock.

It's illogical, and I feel ridiculous even as I do it, but still I kneel and press my ear to the floor. Impossible, irrational, whatever you want to call it—I definitely make out women's voices.

Their words are indistinct, but there's a lilt to them, like poetry, like someone's speaking in sonnets. Or maybe it's that the sound makes me feel the way a sonnet does. I want to lie on the floor, one ear pressed against the cold stone, and listen all night to this siren song.

I want that with a yearning that makes little sense. A nostalgia for something I've never experienced before.

This is impossible. Even if the sounds could travel through stone, the way the house is built on the hill, there can be nothing under this floor but dirt and bedrock. I cannot be hearing people speaking below.

And yet there they are—soft, gliding words. It's the sound of snowflakes drifting from a gaslit sky. Then comes laughter, like a bell, pure and bright.

I jump up, rejecting the madness. I pace as far as I can until the wall stops me, and then I turn and stare searchingly into the empty space.

Am I going mad? From the cat stepping out from its

painting, to ballerinas turned loose in the Musée d'Or-say, to orchestra music playing in the square . . . and now these impossible voices. It doesn't seem possible that hallucinations could feel so real.

I catch my runaway thoughts and surprise myself with a laugh. Too real to be all in my mind—that's just what a madman would say, isn't it?

All right. I'm here and the voices aren't going away, so it seems like a chance to find a possible explanation. Maybe I've misjudged the house's position on the hill. Maybe there's a crack in the stone, or some trick of acoustics.

I'm staring at the floor from an angle, which is how I see it—a rectangular outline in some kind of silver dust. I've seen something like it recently. Then I remember— it was in the calf Remy gave me.

Crouching for a closer look, I see the dust fills a crevice, and I blow on it, trying to clear a space and see if there's a slot of some kind. A latch, maybe, or a keyhole?

All I manage to do, though, is blow the outline out of existence and fill the beam from the flashlight on my phone with a dancing cloud of sparkles—pretty, but useless for my mission.

It seems like a sign that I've done all I can, and a glance at my phone's screen says I've been here longer than I intended. I drag myself from the mystery and the voices, and sprint up the stairs two at a time, like if I don't go fast, I won't be able to pull myself away at all.

It seems to take less time to go up the spiral than down. The trapdoor above is a square of light and reality, and I climb out into the TV room, safe and undiscovered.

The hallway door is still closed, and I yank it open. Simon and Lucy topple into the room, a tangle of limbs and lips.

Simon catches himself and Lucy both before they hit the floor. She giggles as he grabs her waist and sets her upright.

"Whoa! PDA much?"

"Nothing to see here," Simon says casually. "Just blocking the doorway. Make it too awkward for anyone to ask to get by."

"That's very ingenious of you," I say dryly.

"It was a chore," he says with a grave face, "but sometimes you have to suffer to help out a mate."

I look solemnly at Lucy. "Thank you for your sacrifice."

She points at me and wiggles her finger. "You owe me now. Don't think I'll forget."

"I wouldn't expect you to," I say, enjoying how quickly Lucy gets on with anyone. She's perfect for Simon.

We step into the hall, and as I close the door behind me, Remy rounds the corner.

"Are you having the time of your life?" he asks sunnily.

Lucy takes a loud breath like a sob and declares, "I'm having the *worst* time. The absolute worst, most awful time of my life."

Covering her face, she breaks into tears. The genuine shock and dismay on Remy's face is classic. He only manages a distraught stammer before Lucy takes pity on him.

"Gotcha!" She flashes him a grin.

Remy wags a finger at Simon's new girl. "You are trouble, I can tell. But well done, well done." He steps to the side and gestures toward the festivities. "Your reward should be some hot chocolate in the kitchen. It's Rafe's own recipe, spiked with cayenne. Sweet with a kick—perfect for lovebirds."

Simon glances at me, brows raised to ask if I'm good with that, and I tell him, "Have fun, Romeo."

Remy watches with an indulgent smile as the pair goes by, then he turns back to me, head cocked, eyes smiling like we share a secret. "The voices are lovely, aren't they?"

I blank my expression the best I can, trying to look unsurprised. He must mean something up here, something I should know about. He can't mean the cellar voices.

"Like a poem," he adds.

I'm still not sure how I should react. If he's heard them too, does that mean I'm not hearing things, or are we suffering from the same delusion?

But I have to know, and denial won't help. "What are they?"

The question pleases him, judging by his grin, like I've passed a test. "They're Muses."

"Muses?" I echo. I don't know what I expected, but not that.

Remy nods, enjoying my reaction. "Inspiration personified."

I know what the Muses are—they appear in Classical art from Greek statues to the Romantic period, where they're more allegorical. But he isn't exactly reassuring me on the non-delusional front. "There are Muses in your cellar?"

"Of course," he says. His casual certainty catches me off guard. Somehow makes things seem more plausible.

"How did you come to have mythic creatures in your basement?" Not "if" but "how." That's how far gone I am.

"Julien," Remy chides, "they aren't mythic. They're real. And they've always been there. Though, technically, we have a door to the Muses. They don't *live* down there."

"Right. Because that would be ridiculous."

"It would," he agrees, then continues. "I don't know which came first—the Bonheur patronage of the arts or our connection to the Muses. Family lore says the connection goes back at least to the Middle Ages."

"You don't mean Muses metaphorically?"

"I am not given to metaphor at the moment. Not as it relates to the Muses."

I'm not sure how long this candid Remy will stick around before charming, quirky, and unhelpfully enigmatic Remy returns. So I don't waste time.

"Here's where I admit I wasn't paying attention when Rafe and Adaline talked about provenance of *Woman Wandering in the Irises* the other day. How did the portrait come to be in your family?"

His eyes flick toward the media room door then

back to me. "You seemed familiar with the artist Suzanne Valadon?"

"First woman admitted to art school in Paris? Contemporary of Renoir, Monet, and other Impressionists during their heyday?" I give him an "I see what you did there" stare, picturing the drawing on the trapdoor. "Model for some of Renoir's paintings, like *Dance at Bougival*?"

Remy grins. "She's the one. She's my great-times-whatever grandmother. She and Renoir were collegial at one point, but they fell out over ideology, hers being an artistically egalitarian one and his being an elitist exclusionary one."

"Right. Like the five-legged cow thing."

"But she loved *Woman Wandering in the Irises*. It has been passed down through the family, along with the duty of keeping it safe."

I realize I'm staring at the white door at the end of the hall. Remy follows my gaze and smiles slyly. "Would you like to see it again?"

Good sense says I shouldn't. This goes over the line from eccentric to delusional. I know that the deeper I go, the stranger my life is going to get. The most rational part of me says get out while I can.

But something else whispers, *Stay*.

It's the same thing that drew me to follow the sound of dancers on the parquet floor in the museum to see what was there. To find out how much reality there was in my imaginings.

"What do you mean 'keeping it safe'?" I ask.

"It's not like other paintings, Julien. It's quite special,

and it needs protection from harm. So we are charged with its care."

Protective outrage pushes aside confusion. "Why? Who would want to hurt that painting?"

Remy shrugs in that "it just is" way of his. "Why does anyone want to ruin beautiful things?"

I consider the stories that Adaline dismissed. Two artists in love with the subject of the portrait. Maybe her family wanted to hide or destroy the portrait to protect her reputation. Maybe there is some other shadowy reason I can't speculate.

Who is she, this woman who inspired love, aroused jealousy, and needed protection?

"Then why let it go now?" I ask Remy.

"It's time. And I think *you'll* keep it safe at the museum."

"Of course." It's a vow, even though I'm only an intern. Even though I don't know where my career will take me.

We've been moving toward the room as we've talked, and Remy unlocks the door and guides me inside without following.

"Sit. Take your time." He might be grinning, but I only have eyes for the painting. "I'll leave you two alone."

The door clicks shut, and I walk over, hypnotized, to *Woman Wandering in the Irises.*

Warmth seems to radiate from the canvas, reaching across the short distance between us as if the sun that lights the garden doesn't stop at the frame. As if the woman has body heat, a heart pumping blood through her skin. As I study her, she looks back, her lips parted ever so slightly, looking impossibly kissable.

I want to trace a finger across those red lips. What was she saying to the artist? What was she thinking? Was she raising a hand to greet a lover?

She stays still and silent, but the room feels expectant, like the hushed anticipation between the dimming of theater lights and the rising of the curtain. I watch for something, roaming my eyes over her, and when I do, I see the faintest of outlines.

A shimmer of silver.

The canvas buckles near her hand. I hold my breath, afraid to hope for more but pleading for it at the same time. This has to be real. Please let this be more than an illusion. There's a rustling sound, and then one slender feminine finger pokes out. My heart stops then restarts; I have to breathe, but I don't want to risk breaking a moment that feels as fragile as a cobweb.

I lick my lips and wait, not sure what I'll do if enough of her hand appears that I can grasp it and pull her free.

"Come out," I whisper. "Come out."

I move closer, inches away now, so close that my words would stir the wisps of her hair. That sunny warmth spreads over my chest, as if I could wrap my arms around her and hold her against me.

I stare, full of anticipation. "Who are you?"

There's the gentlest swish of a skirt from behind the frame.

"What is your name?"

Then a distant sound, like a far-off bell.

"What are your favorite things?"

There's the sound of merriment, but it's not coming from the party. It's as if the canvas is echoing a sweet, inviting laugh.

I put my hands on the frame. This is as close as I have come to touching her. "What are you like, woman behind the paint?" I ask, and for a moment, I can hear soft breath and the beating of a heart, and I'm sure neither one is coming from me.

The canvas is quiet the rest of the night, and the woman doesn't emerge from the painting any farther. I stay until the party noise dies down, and I'm one of the last to leave. I say goodbye to Rafe, injecting gratitude even though I feel disconnected, as if I'm waking from a too-long nap.

Remy walks me to the courtyard door, where he presses the pink polka-dotted calf into my hands and tells me I earned it.

"I want to see her again," I tell him. "Before she comes to the museum."

He gives me an arch "I thought so" look. It's the look of a successful matchmaker, and I don't care. He asks for my phone and programs his number into it. "I will be your go-between. Like the priest in *Romeo and Juliet*."

He might be joking, but I'm too distracted to interpret sarcasm. "Things didn't end well for that pair. Maybe you could just be my friend."

As serious as I've yet seen him, he nods decisively. "That I will do for you. And for her."

We're no longer calling it *Woman Wandering in the Irises*. It's a she. She's a woman. I want her to step from her painting so I can learn the texture of her dress and the smell of her hair.

So I can look into her eyes. Talk to her. Learn all about her.

Perhaps this is madness, but I'm terribly certain she doesn't exist only in my mind.

6

The following week I have a video conference with my academic advisor for my individual studies class, where he goes over the proposal for my term project, stroking his beard and nodding and muttering as I talk in my living room. Since the proposal is on his screen just below his camera, it gives the impression he's staring right into my psyche.

Finally, he nods. "You seem to have a feel for the subject. *Woman Wandering in the Irises*, with its storied history, is bound to be intellectually engaging, but you bring a personal insight to the topic."

"Thank you, Professor."

"It should make for a compelling read."

"I hope so. I really want to bring the subject to life." *If he only knew.*

"Hmm," says my advisor, stroking his beard again. "It almost seems as though you've seen the painting in person. I didn't think it arrives at the Musée d'Orsay for another month."

"It's not on public display until then, no, sir."

"Ah. You *have* seen it, then? Through your internship?"

There is nothing odd about his interest—art is meant to be seen in person, and the lost Renoir is a sensation. But my previews have been a secret, and I want to keep it that way, like a clandestine affair.

I say truthfully, "No one is allowed to see the painting until the debut. But I do have access to reproductions that you can hardly tell apart from the real thing."

"That should suffice for this stage of your project. We'll meet again next week to talk about your research."

We wrap up our call, and as soon as I disconnect, I grab my bag, making sure I have everything I need for my afternoon at the museum. Adaline is long gone already—our schedules, between work and school, mean that we run into each other more often at the Musée than at the flat.

I'm almost at the Metro when my phone rings—there are only a few people who would call rather than text, and my sister is one of them, especially for anything to do with work, so I never let it go to voicemail during opening hours.

"Oh, excellent," she says when I answer. "I caught you. You haven't left for work yet, have you?"

"I'm on my way now," I reply, hanging back from the entrance to the train so the noise doesn't drown out her voice.

"Would you mind terribly making a detour to meet Claire at the Louvre and have a look at the painting on loan there? It's the Renoir piano girls, the one with the sun damage. It's back from restoration and has already been shipped to the Louvre, but I would feel better if you could give it one final look now that it's been installed."

I'm already detouring to a different Metro stop. "Happy to. But is there a problem?"

"No problem," she answers. But I picture her frowning. "This restorer is the best. I simply want your sharp eyes on it in its new setting. If there's anything we've missed, I'd rather you find it than their people."

"In other words, you're fussing."

She scoffs. "I'm double-checking. Wouldn't you?"

"Of course I would. It's the Louvre."

"Thank you, Julien. Claire is aware the painting has had minor restoration, but not the specifics. If it's been repaired properly, the fix will be undetectable."

"Of course." Sun damage, and its repair, are somewhat routine, but I know what she's saying. Don't draw Claire's attention to something otherwise unnoticeable.

On my way to the Metro stop, I see the usual assortment of street artists who've set up shop along the river to draw caricatures of tourists. I spot Max, one of the regulars, and swing past to say hello. He's one of the best here, and at the moment he's sketching a gangly English boy, who'd clearly rather be anywhere else, as the parents look on, oblivious to his fidgeting. Does it even need saying that this was their idea?

The boy's too-long limbs remind me of a baby horse, and I say this to Max in French as I watch over his shoulder.

"You better hope they don't know *'poulain,'* or I've lost ten euros," he says, but he's laughing.

I laugh too, and go on my way with a parting promise: "I'll cover you if they turn out to be bilingual equestrians."

* * *

Wild horses couldn't drag me into the Louvre after dark.

At the Musée d'Orsay, we only have art painted after 1848—relatively modern in artistic terms. But our sister museum is full of medieval and Renaissance works, from periods that mainly drew from the Bible or other Classical sources. I don't want to run into Salome walking around with John the Baptist's head on a tray, or Prometheus with his liver half-eaten by crows.

The piece I'm studying is a seventeenth-century Georges de La Tour depicting Joseph in his workshop with a young Jesus. It's pleasantly domestic, but they can stay in their frame, thank you very much.

"It's an ironic inclusion as an interior scene, don't you think?"

The slightly smug question tells me Claire picked it for the exhibit—Interiors through the Ages—herself. The assistant curator has the carefully manicured look of a news anchor—sharp skirt, heels, proper blouse, and straight brown hair that falls just so—and she's giving me a preview of the exhibit before we get to the task at hand. When Claire offered to let me take a peek, I couldn't resist.

"It definitely makes me think," I say, though it's more like I'm hoping this painting doesn't come alive, since I'd rather avoid a religious experience in the museum.

In the La Tour, Jesus holds a lit candle for his earthly father, and I peer at it closely, as if the painting could reveal its nighttime secrets to me.

"Well, what does it make you think about?" Claire asks, as if quizzing me.

Before I can form a reply, a sharp, hot pain sears my hand. I gasp and look at my palm, expecting . . . I don't know what I'm expecting, but it's not this.

There, dancing in my cupped hand, is a single flame. A candle flame, like in the painting, as if the fire has jumped from the canvas to . . . me.

My chest seizes tight. Nothing like this has ever happened during daylight hours.

I've just wrapped my head around art coming to life at night and now it can ambush me anytime?

I'd wondered whether something from a painted world could harm me.

Well, now I know—it can hurt like a son of a bitch.

I close my fist around the flame, snuffing it out. Then I slowly uncurl my fingers again, and find my palm is the reddish pink of a bad sunburn.

Claire's gaze drops to my turned-up palm. "Oh, dear. Did you burn yourself?"

Surprise rocks me back a step. "You can see that?"

Her perfectly arched eyebrows knit in a frown. "Your burned hand. What happened? What do you mean?"

Those are both excellent questions. I raise my gaze to the painting, and a fist of shock hits me in the gut. On the canvas, the candle in Joseph's workshop is almost burned out. The flame is now only a guttering spark in the well of wax.

Is that because I put out the flame? Should I have returned it to the canvas like I do with Cézanne's peaches and *Olympia*'s cat?

Did I cause permanent damage to a work of art?

I point to the painting. "The candle flame in the La Tour. It's gone."

Claire glances from the canvas back to me. "Is that a joke? The painting looks the same as ever."

So, Claire can't see the blackened spot, even though she saw the effect of the flame on my hand.

But what the hell does that mean?

I recover the best I can, considering my upside-down world has made another spin. "My apologies, Claire," I say more formally. "I must have confused this with another painting for a moment. How embarrassing."

Humbling myself a little was the right call—she thaws from blast freezer to merely subarctic. "Well, things happen."

"They do. I'll just have a look at the *Young Girls at the Piano* and then be out of your way."

She leads me to the Renoir of two girls sitting at a piano, featured on another wall of the gallery. "I think it looks amazing here."

I smile politely and agree it does. The repairs are

seamless and undetectable. Except . . . when I peer closer, I see one of the piano keys is already fading again.

Adaline is not going to be happy. I glance warily at Claire, ready to assure her the piece had been in pristine condition when we packed it up for transport. But she smiles dreamily as she gazes at the scene. "I love this one. Perfectly on theme. Do tell your sister I'm so grateful for the loan."

Merde.

Claire can't see this new sun damage, just like she couldn't see the extinguished flame on the La Tour. Which leads me to think the damage to both paintings must be related somehow. Or am I the only one seeing this new damage?

When I take my leave of Claire, I double back through the museum, keeping an eye out for any other anomalies as I walk the galleries. Impressionists, Romantics, Neoclassicists . . . No signs of trouble until I get to the Dutch masters.

Rembrandt's Bathsheba in his Old Testament scene has always been a round-bellied woman, but now she looks bloated, her stomach bulging. Close up, bits of flesh are poking out of the frame.

It's grotesque, and like nothing I've seen in my museum.

I picture Cézanne's peach, how I'm able to put it back in its canvas. I glance around. There's no one in the gallery, and perhaps if I can push the protruding bit of Bathsheba back into the canvas, everything will be fine. But there are alarms and security cameras, and this isn't the Musée d'Orsay, where the guards all know me.

Before I can take the risk, a new group of tourists pours into the gallery. I slink into their midst to see the art through their eyes.

Not one person remarks on Bathsheba, or the canvas that for some reason can no longer contain her.

And once more, I don't know if art is losing its mind or if I am.

"The *Young Girls at the Piano* looks fine," I tell Adaline when I reach the Musée, managing not to flinch with guilt. "You'd never know there'd ever been a problem."

My decision not to tell my sister about the fading piano key comes down to the fact that I don't know *what* to tell her. Sun damage no one else can see? Even if she believes me, what can she do? What can I do about it?

Still, I walk the galleries, inspecting every painting for the least sign of trouble. There's nothing—everything here is in perfect shape.

For now.

I have an early class the next morning, and immediately afterward, I take the train from the university to the Louvre. I hardly slept last night. I worried about our paintings in the Musée d'Orsay, but it was the Louvre that kept me wide awake with a kind of inevitable dread.

My instincts didn't lie. Whatever happened yesterday is spreading. More keys on the piano are disappearing, a peacock feather droops in Ingres's *Grande Odalisque*, and the mirror inside a Titian has a hairline fracture.

Bathsheba hasn't fared well either. She's painful to look at. There's a black-and-blue bruise on the rolls of her stomach.

She looks ill, and that thought leads me to a crazy notion—are these anomalies some kind of contagion, spreading from frame to frame? And did bringing that sun-damaged Renoir here introduce some kind of epidemic to the Louvre?

But while the Rembrandt, the Titian, and the La Tour are bruised and cracked and burnt, the Renoir seems to be simply fading again.

Either way, the art here isn't so much coming to life as it is dying.

A pit deepens in my stomach, and I can't exit the Louvre fast enough, hating the sense that I'm leaving the art here to spoil. But a bigger panic seizes me.

I call Remy as soon as I'm outside. "Is the painting okay?" I ask before he even has a chance to speak. "Is she okay?"

"Of course." He sounds startled at either the question or my tone. "Why wouldn't it be?"

"I need to see it. I need to see her."

"Now?"

It's not a reasonable request, but I'm not feeling reasonable. "Yes. If I can. I know it's the middle of the day, but it's important. You said she has to be protected."

There's no hesitation this time.

"Come, then. I'll let you in."

7

I hit the nearest Metro station and take the next train to Montmartre. It's only fifteen minutes, but it's the longest fifteen minutes in my memory, and when I reach my stop, I climb a hundred looping spiral steps to the exit. I start out at a quick walk, but near the house, I break into a sprint up the hilly street.

Remy opens the door before I can text that I'm here. He's dressed casually today in skinny purple pants and a white T-shirt that I'm sure were never peddled in a department store.

"What's wrong?" he asks, as serious as I've ever seen him.

I'm about to do something drastic. I haven't told a soul that I've been living in a mirage since that night the ballerina danced out of the Degas. But Remy said the Muses live below his home. Now I know something is really happening—to me, to the art—and he's the only one I can think of who might believe me.

"This is going to sound completely mental," I blurt out in a rush.

His knitted brows climb into a more Remy-like arch. "*Mon ami*, what besides the sheep on my balcony and a carousel in my living room makes you think I am not accepting of all kinds of madness?"

That excellent point derails my runaway thoughts, which had been centered on convincing him to even listen to me. He closes the gate and says, "Let me guess. The Degas ballerinas are dancing for you at night?"

My jaw hits the paving stones.

I stare at him, dumbfounded. It's as if I've been putting on an elaborate play for the public, and he's pulled back the curtain, revealing the stagehands and sets and all the illusions. I don't have to perform anymore, and it takes a second to figure out what to do instead.

"They danced *Swan Lake* the other night," I confess, pacing the courtyard, and when he doesn't laugh, I tell him everything about the living art. "All of them, or any of them. The Cézannes, the Manets, the Matisses . . . The picnickers in a Monet brought their lunch out of the painting last week. *Olympia*'s cat prowls the galleries. I think she's looking for mice."

Remy does laugh then, not mocking but delighted. "How astounding. The green-eyed monster is eating me alive right now."

"Yeah," I admit. "It's pretty cool, when I'm not worried I'm going completely round the twist." I look at him directly. "It's weird though, right? Does this happen to other people? Does your Monet come alive in the hall?"

Does Woman Wandering in the Irises break free at night?

That's what I really want to ask, but I'm afraid of how badly I need the answer.

"Of course it doesn't," Remy says. "Who ever heard of art coming to life in someone's house?"

"Exactly!" I gesture with open hands to the point he makes in my own argument.

Rather than respond, Remy thoughtfully taps his smooth chin. "I think maybe it is something about a museum. Think of how much planning goes into how and where to display a piece—the frame and the lighting, the backdrop, what's nearby, even the flow of the room. You know this. Art is art anywhere, but the setting affects how it affects us, how we interact with it."

I stare at him, his matter-of-fact explanation as jarring as my first glimpse of the ballerinas. "So you think art can only come to life in a museum? Not in a home or a private gallery?"

He raises his hands in a shrug. "Who can say? Perhaps there are people who enjoy performances of *Swan Lake* in their homes nightly." With a wave, he dismisses that idea as ridiculous. "But no. I do believe it is the museum. This is what I've always believed, and so it must be true. In a museum, you sense the faces looking out of the paintings are just waiting to come alive as soon as the doors are locked."

I'd felt exactly that many times, even before the edges between life and art had blurred. But Remy is right. Only in a museum is there the sense the art has another life when no one is watching.

"I suppose there is a kind of logic to it," I say. "Museums are like churches for art. Sacred spaces, or holy ground or something."

Remy nods excitedly. "Yes, that's it. We come like pilgrims to an abbey to see them."

I feel like I might have a faint glimmer of understanding about what's going on, and that worries me. Am I grasping at straws? "You seem very certain of this when you've never seen it for yourself."

Another dismissive wave. "Do you have to see the sun to believe in it? My family believes it. Sophie believes it. Rafe . . ." He makes a so-so wag of his hand. "The power of art is real, and anyone can feel it, even if not everyone can see paintings come to life. But some people can. The Muses say there are, and have always been, those who can see art live and breathe."

And just as I feared, the explanation is getting away from me again. "Hold up, Remy. The Muses told you this? In the basement?"

He shrugs. "It isn't an ordinary cellar."

"Yes. I gathered that. I hadn't realized how extraordinary though."

"They live and work far beneath Montmartre. I'm a sort of emissary for them."

He might have said "I'm a bike messenger" just as matter-of-factly. I look around the courtyard for a bench because my head is spinning from how quickly my world is changing.

No bench. I have to man up and deal with this on my feet.

"What about that silver dust I saw in the cellar? There was some inside the five-legged calf you gave me too."

"And in the one you won at the party." Remy nods, pleased I am following him, which proves I'm a better actor than I thought. "They give it to me from time to time to pass along."

This is too much. I pinch the bridge of my nose and wonder which of us is the delusional one—him or me. Though I suppose we might both be. Or maybe Remy's delusion is part of mine.

Perhaps he can sense I've reached the end of my tether, or maybe his feet are getting tired, because he puts a hand on my shoulder so that we're both angled toward the house.

"*Mon ami*, we can stand here longer and debate the Muses and madness and the magic of museums, but I think you might rather come inside and see what—who —it is you came to see." The roguish teasing in his voice as he gives my shoulder a shake is more the Remy I'm used to. "A certain beautiful woman in a garden, maybe?"

I run a hand over my chin. "Is it that obvious?"

He nudges me toward the house. "You wear your feelings on your sleeve, as they say."

We go in by the orange door, and he leads me down the hallway, even though I know my way by now. Heat rises in me. The whole house quivers, hazy and warped. There's a strumming in my body, and a whispering in the air that urges me on. Remy unlocks the door to the room where she's kept, and it's torturous to stand still that long.

Then . . .

Then, it doesn't matter—because nothing exists anymore but me and this room and this insanely gorgeous painting that I want to hold and touch. This painting that is perfect—no sun damage, no fading colors, no flowers wilting from the seams.

Remy leaves me alone with the painting, and when I am mere inches away from it, I lift my hand, but I am careful not to touch the frame, or even the canvas. The painting is still a painting.

Until it's not. There's a stretching I feel in my own muscles and tendons, like coming awake at dawn when the first rays of a coral sunrise flare through the windowpanes. A sound goes with it—a sweet morning yawn, delicate arms unfolding from the night, and eyelids fluttering open.

Inside her garden, the woman presses her fingertips against the wall of reality between us, imploring the canvas to yield for her. Slowly at first, then more quickly, she reaches her hand through the paint, spreading her fingers.

I don't hesitate. I reach for her, my fingers touching hers and then sliding around them. Her skin is warm and soft and radiant.

And confident.

There is a boldness in her touch that makes me feel like I can do anything, and the things I've done, I can do better.

I press her soft hand to my cheek; her palm is so warm, so tender on my face. I want her to come all the way out, to talk to me, to tell me who she is.

Holding her hand, holding her painted gaze, I speak the first and only thought I have. "I want more than anything for you to be at the museum. I can't wait to meet you."

"It is the same for me with you," she whispers from beyond the canvas.

8

I carry her words with me, through waking and dreaming, over the next couple of weeks. There are exams to get through, grades that hardly matter, since I've already been accepted to graduate school here at the university. The most important thing, scholastically, is my project for my independent study.

The most important thing on my mind, personally, is getting to the museum.

Bless whatever neuron came up with the brilliant idea to do my project on the Renoir, because the overlap of those two things may well be the difference between graduating with honors and without.

Today is the day.

I force myself to keep a normal pace on my way to work, just to prove I have some self-control. And also, the woman can't come out of the garden until the sun sets. So, there's that.

I let myself into the Musée d'Orsay's administrative wing with my key card and make for the nearest stairwell, taking the steps two at a time to the first floor, where she—the only "she" who matters—is already in place, ready to welcome visitors.

The crowd surprises me, though it shouldn't. Tourists and locals alike pack the entrance to the gallery that showcases *Woman Wandering in the Irises*. It's not quite *Mona Lisa* level, but it's more traffic than the Musée usually sees.

It feels like the floor of a concert venue, everyone sweaty and elbowing each other, angling to get closer to the rock star. Everyone wants to see the lost Renoir.

Then—there she is.

My heart stutters, and a flush heats my face and neck. I want to push through the crowd to reach her and run my hands over her painted body. I want her to see me, and only me, amid the chaos.

I want her to like me.

I want her, full stop, and that's an exceedingly uncomfortable thing to admit about a painting.

Only, I'm no longer pretending that's all she is.

I leave her to her adoring public, calmer now that I've seen her here. Now that I know she's in the building. I even manage to get some work done, and to say good night to Adaline when she leaves, and to behave like a human being and not an instinct-driven hormone machine raised by wolves.

Finally—*finally*—the museum closes. Gustave patrols, and another guard keeps watch on the monitors at the security desk. *Now* the waiting gets tough. The sun sets late in the summer, and I'd wrestle it down beneath the horizon if I could.

My phone chirps at sunset, and I pack up my messenger bag and make a loop through the galleries while I wait for full dark. Anticipation has sharpened my senses, and as I near her gallery, a dress rustles. Quickening my pace, I arrive as she steps out of her frame.

It's as natural and effortless as if she does this every single night. Her long cream dress skims the floor, and she shakes out her curls, a Botticelli Venus emerging from the ocean, sun-kissed skin and tousled hair. Her chestnut hair is long and luxurious, enticing me to touch it, hold it, wrap my fingers around its silk.

She hasn't noticed me yet, doesn't realize I'm watching as her paint turns to flesh. As she takes on shape and skin and breath and life.

I would be shocked if I wasn't used to paintings coming to life. What I am, though, is awed.

Awestruck by her beauty and her wonderful *realness*.

She turns, and her eyes fall on me for the first time. They are the fierce blue of a revolution, a color to rally flagging armies. They stun me.

Then she speaks. In English, her accent warm, her voice sounding like a poet. "I'm awfully hungry."

I laugh in surprise. I didn't dare imagine what she might say first, but not something so pedestrian.

But I like it, and it makes answering easy, bypassing nerves and vaulted expectations.

"It's probably been a while since you had a bite to eat."

She nods with a wry arch to her brow. "More than a hundred and thirty-five years."

"I know where there's a great *ile flottante*," I say, thinking of the nearby café that serves the floating meringue in caramel. Then I follow the thought through, and wince. "But it's closed."

"Maybe you can bring me one tomorrow?"

"Sure." I would bring the Eiffel Tower to her if she asked for it. "It's the best in the city."

She nods. "I do love sweets."

"Fortunately, we have plenty of those here in Paris." I remember I have half a sandwich from earlier, and it's not a courtly gesture, but it solves her problem.

I pat my messenger bag. "I have some of my lunch in here. It's just a sandwich, but it's pretty good."

She eyes my bag hungrily, like she might take a bite out of it instead if I don't hand over the food. "Would you mind terribly?" she asks, then recovers her aplomb. "I mean, may I have it?"

"Absolutely." I sit on the wooden bench, and she sits next to me. The skirt of her dress spreads out and touches my leg.

She's real. She's here. And to say she's beautiful would be to call the Alps tall or the ocean salty.

I unwrap the sandwich and hand it to her. When the food reaches her lips, she rolls her eyes in pleasure.

"This is perfect," she says.

"I can bring you one of your very own tomorrow. Is there something you'd like?"

"Anything. Anything is good."

She takes another bite, then holds up a "one more thing" finger until she can swallow. "I meant that. *Everything* is good. Bring me one of everything."

Her voice is ravenous. No, *she* is ravenous. As she chews, she looks around the gallery with lively, hungry eyes. She glances at the messenger bag at my feet, as if she's able to notice them now. She inventories my shoes, my jeans, my button-down shirt, and she can probably see the flush rising on my neck when she gets to my collar.

"I don't know what to call you," she says.

"I'm Julien." I offer my hand to shake, and she takes it. I let the last of my doubt run out on a sigh. Her touch is real. *She* is real, from the hair that falls past her shoulders to the folds of her dress to the slim silver bracelets she wears, each one the width of a few strands of thread.

"You can call me Clio," she says.

"Clio." Her name is like a bell, clear and pure. "Clio."

"It's better like this, isn't it? When we are on the same side of the frame?"

I laugh softly. "I couldn't agree more."

"I'm free." Her voice breaks a little, as if her throat is tight with tears. She sighs and stretches her arms overhead. "And it feels *spectacular*." She leans her head back as if she's on a beach letting the sun warm her face. "Ah, you have no idea what all those years inside a painting will do to a body."

Eyes closed, she shifts her neck from side to side, and I want to offer to rub the kinks out of her muscles, if only for an excuse to touch her. She turns to me, her wild blue eyes lit up like she's ready to misbehave. Whatever she's about to suggest, I'm down for it.

"Would you like to show me this museum, Julien?"

I can't help my grin. The suggestion isn't improper, but it's the way she says it. Like nothing could be better than the two of us, nearly alone, in the Musée d'Orsay.

Standing, I offer her my hand. "I would love nothing better than to show you this museum."

She looks tickled by the gesture. It goes with her dress and her era, but she doesn't seem as prim as I thought women were a hundred and thirty-five years ago. Still, she takes my hand, and as her fingers touch my palm, a tremble sweeps through me—up my arm and through my whole being.

I don't move for long seconds that contain lifetimes.

The painted woman is real. Is holding my hand. Is touching me. Her fingers wrap delicately around mine as she stands in front of me, alive and in the world.

And it feels spectacular.

Flesh and bone, warmth and sparks.

So many sparks race across my skin at the simple clasping of our hands.

If holding hands is a gateway drug, I'm already addicted.

We wander through the galleries of my home away from home, past the paintings that are almost like family. She trails her hand along the canvases, brushing pastel bathers on beaches, bowls of peaches, and moonlit stars. She traces her fingers over vases of flowers, Tahitian women on islands, and cabarets in Montmartre.

I would tell anyone else to stop. But there is reverence in her touch, something loving and tender.

When she reaches a painting of Monet's *Rouen Cathedral*, she stops to consider it.

"I want to go there," she announces, with some of the same longing as when she said she was awfully hungry. "I want to see the real cathedral. Have you been?"

"Yes. I'm studying art history, and I've visited a lot of the places the artists here painted. Rouen, Arles . . ." I watch her for a reaction. "Even Monet's garden."

Her eyes widen. "You've been to Monet's garden? The real one?"

I laugh once. "Is there another one?"

"What is it like now? Tell me everything."

There it is again. *Everything is good. Bring me one of everything.* She's as hungry for the world as she was for my sandwich.

I search for words that are up to that hunger. "It's a paradise of colors and scents and sounds. Like art made real. Walking through it is like strolling through a field of inspiration, where you can reach out and pluck an idea as easily as a flower."

Then I hear myself, and stop with a grimace of embarrassment and chagrin. "That sounds unbelievably pretentious, doesn't it?"

"No. It doesn't. It sounds . . ." She looks again at the Monet, laying her hand against it to frame the doorway of the church. "It sounds like something I'd want."

The way she says "want" is wistful and pained. It's a wish from a woman shut away for too long.

Are the other people in the paintings trapped too? The idea never occurred to me. There's something different about Clio, a vivacity I haven't seen in the others. They seem content to do what they do, in or out of their frames. At the risk of a terrible pun, they strike me as rather two-dimensional.

Clio is something else.

I have so many questions. I want to ask who she is, where she's from, but the moment is delicate, and I don't want to break it.

"Do you want to see my favorite Van Gogh?" I ask, changing the mood and the subject.

"Yes!" She's smiling again, sparkling again. "I definitely want to see your favorite Van Gogh, Julien."

The sound of my name on her lips makes me want to touch her arm, to take her hand. I don't do either of those things, or anything else my mind suggests. She'd been desperate to come out of her frame. I'd hoped—all right, assumed—her reasons were the same as mine. That we both wanted to see each other. Touch each other. Do other things with each other that I wasn't going to admit to fantasizing about doing with a woman in a painting.

But now I don't know if she wanted to come out for me or to be free of her painted chains, so I keep my hands to myself.

I take her to the wing on the second floor and show her Van Gogh's *Starry Night*. In it, a couple walks along the River Rhône under a sky full of sparkling stars while sailboats bob in the water. Clio gazes at it for a moment, a hand pressed over her heart, then she closes her eyes. When she opens them again, she reaches for the painting, her touch as soft and light as a murmur on the waves.

"Is this one of the places you've been?"

"Yes. Van Gogh painted this by the Rhône in Arles. That was a family trip, though, and I was too young to remember it."

We lapse into silence side by side as we admire the painting. She shifts her body closer to me. This near, she's intoxicating. "Then we'll go together someday," she says, surprising me again.

I glance at her and find her looking back at me. That word, "together," does a number on me, especially combined with "someday," which implies a future date. A future *together*.

"Anytime, any day," I promise. I don't examine how or when. I just pretend it would be possible and then enjoy the heady, swooping feeling that maybe she likes me too.

After a long, sweet moment in front of Van Gogh's *Starry Night*, she grabs my hand and says, "Show me more."

I do, and we don't stop until she has seen haystacks and operas, mirrors and pheasants, doctors and patients. When we come back to her gallery, it's nearly midnight. I hate that I have to go home, and I'm dragging my feet to draw out the night.

We pause outside her gallery as if I'm walking her home from a date. She studies me, head tilted in speculation.

"You love them all," she says—not asking, but confirming—and I nod.

"Yes. I do."

Her head tilts the other way as she asks, "You've been coming to see me, haven't you?"

I'm not surprised she knows, but I have so many questions.

"Could you see me? Hear me?" I ask.

"You're the first thing I've been able to see or hear on the other side of the frame," she says. I can't tell if that's frustration or relief in her voice. Maybe both. "I saw you in that room. You heard me, didn't you?"

"Yes," I say, remembering every encounter with her at Remy's house.

"I wanted to come out sooner." There's so much longing in her voice now. Is it longing for what could have been? For the years she missed?

She moves a step closer, until we're inches apart. "As soon as I saw you, I tried to get out. It was the closest I've ever come to managing it." She gestures to our surroundings. "Until now, obviously."

"I'm glad you're able to come out now."

"Me too. You're not like anyone I've ever met. You asked questions about me. You *talked* to me and made everything better while you were there."

I smile slightly. "I was thinking the same thing about you."

For a moment, the question flashes through my head like a neon sign—*what are you thinking?*

It's a valid question—how can I be so attracted to a painting?

But perhaps the answer is in front of me. She's not a painting. She's a person.

And that's really all that matters, I suppose.

"'What are you like, woman behind the paint?' That's what you asked me."

"You remember," I say. I'm sure she's some sort of enchantress, and she has put me completely under her spell. "Who are you?"

"I'm Clio. I'm just an ordinary young woman."

"No . . ." I reach up and brush a wayward chestnut curl behind her ear. "Who *are* you?"

Her gaze dances away and then back, and then she grins. "Julien . . ." she tsks, and it's the sexiest thing ever, her chiding me in that shy but bold, joking but not kind of way. "I have to keep *some* secrets. You don't want to learn everything about me on the first . . ." She seems at a loss for the word she wants. "What do you call it these days?"

"Date?" Hoping she feels the same way, I trail the back of my hand down the silken skin of her arm and say, "First date?"

"First date," she echoes as if trying on the words. "Yes, that's what I mean. I quite like the sound of that." She tilts her head the other way. "How does this compare? Was touring the museum a good first date?"

"The best ever," I tell her.

She nods decisively. "And for me as well."

The admission makes my head spin, and I look at her, feeling helpless and wobbly and really, terribly happy. I save some questions for later, and shake my head, bemused. "Where have you been for the last century?"

She points to the gallery where her gilded frame rests. "On the other side of that painting."

We're back to her frame now, and I regard it with curiosity. "What's on the other side?"

"Tulips and hollyhocks, pansies and irises." Her voice is pure, her French is impeccable, but she doesn't have the accent of a native. She doesn't have any accent.

"You don't sound like you're from here."

"You doubt my French?" She places a palm against her chest as if mortally offended.

I hold up my thumb and forefinger a scant inch apart. "Maybe a little."

"Do you think I'm French?"

I shake my head. "I don't know *what* you are. Or who you are. At least tell me where you're from."

She shakes her head. "You'll come back tomorrow?"

"For our second date? I wouldn't miss it."

"Promise me?"

I pause, considering her pinched brows and the shift in her tone, and my nod is weighty, a vow in itself. "I promise."

She places her hand on my cheek, just where I'd held it that day at Remy's, and trails it along my jaw as she steps away. "Then I will see you tomorrow, Julien."

"Tomorrow," I echo. She walks back to her painting but stops and turns with her hand on the frame as if remembering something. Before she can speak, I say, "And I'll bring food. One of everything."

"Julien, no!" she exclaims. "I didn't mean everything all on the same day!"

I tease, "You should say what you mean, Clio. Now I will have to eat all the sweets myself."

She shakes her head with a little roll of her eyes.

"Then I promise to taste one of whatever you bring." So much is conveyed in the flick of her gaze, the saucy hint of a smile on her lips as she steps into the frame. "In which case, I am eager to see how you plan to indulge me."

Her demeanor changes slightly as she settles into place, softens to something sweeter and terribly earnest. "Also, *thank you*, Julien."

She says it with such appreciation, as if I've accomplished some tremendous deed for her. Anything I've done seems inconsequential next to what she's done for me.

I don't simply mean the wild beating in my heart, or the sizzling of my skin. But what she's done for my mind—she's proven I'm not mad.

Not in the sense that I can't tell reality from fantasy.

But maybe I'm mad in another way.

Because one date, one night, one stroll through the museum by her side and I'm absolutely mad for more of her.

"Good night, Clio."

She blows me a kiss then pulls up the gauzy hem of her skirt, the lace edges brushing against the painted irises, until she is immobile once more, leaving me dizzy with want.

I start home in a haze, feeling like I'm drunk or dreaming. Clio is imprinted on my skin; I feel faint traces of her. I'm so absorbed by the lingering sensation that I don't notice the man sprawled on the museum steps until I'm almost past him. In a worn sweatshirt and jeans, he could be a vagrant or an artist—or both. Once I see that he's lounging and not injured, I continue on my way, wrapped up again in the vision of Clio and the promise of seeing her again.

9

The next day takes a century.

Classes go on like dreams I can't wake from.

Time taunts me.

Every instant I resist looking at the time on my phone, I'm battling my own impatience.

All I want is to see her again.

And when time finally takes pity on me, and the sun mercifully dips below the horizon, I go to the museum.

The only place I want to be becomes the only place that exists for me as I wait in the gallery, her gallery, for the last straggling patrons to leave. I keep my sketch pad out as an excuse for the security guards, but after their obligatory check, I put it away. I want to capture Clio with my mind because I'm sure my pencil isn't up to the task.

At last, the young woman emerges from the garden, and my heart slams against my rib cage with excitement.

"Fancy meeting you here," she says with a cheeky grin.

I offer her my hand again, and she takes it. "I hope I didn't keep you waiting too long," I tease.

"Only all day," she answers in the same vein.

I laugh, she smiles, and we both look at our clasped hands then back up at each other. As our eyes catch, my smile slips away, but not my pleasure in this moment. Her mouth softens too, and mixed with the sparkle of humor in her eyes, there's a hint of desire.

It spurs me on, and I lean closer, dusting a soft kiss against her cheek. "Hi."

"Hi." Her voice is breathy and beautiful, and I'd wait another endless day to hear it again.

* * *

"Look! The sheet is messy on Olympia's bed." Clio points to Manet's *Olympia*, where a small bit of white satin fabric hangs out of the canvas and over the gilded frame.

I feign an aggravated sigh. "I tell them to clean their rooms and put their toys away, but they never listen to me."

"May I do it?" Clio asks.

"Be my guest."

She hands me the takeout container with half of the *île flottante* still in it. The meringue had sunk into the caramel by the time Clio emerged, but she declared it delicious, which is all that matters.

It's frightening how quickly pleasing Clio has

become all that matters to me.

She gathers up the runaway sheet, and I notice I'm holding my breath, worried it won't return to its spot, thinking of Rembrandt's Bathsheba, bulging from the canvas. But the bedsheets behave, and Clio tucks them neatly into place.

Over the days, I've kept alert for any sign that the aberrations at the Louvre might have spread to the Musée d'Orsay. But our paintings seem healthy, and they respond to my touch whenever I replace a piece of fruit or shoo the cat into her home.

"There." Clio brushes one palm against the other. "All done."

"Wonderful. It's so hard to find good domestic help these days."

She laughs and reclaims the dessert container before we continue on. It's strange to have company on my nightly amble through the galleries, but it's wonderful that it's her.

"Does this happen a lot?" she asks before we're far from *Olympia*.

"Every night. The paintings are terribly lazy. They make a mess and expect me to straighten up after them."

Clio gauges my tone of fond exasperation and ventures, "But it's more like they're playing perhaps?"

"That's it exactly." Their antics at night are like those of naughty children. No, not even naughty—just mischievous, like students restless from being cooped up all day. "They seem to be having fun."

"But you still pick up after them?"

"Of course." It never occurred to me not to. "I'll

always care for the art."

She nods. "You are a caretaker," she says, like that settles it. She has another bite of the meringue then offers some to me. I take the spoon from her and eat a piece.

Then I hand the *ile flottante* back to her and glance at my watch. It's almost eleven—the paintings have more of a rhythm than a schedule, but the dancers are usually timely.

"Are you ready for our second date?" I ask, hinting that I have a plan.

"This isn't it?" she asks, that playful glint in her eyes. "The lovely dessert and the stroll through the museum? Because this has been a pretty good date. At least, where I come from."

"There's more. I have something else in mind. I'm wondering if you would like to go to the ballet with me."

"The ballet?" She sounds interested, but then, disappointed, she shakes her head. "I can't leave."

I quirk up my lips, having a little fun with her. "I'm thinking more of a command performance."

"Color me intrigued," she says, all flirty.

"Intrigued is a good look on you," I toss back.

"You look good too."

Sparks tear across my skin again. Flirting with a painting. This is my new world order.

And I like it.

"But you won't distract me, Julien," she admonishes me. "A command performance, you say? Show me now, or I won't believe you."

"I hope you'll believe your eyes."

Relishing the moment, I take the empty takeout container from her and drop it in the recycling bin on our way from one gallery to the other.

We cross the cavernous main hall to where my dancer friends hang out. I tap twice near the frame of the Degas, then the girl in white squeezes her way out of the paint.

"It's you!" she exclaims. "How nice to see you."

"Hello there." I'm not surprised she's the one who answered. I saw her out on her own first, and she's been more interactive than the other art. "How is your foot?"

"All better. See?" She balances on one leg and rotates the other ankle.

"Glad to hear it." I sense Clio watching the exchange with avid interest, but my vibe with the dancer is unquestionably platonic. "I didn't introduce myself the other night. I'm Julien, and this is Clio."

The dancer curtsies with a giggle. "Hello, Julien and Clio. I'm Emmanuelle."

"A pleasure to meet you, Emmanuelle." Clio nods, and her smile is as warm as ever—at least while she's out of her frame. The contrast between her manners and the little ballerina's strikes me—a dynamic from another era. Clio is forthright, and I love that about her, but from her clothes and manners, she's definitely a lady, no matter what social status she might have been born into. She also blends seamlessly into *this* time, picking up mannerisms, ways of speaking, things like that. It's fascinating to watch her soak up the world around her like a sponge, to assimilate it.

Her ability to adapt lights the flame under my curiosity, and I'm going to get distracted if I don't bank the fire and stick to my plan.

Emmanuelle motions for her friend from the painting to join her, which she does, in a flutter of white tulle. Another moment and there are ballerinas everywhere, wriggling out of frames, stretching, and greeting each other with kisses on cheeks, and then a voice calls, "Places, places!"

I steer Clio to a bench where we watch as the Degas girls begin the finale of *Swan Lake*. Dancers in pale shades of pink and blue and white become graceful birds as the drama plays out with Emmanuelle and her friend dancing the parts of Odette and the prince confronting the evil sorcerer. There's no music but the tapping of their toe shoes on the parquet floor, but it's easy to imagine an orchestra, maybe Tchaikovsky himself directing. Why not? Art crosses all mediums.

Some things can't be confined to one time or mode. Music. Movement.

Moments where the universe slows, narrows down to the sliver of space between two bodies.

As the painted women dance, Clio's soft, slender fingers inch across the bench toward mine. I catch the motion out of the corner of my eye, her edging closer to me, and it sets off a rush of heat from my chest outward.

She sparks a thrill in me that zips along my nerves all the way to the fingertips almost brushing hers.

For the longest time, I admired her from afar. Falling for her without knowing a thing about her.

What could that be but a silly infatuation?

But now, two nights in, nothing about this seems foolish at all. It feels like she wants to hold hands because we have talked, we have wandered, and we have watched art together.

I finish the thought, reaching for her hand, sliding my fingers through hers.

At her soft gasp, I smile privately. I squeeze her hand a little harder, and she squeezes back.

When I turn my head slightly to glance at her, Clio is watching the performance, but I sense her attention sliding my way as she nibbles on the corner of her lips. All I want is to lean in and kiss that corner then the rest of that pretty mouth.

But that would be rude to the dancers.

The finale is enthusiastic, and when they're finished, we break our handhold to clap. Clio shouts "Brava!" as the corps take their swanlike bows then leap back into their frames.

The stillness is jarring after the gallery had been a pastel whirl of arms and arabesques a moment ago. Knowing how Clio felt while trapped in her frame at the house in Montmartre, I watch an immobile Emmanuelle and wonder what happens to her during the day. Is she a spirit yearning to escape a bizarre eternity of paint, or is she simply a shadow—a representation of the girl she once was?

I'm still mulling over the question as Clio and I resume our walk through the galleries. She is so vastly different from them, but I still don't understand how or why.

"Clio," I begin, uncertain how to ask this or if I even should. "When we held hands just now, you felt real to me. You've never felt anything but completely real to me. Hell, you *are* real."

"Well, thank you," she says drolly. "I can't argue against that."

I drag a hand through my hair. That was not the best start. Maybe this will ruin the mood—no, it will definitely ruin the mood—but I have to wrap my head around what I'm dealing with. I want her to help me so that I can better care for the paintings—in the general sense, and in light of the plague of art anomalies at the Louvre. I don't know if I can do anything about the art there, but I want to protect what is here.

Most of all, I want to know how to protect *her*. And I can't do that if I don't understand her.

"What I'm trying to grasp is whether you are the woman Renoir painted? Or are you—I don't know—a version of her that lives on in the art?"

"Am I like the other paintings? Paint coming to life at night?"

I grimace at her tone—not chilly, but definitely . . . tepid. A sharp contrast to how she was when we were holding hands. That moment already seems like forever ago. "You make the question seem rude when you say it like that."

Her mouth pinches, and she doesn't meet my eyes. "It's complicated." Then her nose wrinkles, as if she can't help but let me see her feelings. Tepid isn't in her design. "The essential nature of one's being doesn't seem like a topic for a second date."

She's right, and my steps stutter as that sinks in. We *haven't* known each other as long as it feels like we have.

Perhaps I've assumed too much from the moment we shared while watching *Swan Lake*. Taken too many liberties.

Then again, what is the right number of dates before you can say to someone, "I think you're real, but I need to understand how that can be"?

Thing is, I never questioned her personhood, even when she was at Remy's home. Maybe that's my answer and I should trust my instincts.

"I can tell it's complicated, and that's why I ask. You seem different than the rest of the art here, and it's the paintings that I'm wondering about. They don't seem trapped or unhappy—or anything, really—and they hardly talk. I think Emmanuelle has said more to me than the whole of the other artworks combined. They don't notice me at all, mostly. They go about their patterns like spirits reliving an event. So, I have to wonder . . . are they?"

"Are they what?" she asks, confused.

I force a laugh. "Ghosts."

She doesn't laugh at me, so that's good, and she shakes her head solemnly in answer. "But I have heard that the ghosts of great artists tend to haunt cafés."

"Really?" I can't tell if she's joking.

Her straight face breaks into a teasing grin. "Since that's where so many writers, artists, and poets hang out."

I chuckle at the joke, but also in relief that I haven't ruined things with us, either tonight or altogether.

Clio continues her thought, glancing around the grand gallery. "Though you'd think they might frequent museums too. To see if they approve of how their masterpieces are being treated."

I wince. "That is a terrifying thought. Please don't tell me to expect a visit from a displeased ghost with an artistic temperament."

Her laughter chimes like a bell in the vaulted ceiling of the hall. "Then I won't tell you that."

I don't pursue an answer I don't want. We walk a little farther and then she stops to face me, her expression serious. "When the paintings come alive for you, you see what some people sense when they say that art is immortal. The artist lives on in their work, and a bit of what they paint lives on too. But only as art. You could say that the painter catches a *moment* as much as a person. The subjects don't spend their days wandering beyond the frame. They aren't alive on the other side."

But she is.

"You exist as more than a moment though," I say, and her eyes flash and then widen. Have I stunned her with my insight, or is she just pissed that I've brought the question back to her? I don't know, but I hold her gaze as I push my luck. "You are more than a moment, Clio."

She swallows and nods. Her nose turns red as if she's about to cry. It's adorable, but I don't want her to be sad, so I reach out and put my hands on her shoulders, rubbing her arms. "Hey. I've always felt that you were a person—a real woman in the irises. That's why I said you feel real. Not just to me, but real in and of yourself. And that's what I can't make heads nor tails of."

Her breath catches in a humorless laugh. "You don't know the half of it. That's why I asked about Monet's garden the other night." She lets out a long, heavy breath, like this is hard for her. "Because I live in the painted one—all the time."

I flinch from surprise. How is that possible? "You . . . you . . . you live in Monet's garden?" It's hard to form a coherent sentence when I'm struggling to wrap my head around the idea.

"That's where I was when Renoir painted me, so that's where I am in the frame—a painted version. That's where I sleep." The way she says it, it sounds like a prison sentence. "That's where I've been for all this time."

"That sounds beautiful and awful at the same time."

Her eyes are full of sadness. "It is. It's gorgeous, but it's lonely."

I can't even imagine what she's feeling. I'm in awe that she hasn't gone mad, alone in a painted garden for a hundred and thirty-five years. But how? Was it an accident?

Maybe the story is true. Perhaps Renoir was in love with her, but she didn't feel the same, so he locked her away in a painted cage.

"Did he trap you?" I ask, my mind racing. "Renoir?"

She sighs and shakes her head. "There were things we didn't agree on, certainly. But no."

I begin to ask another question, but she places her hand on mine, and I wait.

"Julien . . ."

Everything stops—breathing, heartbeat, brain function. The universe narrows to only her as she says, "I don't actually want to talk about Renoir right now."

"Me neither."

"Ask me what I do want to talk about," she says.

"What do you want to talk about?" I oblige, matching her lighter tone.

"I don't want to talk at all right now."

She reaches for my hand and slides her fingers into mine.

I let go of all my questions. They fall from my mind like marbles scattering, and I smile at her, weaving my fingers through hers. "Funny, I don't want to talk either."

Her grin is delicious.

With a gentle tug, I bring her close. She slides against me, fitting perfectly. I lift my free hand, brush the soft tendrils of hair from her face, then ask her softly, as if anything louder would shatter the moment, "May I?"

"You may."

I thread my fingers through her soft hair, shut my eyes, brush my lips over hers, and kiss this woman who was a painting and who will become one again.

Now, though, in my arms, she's the most vibrantly real thing in my world.

She tastes like a song, like a perfect summer day. She shivers as I touch her. It's so sweet and so sexy at the same time. She's warm and lush, her breath shuddery as I slide my lips across hers. A tiny gasp is the first sound she makes, then a soft, enticing *ohhh*.

I don't stop.

I don't want to.

Nor does she.

I hold her face in my hands, exploring her lips like it's all I've wanted to do all day, all night, all year.

Perhaps it is.

Because this kiss feels like it was always destined to happen.

Like our lips were meant to touch.

Soon, she's snuggling closer, exploring too, her tongue skating over mine.

My head goes hazy, and my heart is beating so damn loudly, she must be able to hear it. The guards on their rounds and the stars above the city can probably hear it too.

And in these delirious kiss-drunk moments with Clio, I don't care about anything at all but the taste of her, the feel of her—the sound of her as we lose ourselves in an intoxicating kiss after midnight, surrounded by nothing but vaulted, echoing halls of endless, ageless beauty.

But even the best things must end.

After a time, we break the kiss, and she simply smiles at me with bee-stung lips then gestures to her home.

"See you tomorrow?"

"Yes, you will."

"What will you do during the day?"

I don't have to wonder.

I'll spend it waiting for the night.

10

And the nights are worth the wait.

For the next few days, my life seems to pass by in a dream state. A trance of fantastic first, second, third, and fourth dates.

Sunlit hours pass molasses slow, and evening hours race by like they have somewhere to be. One moment follows another too quickly as Clio and I wander through the Musée d'Orsay enjoying each other's company.

We eat, dining on sandwiches, bread, and croissants.

We talk, discussing art and music and ballet.

And we ramble too, chatting about little things, the smell of flowers, what color would have been better on that bridge Monet painted, and if the Moulin Rouge is as fun as the paintings make it appear.

And we kiss. I lose track of time in our kisses, stolen in alcoves, stairwells, quiet corners far away from the prying eyes of Van Goghs and Toulouse-Lautrecs, those Peeping Toms.

We kiss like it's the only thing we've wanted to do all day.

We kiss good night like it's all we'll want to do tomorrow.

And it never gets easier to say goodbye to Clio at the edge of her frame.

Despite the impatience that runs like white noise through my day, there are still things that need doing. I'm not *merely* a guy infatuated with a beautiful, lively mystery of a woman in a painted garden. I'm also a university student and a museum intern.

So I put some effort into being more present at school and work. Of course, since my independent study project and my duties as docent and guide at the Musée d'Orsay both center around *Woman Wandering in the Irises*, I can't totally leave her behind. Which is a good thing, since I don't want to.

On the fifth day since I met Clio—because that's how I tell time now—I drag myself to an early lecture on campus and then a meeting with my faculty advisor. Ironically, he cautions me not to rely too much on indirect sources for my research—I'm not sure I can get any more direct than to be dating the subject of the painting itself.

With that done, I head to the museum for a full schedule of tours. Along the familiar route, I pass an art gallery where a Jack Russell terrier snoozes in the front window, stretched out between the clawed feet of an antique chair. He's fast asleep, so I don't slow to greet him, but I do spot my friend Zola coming from the opposite direction. She's the spitting image of Zoe

Saldana, so much so that I've seen tourists do double-takes in the street, which always makes me chuckle.

Zola owns the gallery along with her wife, who is a renowned art authenticator. She's done work for the Musée d'Orsay as well as museums around the world.

I wave, and Zola grins when she spots me. "You caught me coming back from my coffee break," she says, a gleam in her eyes.

"What's today's verdict?" I ask.

She shows me her phone and her latest blog post, featuring an image of two tiny pink-and-blue espresso cups from Ladurée, turned upside down.

I cringe in exaggerated horror. "Not the vicious two cups down." It's not the worst rating on Zola's coffee blog, where she reviews espressos at cafés all over the city, but it's pretty bad.

"Ladurée's espresso was simply awful."

Shaking my head sadly, I put a hand on her shoulder. "Zola, how many times do I have to tell you? All the coffee in France is wretched."

She gazes heavenward. "I dream of a day when our espresso is as good as our chocolate."

"Keep dreaming."

I gesture to the shop, where I saw no sign of Zola's wife when I looked in on the snoozing pup in the window. "Where's Celeste today?"

She waves airily. "She got called to consult on a suspicious painting. All very hush-hush," she adds, leaning in like a conspirator.

"I hope that means you'll tell me when you can."

"*Naturellement.*" She winks. "And speaking of paintings, how is your Renoir doing?"

No need to ask which one she means—Celeste verified *Woman Wandering in the Irises* for us. It makes me feel related to her and Zola somehow. Two more people tied to Clio's painting.

"She's amazing." And that feels amazing to say, as if I have a wonderful secret.

Which I do.

We exchange *bonjours*, and Zola heads into the store while I continue to the corner and turn onto the museum's block. Greeting some of the staff taking their lunchtime smoke breaks, I dart into a side door to the offices and snag my name tag.

Adaline pops her head out of her office door as if she's been waiting on me. "Hey, Julien. Got a minute?"

She looks worried. There's tension between her brows that matches the tightness in her voice.

"What's going on?" I ask.

Gesturing for me to follow, she ducks back into her office and closes the door before she speaks. "*The Boy with the Cat* has sun damage now too."

"It never even sees the sun." That's another one of our Renoirs here, and like the *Young Girls at the Piano* at the Louvre it's always protected from damaging UV light.

"I saw it today when I was out on the floor. And the restorers are coming right after they visit the Louvre." Adaline falls into her desk chair and rubs her hands over her face "Claire called me today. The sun damage is back on the *Young Girls at the Piano* too."

Back.

I sort through the timeline in my head. The damage had been repaired before the painting went to the Louvre, but when I'd seen it there, the fading had returned, but Claire hadn't been able to see the damage.

And now, a few weeks later, she can.

What does that mean, that other people can see what only I had been able to see before? Nothing good, I'm sure.

"I have no idea what is happening," Adaline says.

From what I can tell, two vastly different things are happening to the art. There's the simple fading of the Renoirs that appears like sun damage. Then there are the more drastic, more destructive changes to the others, like Bathsheba falling to pieces, like the flame in the La Tour.

I dread asking my next question, but I have to know. "What about *Woman Wandering in the Irises* though?"

Adaline breathes deep and her shoulders relax. "Perfect. Thank God."

"That's good." I'm dizzy with relief. It seems selfish to worry more about one painting than all the others. But Clio is different, more than paint and canvas. She's the woman I want to spend my nights with, and she's alive in that painting. "And I'll be sure to check the other Renoirs in the museum for sun damage," I say, then I rush off for my scheduled tour.

I meet the group on the main floor and guide them through the galleries, stopping at the featured paintings. One of them is another Renoir, a portrait of a woman, *Gabrielle with a Rose*. She is half-dressed, wearing a shawl over her shoulders, holding a rose near her ear.

As I promised Adaline, I scan quickly for any sun damage, and my heart catches when I see that a tiny sliver of her painted shawl has turned pale.

If this follows the pattern, then in a few days, Adaline will be able to see the fading too. First things first—I force myself to focus on the tour group here in front of Gabrielle.

"Renoir painted until late in his life, and this is one of the last masterpieces he created," I tell them. "By that time, he was crippled with arthritis." Curling my fingers into claws, I demonstrate. "He strapped the paintbrushes to his wrists and painted like that because his fingers were too gnarled to hold the brushes anymore. And yet, even with his damaged hands, he still crafted such works of beauty."

I take a step back and let them admire the painting before we move on to the next. One of the last on the tour is Van Gogh's *Portrait of Dr. Gachet*.

"This is the physician who treated Van Gogh in the final months of his life. This is one of only two authenticated paintings of Dr. Gachet. The other sold for more than eighty-two million dollars at auction."

That's always a good note to end on, since the price of art at auction is a topic that baffles but intrigues people. It usually provokes some animated conversations after I thank everyone and wish them a good day.

Today is no different, as two Americans stand in front of the red-and-blue Van Gogh and marvel at such a price. I'm about to leave them to their debate when a man clears his throat loudly enough to interrupt the couple.

"Great art demands a great price," the man says.

I search out the voice and am surprised to see Max, the artist I pass almost every day drawing caricatures by the river. "You have to be great—have great talent—to make art that matters," he adds.

I don't know Max well, but this doesn't sound like the guy who joked about horses the other day. The pair in front of the Van Gogh do that smile Americans do when they don't know how else to respond and then make an awkward exit with the last of the tour group.

Max, though, strides over to me and lifts his chin defiantly. "Your painting is a fake."

I blink, unable to put that into context. "I'm sorry?"

"*Woman Wandering in the Irises*. It belongs to *my* family." He stares at me with unflinching eyes, and a thick curl of dark hair slides onto his forehead. "To my parents."

"Whoa. I don't think so." I want to ask how a street artist could even own a Renoir, but I suppose that's elitist. For all I know, his family could be reclusive millionaires, collectors who live in a castle full of Dr. Gachets. In his ratty sweatshirt with worn cuffs hanging down to his fingernails, Max could be some kind of family rebel, I suppose.

Sweatshirt. The other night, leaving the museum after my date with Clio, didn't I see a guy in a sweatshirt and jeans lounging on the steps? It certainly could have been Max. But why? Had he been watching me? Or was he staking out the museum?

He's definitely confronting me now, tapping a black leather folder he's carrying. "I have the papers to prove it," he says.

That shakes me out of my dazed confusion. "How come you've never mentioned this all the times I saw you by the river? You knew I worked at the Musée, and it's been in the news that the Renoir was coming here. Why are you just bringing this up now?"

"It was not part of our conversations," he says. His voice is off somehow, like the words and cadence don't quite fit. "And if you'll just introduce me to your sister, I can resolve the matter with her."

Adaline has enough worries at the moment. More than that, though, there's the queasiness that sets in at the thought of Max—of anyone—taking Clio away.

Her painting is mine to keep safe. Mine to protect.

I motion for Max to follow me to the stairwell where we'll have some privacy, and I channel that desperate feeling into a voice of steady authority. "Show me the papers first," I say when the stairwell door closes behind us. "Then I'll take you to the curator's office."

Max still holds the folder against his chest like we're in a standoff. "It was ours," he insists. "It was stolen during the war, and we've been searching for it since then."

Reaching inside the folder and using only the tips of his fingers to handle them, he pulls out a sheaf of papers and hands them to me. A quick scan shows they claim his family bought the painting from Remy's family before the Second World War.

When Max leans closer to look at the papers alongside me, his breath smells like heavy rose perfume, like how I imagine the girls at their vanities in those Renoir paintings smell.

Max nods to the papers. "I would like to show Ms. Garnier the documents."

I'm not an expert on authentication, so even though it's the last thing I want to do, I lead him downstairs to my sister's office and introduce her to Max, who corrects me to say his name is Maximillian Broussard. He launches immediately into an impassioned assertion of his family's ownership of *Woman Wandering in the Irises*, and all I can think is, *You don't own Clio. No one does.* No one can claim her, and I vow to make sure that stays true.

As he talks, all I can think about is the woman I kissed last night, how warm and sensual she is, how clever and fun, and how sad she is at times . . . sad to be trapped.

I cannot let this man take her away.

I can't let anyone get their hands on Clio. I have to protect her until I can figure out how to help her.

Free her.

It's the first time I've let myself think it in so many words. But if she's trapped, then it stands to reason she can be let loose. I haven't a clue how, but I won't figure it out if Max or anyone else takes the painting out of the museum.

Adaline stands, looking remarkably poised and confident, considering the acquisition of *Woman Wandering in the Irises* might be the pinnacle of her career so far and this man is questioning it.

"Mr. Broussard," she says, "the museum has researched this painting's ownership thoroughly, but we treat provenance claims quite seriously. I will certainly look into this and be in touch after I confer with the board."

Opening the door, she flicks her gaze toward me, and I see a bit of "holy shit" when our eyes meet. It doesn't come through in her voice though. "Julien, can you show Mr. Broussard out?"

"Of course, Adaline," I say with the same formality— stiff upper lip and all that.

I guide Max upstairs, out to the gallery floor, and then to the main exit. "I am sorry to be the bearer of such bad news," he prattles, not sounding sorry at all. He leans closer and speaks in a low voice, the cloying rose perfume thick on his breath. "But some women can just be trouble, and they shouldn't be let out."

As he clips the ends of those last words, it's as if some force has vacuumed up all the sound, so there's only Max and me. *He's not just here for the painting.* He knows about the woman in the irises. But how? I suspect he's been watching me, but how could he spy on Clio as anything other than a painted figure in a frame?

I'm stuck with that thought as Max leaves. But once he's out the door, I step outside and watch him walk away from the museum. After he heads across the street, I follow him. He settles back into the green-slatted chair in front of his easel where he usually is, where he paints his bloody caricatures, then pushes up the cuffs of his sleeves.

When I see his hands, I nearly stumble. His fingers

are curled inward, the nails scratching his palms, bent up and seized.

Like Renoir's.

Then, he cracks his knuckles and turns his TEN EUROS sign around, and his hands are back to normal. Young, flexible Max's hands.

Clio's words about the ghosts of great artists come back to me. *Though you'd think they might visit museums too.*

What if she wasn't joking? Could the ghost of Renoir be inhabiting Max the street artist?

I walk over to Max as he reaches for his pencils. Grabbing the other green chair, the one his customers sit in while he does their caricatures, I plunk myself down.

"You seriously want your picture drawn?" He laughs a little, sounding like Max again, the street artist drawing exaggerated sketches of tourists.

"What was the deal with that back there?" I ask.

He frowns, and it looks genuine. "What back where?"

"Hello?" I gesture across the street. "In the museum?"

The side-eye looks authentic too. "I've been here the whole time. What are you talking about?"

"You were just on my tour," I press him, less because I think he's lying and more because I suspect he's not. "You had all those documents for the painting."

Max laughs. The dour guy he was a few minutes ago has vanished. "I don't know what you've been smoking, but can I have some of it?"

I stand and run a hand through my hair. I excuse

myself then walk across the bridge, trying to make sense of this newest wrinkle. Just when I've settled into the idea of living art, I learn that ghosts might be real too. The rose perfume smell, the hands—are those signs of ghostly possession?

No clue.

No bloody clue at all.

Who would know?

The only person I can think to ask is Remy. If there's anyone in Paris who might have something useful to say about ghosts, I'm betting it's him.

As I walk along the river, I ring him and launch into everything about Max.

"Interesting," he says pensively, and that's interesting too, since Remy is usually buoyant and bursting with words.

"Why is that interesting?" I press as a riverboat cruises by in the water below.

"My sister and I have been doing a little digging into forgers. We've gotten word that someone is back in business."

"Someone?" I ask, tension in my voice.

"Julien, let me call you in a bit."

"But . . ." I sputter, feeling desperate, needing to know what I can do to keep the *Woman Wandering in the Irises* safe.

"Good things come to those who wait," he says, and that's the Remy I know.

He hangs up, and I heave the most massive sigh as I stare at the screen.

With nothing to do but my final tour for the day, I

return to the museum, chat up another group about Renoir, Van Gogh, Monet, and more, and shortly after they disperse, Remy's name lights up my screen again. I duck into a stairwell.

"Can you get to the Marais in twenty minutes?"

"Sure. What part?"

He gives me an address. "Sophie has been casing a shop that may be a new forgery operation. And we think that's where that guy doctored up those papers your friend brought you today."

A thrill of excitement and relief whips through me. "I'll be there right away."

"And Julien? Bring that calf you won at the party. You never know when the Muses' dust might come in handy."

Ending the call, I grab my messenger bag containing the calf, head out the side exit, and dart into the nearest Metro.

11

The address is on Rue des Rosiers. The area is arty and fashionable, and I pass familiar shoe shops selling short boots with high heels, and stores hawking expensive tailored shirts for men. Along with fashion boutiques, this arrondissement is home to several museums and galleries, so I know my way around. I particularly like the Jewish deli—it's housed in an old dress store where blue mosaic tiles read "LES JOLIES JUPES" above windows now full of rugelach and challah bread.

I walk past a falafel shop where Simon hangs out in the evenings, holding court at one of the red vinyl booths, but it must be too early, because I don't spot him now.

The app on my phone tells me I've reached my destination, a vintage shop, the kind with a pastiche of goods from black lace skirts to silver tea sets to sky-blue vanities.

I grab the door handle and pull, but it's locked, and

then I notice a sign that says BE BACK IN FIFTEEN MINUTES.

I stare at it, befuddled for a moment, then turn around, scanning for Sophie. Behind me, the shop door opens, and a hand grabs my arm, and yanks me into the dim—and *closed*—shop.

Remy's sister lets go of my arm and shuts the door, then motions me back a few steps where we can't be seen through the front window.

"Did you break into this shop?" I ask.

Sophie waggles her hand in a so-so gesture. "I hid behind a dresser when I saw them put the rugelach out in the deli." Sophie points across the way to LES JOLIES JUPES. "I've been keeping an eye on this place since Remy and I caught wind of a potential forgery scheme. The other day I spotted the guy with the hair"—she mimes Max's flop of hair on her forehead—"come around. And I've been watching the shop since then to figure out when to slip in. The secret lies in the rugelach. As soon as the rugelach goes out over there, the shop owner *here* closes the store for fifteen minutes, has some with an espresso or sometimes a cigarette, and comes back. We have about ten minutes left before she returns."

"And who is she?"

Sophie takes her phone out of her jeans, unlocks it, then shows me the picture at the top of a news article from *The Guardian* about a year ago. A man and a woman are in the photo, but I don't bother to look closer because the headline rivets my attention.

"Forging Generations: Father and Daughter Con the Art World."

Their names are in the caption: "Oliver and Cass Middleton under investigation in fake Gauguin scandal."

The article dates from when they were nearly caught in a scheme involving a fake Gauguin. In the end, there wasn't enough evidence, and the case was dropped and the pair disappeared.

"You're joking," I accuse her.

Sophie swings the phone around and enlarges a different picture, showing that to me next. "No joke. That's who I saw walk right past me. Cass Middleton, in the flesh."

"So, we broke into the Middletons' shop. That's just great," I say, because running afoul of world-renowned con artists was not on my to-do list today.

"Technically, *you* didn't break in, I did. Though, *technically*, I didn't either. I was in, and I just *stayed* in."

"I don't know that master criminals are going to appreciate the difference," I comment, but I'm hardly running out the door. Is it strange that I am more afraid of Clio being stolen away from me than I am of being caught by these fraudsters? "Let's get on with it."

She leads me deeper into the store. The place is large, and the path through gilded mirrors and pastel hatboxes meanders like a maze.

At last, Sophie points to a door with peeling paint and a long scratch near the keyhole. "I already tried the door, and it's locked. But do you smell that?"

As we get closer, something familiar tickles my nose.

"India ink?" I ask. I'm not an expert, but I know it makes new documents look old.

"See? That's where they must have been dummying up the papers so your pal could claim *our* Renoir was his. And that *irks* me."

Irk. Such a funny word for such real vehemence. "You're not indignant just because it's a crime, are you? You feel a true connection to the painting, don't you?"

She rolls her eyes, then counts off on her fingers. "I'm indignant for many reasons. One. Because forgers suck. Two. Because my great-great-great-however-many-greats grandmother asked our family to keep that painting safe because of the curse on it."

"A curse?" I echo. What the hell? My skin prickles with this new intel. Is Clio trapped because the painting is cursed?

"That's why we had to keep it away from Renoir's family all these years. To protect the woman in the painting."

Some women can just be trouble.

Yes, Clio needs protecting.

And now it's my job, too, to look out for her. Because of everything I feel for her.

"What is the curse? This is the first I'm hearing of it," I press.

My head spins. Hell, it swims with facts and suppositions. With magic and mystery.

"I don't entirely understand all of it. But there's clearly some sort of curse on it to keep the woman trapped in it. I suspect it's because Renoir and Valadon didn't see eye to eye on something. Renoir believed art and inspiration were only for great artists," she explains. "Valadon didn't, and the Muses don't either."

Just when I think I've found the pattern, some random new piece drops in. "So . . . they talk to you too, the Muses?"

"Duh. How else would I know these things? The Muses believe that one day there will be an age of great artistic creation and expression." Sophie spreads her arms wide like she's embracing the invisible masses before her as she orates. "An artistic revolution that's for everyone." She points at me. "That's where inspiration comes in. Where *you* come in."

"Me?" Pointing must be contagious, because I tap my chest with my finger. "How so?"

She sighs loudly, impatiently. "The Muses have always been eternal, not mortal like we are. But they believe a human muse will come along, and that will mark the start of this new age." She taps me now, right on the sternum. "That's you, doofus."

Human muse? What now? "Sophie, what are you talking about?"

She throws up her hands and looks at the ceiling. "Didn't my brother tell you all this?"

Frustration gets the better of me, and I snap, "No one has given me a complete answer about anything!"

She cuts her eyes my way. "Then I will. The Muses have been expecting a human muse, and when they saw you hanging out with the Degas dancers one night, they figured out that you were the one. The one they've been waiting for. But since you're the first, you'll have to figure out for yourself what that means. Now, let's get into that room."

She says all of this as if she's giving me directions to Notre Dame from here. *Turn down this road, cross this bridge, and there you are—a human muse.*

I look from the locked door to Sophie and back again. I picture Max taking the papers out of the black leather portfolio earlier. The ink must have barely been dry, and he was trying to steal the painting.

Sophie says quietly, "I'm not putting you on, I swear. If you won't believe you're a human muse, then at least believe that you're the only one with the power to keep that painting safe. Perhaps the power to break the curse."

I pinch the bridge of my nose, wondering if this is any stranger than seeing Degas' ballerinas performing in the gallery or entertaining the idea that the ghost of Renoir is inhabiting Max.

I picture Clio looking up at me, picture her face as she edges around the subject of being trapped in the painting. She's as alive as I am, and if buying into this human muse business lets me save her, how can I reject the idea completely?

If I'm the only one who can keep her safe, then dammit, I'll have to do it.

Break the curse and set her free.

Looking over Sophie's shoulder to the door, I focus on the immediate and concrete problem. "The door is locked. We'll have to find another way in."

Her eyes are intense as she stares at me. *"You're* the

other way. You brought the calf, right? With the Muses' dust in it?"

Just go with it and remember it's for Clio.

I take the pink polka-dotted calf I won at the party from my messenger bag and hand it over. Sophie takes off the cap from the calf's fifth leg and taps some of the silvery dust into her palm. "Now, draw a key and touch it with the silver dust."

"Right, sure. No problem," I say with an eye roll.

But her expression is dead serious. "Please."

The sound of her voice does me in.

There is no joking, only earnest gravity. As I take out my sketch pad and a pencil, I remember how I'd rubbed my silver-coated hand across the page where I'd drawn *Olympia*'s cat and found a black cat's hair. I'd dismissed the oddity and forgotten about it, but maybe . . .

The lock on the door is the kind that takes an old-fashioned skeleton key. I put my pencil to the paper and draw a precise, pristine skeleton key.

When I tear out the page and put away my sketch pad, Sophie holds out her cupped hand full of the silvery dust. I dip my finger into the dust as if it's finger paint and then trace the outline of the key.

There's a silvery glimmer like sunlight on fish scales as the paper quivers on my flattened palm. A moment later, the weight changes, and instead of a sketch, I'm holding a key.

Exactly what I need for the lock.

12

The key has weight and shape, and when I bring it to my nose, I smell rusty metal. I want to laugh in amazement, cackle with glee.

I have officially blown my own mind.

Yes, I've put things back into their frames. But I just took an idea and made it into a thing.

A thing I need to put to use before the forger-slash-shopkeeper comes back.

Sophie's already at the door, gesturing for me to hurry. I fit the key into the lock, and it works perfectly.

The backroom is dim but not dark, and Sophie closes the door once we're inside. I tuck the key into my pocket and take a look around.

The room is the size of a large closet, and the faint light comes from atop a desk with a vintage green-shaded banker's lamp that could have come from a vendor in the store. The large ornate wooden desk stands proud against one wall. A cabinet is wedged into the corner.

Sophie is off and running, foraging through papers, wax seals from various art galleries, stationery from state-run museums, invoices of sales. All the tricks of the forging trade are here. One of the drawers is full of stuff to make the papers look older, like they have a history. At least convincing enough to fool the eye.

"Floppy Hair just picked up the documents today," says Sophie. "There has to be some evidence of what they were doing." She stops rooting around and looks at me expectantly. "Hello? We don't have all day. Try the trash can."

I stoop to pick through the trash. One minute I'm creating a key from paper and pencil, and now I'm pawing through someone's litter. "Nothing here but a few apple cores and some rubber bands."

"There has to be something. A slip of paper, a practiced signature . . . You saw the finished documents, Julien. Find something that looks like a first draft."

I rifle faster through the papers on the desk, then the papers in the drawers, then the papers in the filing cabinet. Nothing.

Then I catch a glimpse—a bit of paleness in the shadows. A handful of pages have slipped into the steep valley between the desk and the filing cabinet. I slide my hand along the desk legs, grab the pages, and pull them out. They're rough copies of fakes, first attempts at forged documents. My heart springs like a jack-in-the-box.

Because this is the evidence, the proof that Max, the street artist and, it seems, the host to Renoir's restless spirit, presented nothing but fake documents to the museum. He has no claim on the *Woman Wandering in the Irises*.

Sophie cocks her head like a dog alerting to a sound. Then she hisses, "Hide the papers. Put them in your trousers or something."

"Why don't I just put them in my bag?"

"Because someone could ask to search your bag." She goes soundlessly to the door. "Just hurry. And think of a good lie while you're at it."

She opens the door while I still have my hand down the front of my jeans, making sure the folded papers won't go anywhere awkward. "Hey!" I whisper.

"Hurry!" she hisses back.

I do, leaving the office and clicking the door shut behind me. I walk past old phonographs and stiff ballet slippers into the main path through the store, where I come face-to-face with one of the most cunning art forgers in the world.

13

Cass Middleton has wide-set eyes and an athletic build. With her tan and her blonde hair pulled back high in a ponytail, she looks like she could compete in beach volleyball, which makes me wonder if she's spent the last year lying low here or somewhere much sunnier.

I don't wonder about it long, though, because I'm worried about getting out of the shop without letting on that we were poking around, investigating her criminal activities.

"*Bonjour,*" she says. "Are you looking for something in particular?" Her voice is amiable as she speaks to us in French, a shopkeeper who doesn't want to lose a sale. But her gray eyes are sharp and piercing, like she smells a thief—or two.

I don't have a plan, but I improvise one in a hurry. "Sorry. I don't know French," I say, widening my eyes and adopting a flat, broad American accent. People are used to clueless tourists.

Cass Middleton repeats the question in English, in

her native British accent. "Were you looking for something in particular? Our store was closed for a few minutes, so I didn't expect to see anyone in here."

"Oh, gosh," I say, widening my eyes in innocence. "I didn't realize the store was closed. I just tugged on the door, and it opened right up." I laugh as I wave toward the street.

Something wiggles in my pocket where I stashed the key.

That's . . . unexpected.

It's moving around in there.

Awesome.

I turn quickly to the nearest display, arranged like a lady's dressing table, and grab the purple hat perched on a lamp. "We were looking at this hat. It's just the kind of thing we hoped to find in the Marais." I make sure to butcher the pronunciation. "Right, sis?"

Sophie nods, doing a good job of looking overwhelmed by all the Frenchness around us.

"It's a lovely hat," Cass says as the key wiggles a little more. "Shall I wrap it for you?"

"Yes. That would be great."

"I'm glad you enjoyed looking around," Cass says, appraising me with her stone-gray eyes. "My family and I pride ourselves on our unique items." She heads to the register and rings the item up. I drum my fingers against the counter as she wraps the fake gift, purchased by a real thief, from one of the preeminent fake artists of the last few years.

A real thief with a key shimmying in his pants.

I dip my hand into my pocket like I can settle it down. But then, it's gone.

Now you see it, now you don't.

Or rather now you feel it, now you don't.

I root around surreptitiously just to make sure, but nope. The key has vanished.

Good riddance, I say.

When Cass hands me my package and says, "Come back," I finally make my escape with Sophie, some euros poorer, but with proof of the fraud that will keep Clio's painting safe.

I wait until we're a block away from the shop before I turn to Sophie and say, "I thought your brother would be here by now."

She points down the street, and I look to see Remy walking toward us. "Did you find them? The fake papers?"

"Julien found them," Sophie gushes. "And you'll never guess what else."

I jump in before this becomes a game. "*What else* is what *I* want to know," I tell Remy. "Any other bombs you want to drop besides how I'm supposed to be this . . . human muse?"

Remy, no surprise, doesn't look repentant. He just glances at Sophie and asks, "You told him?"

She folds her arms, her chin jutting out. "You didn't."

"Yeah. It was the perfect timing, really, finding that out while we were breaking into an art forger's shop."

"Well, it was," Sophie insists. "Otherwise you wouldn't have been able to make the key to let us in."

Remy's gaze bounces between us. "I think I missed quite an adventure."

"I'm sure Sophie will give you all the details," I say, "since you tend to leave things out."

He laughs first, then catches the look on my face. "Julien, you're not seriously mad, are you?"

I sigh—one of Sophie's loud, *meaningful* sighs. I'm more irritated than angry. "You couldn't have said something the night we talked about all this at your home?"

"Would you have believed me back then?" he asks, about as serious as I've seen him.

"I don't know," I answer truthfully.

"I thought it would be too much at once," he explains, a note of apology in his tone. "I was worried you'd just walk away, and we need you."

Before I can reply to Remy, my phone rings, and when I look, I see that it's Simon. He rarely calls when he can text.

"What are you doing in the Marais?" he asks immediately.

"How do you know where I am?" I demand.

"Look falafel-ward."

I glance across at the falafel restaurant and see Simon give me a cocky wave through the window.

"Be right there," I tell him, then I hang up and turn to Remy. "Listen, I'm going to get something to eat and then give these papers to Adaline. She's really worried about the Renoir."

Remy frowns, looking like he might try and explain again, but I wave it off. "Don't worry about it. But maybe you should write up a user's manual, because this on-the-job muse training is the worst."

Remy gives me one of his open-handed shrugs. "You're the first one. Maybe you should write it yourself."

"Maybe I will."

I say *au revoir* to him and Sophie and head into the falafel house. I also pull the papers out of my jeans and look at them again.

"Hands in your pants again, Garnier?" Simon calls to me from his throne booth in the middle of the restaurant.

"Some days I just can't help myself," I say as I slide onto the bench across from him, dropping the bag with the hat next to me. Lucy is here too, sitting against him, two jigsaw pieces with interlocking edges that fit just so.

"What have you got there?" Simon asks, nodding to the papers in my hand.

"It's complicated."

"But is it interesting?" Lucy's voice is a purr, and her green eyes are the perfect complement to the emerald streaks that curve like streams down her cascade of dark hair. "Complicated can be dull. Or complicated can be fascinating."

"More of the latter," I tell her.

Simon slaps a hand on the table, decreeing, "Well? Let's hear it."

Where should I start? Muses. Dust. Paintings that come alive. The voices I heard in Remy's cellar. Voices that sounded like poetry, like history, like music, like art.

"Do you believe in Muses?" I ask Simon and Lucy.

He pulls her closer, which I didn't think was possible. "I believe Lucy is my muse," he says, then ducks in for a quick kiss.

"And what does she inspire you to do?" I ask, ignoring their sappy grins.

"To order falafels," Simon says. "Want one?"

"Sure."

He raises a hand, and the waiter appears as if by magic.

Magic. The word rolls through my brain like a marble in a tilting maze. There is magic in Paris. Magic in art, magic in dust, magic in my hands. I can't help the grin that spreads, big and wide, over my face. These things are real, and they're magic, and they're happening to me.

Clio is real, and *she* is happening to me.

But there are also curses, and art getting sick at the Louvre, and Renoirs fading from sunlight they never see. If there's good magic, wouldn't there be bad magic too?

After we order, Simon returns to the question. "So, Muses. You mean the nine ladies who inspire artists, writers, musicians, and so on?"

"Yes. Those Muses."

"Sure, I believe in them," he says, surprising me a little.

"As you should," Lucy offers. "The Muses are powerful women."

I chuckle silently. Not all muses are women. "No argument from me."

There's a pause while I tap my fingers on the table, wondering how much of the truth I can share. The thing is, I have to tell somebody *something*, even just part of it, or I'll burst.

"So," I begin, "there's this guy who came into the museum claiming to own the Renoir painting we just hung, when he clearly doesn't. So I followed him out of the museum, and, long story short, I found these documents." I put my hand on top of them on the table. "They're versions of the fake papers he offered Adaline as proof that he owns the painting."

"Look at you." Simon grins as if he's proud of my cunning. "You've gone from cat burglar to detective."

"I'm just full of special skills. Speaking of," I say, "can you put yours to good use and research someone for me?"

"Anything for a cat-burgling detective."

I give him Max's full name and ask him to research his family, who they are, where they've lived, what they've done, and any notable details about them.

"Do you want us to follow him too?" Lucy asks, and her eyes light up, mischief in full bloom. She turns to Simon. "Wouldn't that be fun?"

"What I did for my summer vacation," Simon quips, narrowing his eyes and shifting them back and forth. "Espionage."

"Actually," I say, my thoughts racing, "that's not a bad idea." Sophie seems to be doing Remy's legwork. Simon can help me with mine. "That would be great if you would."

The waiter brings our food, and we eat. Then I remember the hat, and on impulse, I ask, "Lucy, would you like a purple hat?"

"I would *love* a purple hat," she says, and then coos when I hand it to her. She models it, tilting her head just so.

"That hat is turning me on," Simon says, which is my cue to leave. I place some euros on the table, and the pair of them barely seem to notice.

Walking back across the city, I rehearse a slightly more detailed version of what I told Simon about my discovery of these papers, because obviously I'm going to have to tell Adaline *something*, even if it's half-truth and half-fable.

But overall, I count the day a win.

Especially since Clio isn't going anywhere.

14

I spread the desserts out on a bench in one of the galleries. Using it as our table, Clio and I sit on the floor in front of Monet's picnickers. They have their own alfresco meal inside their frame but watch us with smiling eyes.

"This apricot tart is pretty much the best thing I've ever had," I tell Clio as I show her everything I've bought.

"Better than chocolate? I don't know, Julien. That's a tall order. Chocolate is pretty decadent."

"Mark my words. You'll be moaning in pleasure once you try it."

She arches a most flirty eyebrow. "Moaning in pleasure? All from a tart?"

And this is an opportunity if I ever saw one. "Take a bite, then, Clio," I say, my voice lower, a little smokier.

With her gorgeous eyes on me the whole time, Clio tastes it. "Mmm," she says, murmuring around the fork, then handing it to me when she's done. "That is decadent. I can't resist sweets."

I set down the fork, push my palms against the floor, and lean into her, closing my eyes, dusting my lips across hers. Tasting her sweetness. She moans, a soft little sound, but still an enticing one that makes me feel dizzy everywhere, that makes my head go hazy. She inches closer, kissing me back with more fervor, her tongue sliding between my lips.

Oh yes, I like this side of Clio.

I like her exploratory nature very much. The way she wants to kiss every night.

Her hands slide up my chest, then she ropes them around my neck and brings me closer as she deepens the kiss.

She flicks her tongue across my lips, and my skin sizzles everywhere from this passionate side I'm learning she has.

And it's a side that works for me. Oh hell, does it ever work for me. I nip at the corner of her mouth, then crush her lips harder.

Moaning in pleasure indeed.

Both of us.

Sighs and murmurs and soft groans fall from our lips, and for a few delirious seconds, I imagine sliding her under me, kissing her till her lips are bruised and bee-stung, till she's arching against me and moaning in so much more pleasure. Asking for me to make love to her right here, in front of the Monet. And honestly, having this woman in a museum might very well be the ultimate fantasy—her and art.

A shudder jolts my spine as I imagine bringing Clio to new heights here in front of priceless treasures.

Perhaps I have an art kink.

An art and Clio kink.

Someone chuckles.

I break the kiss, and both of us swing our gazes to the picnickers in the frame. Their smiles have turned into laughter.

"I guess we're putting on a show," I whisper, smoothing my hands over my shirt, like that'll knock the desire right out of me.

With a wicked grin, she runs a hand over her hair. "Not a bad idea," she murmurs.

I clasp a hand to my chest. "My, my. Someone has a naughty side."

She simply wiggles her eyebrows. "Perhaps I do."

I can't resist. I lean in to brush a kiss against her cheek, skating toward her ear. "And I love it."

"Good," she answers. "Also, you were right."

"About the tart?"

"Yes, it made me moan in pleasure."

I shoot her an appreciative stare. "Then we should have tarts every night."

A flash of sadness crosses her eyes, maybe remembering her sentence, but then it's erased. Her blue irises glint with mischief now. "I like that plan." She squares her shoulders, gesturing to the food. "Now, stop distracting me with your fantastic lips. You're such a show-off when it comes to your kissing talents."

I laugh loudly. "Oh, shall I keep them to myself? Along with my other talents?"

"You better not. I want to know those talents," she says.

And my God, if this woman was going to my head before, she's carving out a permanent spot in it right now. Her directness and her confidence are so alluring.

"But I want more food before you introduce me to all your other talents," she says.

"Fine, fine," I say in mock annoyance as I shift my focus back to the spread. I show her the fruit crumble. "You know what the best part of a berry crumble is?"

"No. What's that?" she asks with an impish grin.

"You've got your five-fruits-a-day requirement right there. Blackberries, raspberries, strawberries, and blueberries . . . Well, four fruits. But close enough."

She smiles and tries the crumble. "I feel so healthy right now."

I point to the macaron I picked up at Pierre Hermé. "Now, this guy is one of those rock-star pastry chefs."

She raises an eyebrow. "What does that mean? Rock-star chef?"

True, there were likely no famous chefs and certainly no rock stars in her day. "He's written books. His stores are a must-see for tourists from all over, and the lines go out the door. He mixes absurd flavors together, and people love it." I pick up one of the macarons along with its napkin and slide it onto her palm. "I got you a grapefruit-wasabi macaron. I figured you had probably never tried that combo before."

She takes a bite, and maybe a second later, her eyes go wide and water. "My nose is on fire," she says, with a laugh.

"Maybe they skimped on the grapefruit and just put wasabi in."

"Oh, there's definitely grapefruit flavor in there too," she says, dabbing at her streaming eyes, but she's grinning. "The tartness makes my tongue curl, and the burn makes my palate sting, but it was still delicious."

I grin at her description. "You should do food reviews."

She laughs. "What's your favorite food?"

"Me? I like everything. But you can never go wrong with pizza. Or fries. Or chicken. Or roasted potatoes. Or sandwiches. I can pretty much eat all day."

She laughs and leans closer to pinch my stomach. "But you hardly seem like you eat all day."

I laugh too, because I'm ticklish, then catch her wrist. Only, instead of pulling her away, I hold her hand against my side for just a moment. "I walk a lot," I say when I let her go. I like her touch, like even better that she initiated it. I distract myself by telling her, "Walked a lot today, actually. All over the city. Crazy day," I add, shaking my head.

"Why? What happened?"

"More like what *didn't* happen. First, this guy showed up claiming he owns your painting." Clio's eyes widen, her brows climbing. "But the same guy is connected to a pair that have been acting suspicious in Le Marais, so my friends had been tailing them, and when we put our information together, we figured out they've been forging documents."

I notice her expression and realize she could use some reassurance. "We found the fake papers, though, so that's not an issue anymore. But Sophie and Remy—my friends—think there's a curse on your painting."

"A curse. Interesting." The vulnerability in her rounded eyes fades, and she's veiled and private again.

I've learned that pushing her when she gets enigmatic like this does no good, and I haven't gotten to the best part yet. "But wait, there's more." I allow myself a tiny dramatic pause. "I found out that I can draw things and they come to life."

With that, she's lively again, eyes bright, voice rising with excitement. "Show me! Show me now."

"Really?" Her enthusiasm surprises me.

"You think I don't want to see that?"

That's just what I think. She's seen much more impressive things. She *is* one of those things. But I don't remind her of that when she's looking so eager.

I reach into my messenger bag for my notebook, pencils, and the pink polka-dotted calf. "Okay, what do you want me to draw for you?"

"Hmm. Not flowers. I've seen plenty of those. And with all this deliciousness"—she sweeps her hand toward the food—"we don't need chocolates."

I glance at her slender neck. "A necklace, maybe?"

She looks sharply at her bracelets, one on each wrist. There's barely any space between the metal and her skin, and I don't see a clasp on them. "I detest jewelry."

"So that's a no on flowers, jewelry, and chocolates for you."

Suddenly, she sits up straighter. "Wait! I've got it. Do you know what I desperately want?"

I know I want to give it to her. "Tell me."

"A new pair of shoes." She pulls up the hem of her long skirt, revealing a pair of formfitting beige slippers. "I want something fun. Something modern. But I have no idea what's in style. Do you?"

Shaking my head, I chuckle at the idea. "I don't really follow shoe fashion. Or any fashion, actually." Then I remember, vaguely, the shoe store window in the Marais earlier, and I take up a pencil. "What about some short boots?"

Clio's eyes twinkle with delight. "Yes, boots." She taps her chin. "Can they be red? A cherry red?"

"Like your lips?"

"Julien," she says playfully, but she's not embarrassed so much as . . . enticed.

"Well, that's an accurate description of your kissable lips."

"Cherry red after you've kissed me senseless, maybe, like you do every night," she says, in a feathery voice that makes me want to say screw the drawing, and just screw . . .

But I'll take my time with her.

I'll be a gentleman. I sense she needs that. *Time.*

And I want to give her more than just shivers, more than just bee-stung lips. I want to give her wonderful nights.

And shoes.

I want to give her shoes.

I press a soft kiss to her lips, then focus on the artistic mission at hand.

I start to draw. "I have to warn you though. They'll only last for a few minutes. That's how it went with the key and cat hair anyway," I say, flashing back on the first night the cat hair appeared, then vanished. The same lifespan applied to the key. So I've got to imagine these shoes will be temporary too.

Imagine.

Seems so much of my life is imagined. But yet, it's as real as the shoes are about to become.

"Then I will enjoy them for all of those minutes," she says with a grin.

I sketch out a pair of shoes, with Clio giving me directions like I'm a police sketch artist. Redder, higher, and not such a pointy toe. "Like this?"

"Perfect."

"Here goes." I tap out a sprinkle of the Muses' dust onto the drawing and trace the shoes with my fingertips. Seconds later, they become three-dimensional.

Clio brings her palm to her mouth. "That's amazing." She takes off her slippers and pulls on the boots, then stands and twirls, holding up her skirt to show me the shoes.

"They fit perfectly," she says with wild delight. "I feel like Cinderella."

And I feel like a rock star. "You look stunning and ready for a night on the town as a modern, stylish, sexy Cinderella."

"Ooh, where would you take me?"

I stand and pretend I'm appraising the ensemble, though I'm really just enjoying the view of her. "I'd draw you a pair of jeans, a tank, and I say you're ready to go clubbing with me in Oberkampf."

"I love dancing." She catches my hand and steps close, into a ballroom dancing pose, and pulls me into a few steps. She quickly stumbles, though, and catches herself with a giggle. "I never said I was any *good* at dancing though."

Smiling, she does a turn on her own, her skirt rippling out. I am sad not to have my hand on her waist anymore, but happy to see it looks like she feels the same way.

"I've always been better at painting," Clio says, spinning more slowly. "Or, at least, having an eye for paintings. Like that one."

She stops turning and points to a Monet, an image of a street celebration in Paris in the late 1870s. "I remember when this was first exhibited."

"What was it like? Seeing this for the first time? Before Monet became, well, Monet as we know him today."

"It was heaven." Her lips part as if she's about to say something more, but she stops. Her question, then, seems to change its course. "What did your friends tell you about this curse?"

"Not much. They—Suzanne Valadon was their great-great-great-grandmother or something—only said that Renoir cursed your painting. There wasn't time to ask more than that, so I don't know how, or even if, artists can curse a painting."

I end with a shrug, as if it's not a big concern of mine, but I'm watching her closely as she silently looks at the calf then back to her shoes. I give her the chance to say more, but she doesn't.

"Is there a curse on your painting, Clio?" I ask gently. "Is that why you're trapped?"

"My shoes are starting to disappear."

I take her elbow so she doesn't trip again as the shoes dissolve into dust then vanish. Her feet are bare now.

She wiggles her toes. "I miss my shoes. I'll have to ask you for a new pair every night."

"I'll happily draw you a pair every night, then."

She's quiet again as she laces up her slippers. I care too much about her to be impatient but also too much not to try to understand her. "You're different than the others. You were trapped until you came to a museum, but now that you're alive again, can you just leave? Walk out the doors?"

"I think I probably could." She's pensive about the idea. Me, I hate everything about the thought of her leaving here without me, but I'm trying to figure things out. "In fact," she goes on, "I bet you could hold the door open for me, and I'd be on my way." I hold my breath until she shakes her head. "But I don't actually want to leave right now. I don't want to go back."

I'm lightheaded with relief, but then I wonder what she means by "back." I would think she'd walk out into the twenty-first century, that she'd stay in this time and place. Does she mean she'd be transported somehow to where she started, if not *when*?

Instead of pursuing that down a hypothetical and possibly depressing avenue, I use it as a chance to ask more about her—what's made her into the person she is now.

"So, what's 'back'?" I ask as conversationally as I can. "Where are you from?"

She waves a hand as if she's dismissing the question.

"Do you have a family?"

"I was very close with all my sisters. But we worked all the time."

"What kind of work?"

"This and that," she says in that evasive way she sometimes has. She seems to want to be close to me, to flirt and talk and play and kiss, and to invite me to share all of that with her, no-holds-barred. But talk of her history, of her story, makes her dart and dodge. "That's why I don't want to go back just yet. I'd just have to work again. I got tired of working."

It seems too cruel to point out that wherever her home is, it likely doesn't exist anymore, at least not as she remembers it. Her sisters aren't waiting around for her to pick up the household chores.

"Besides," she says, and her eyes are playful now, "the other reason I don't want to leave is I rather like this handsome man who visits me in the museum."

That decides it. No more questions about where she would go if she walked out of the museum. I grin and let myself be buoyed by the effervescent humor in her eyes.

"Is that so?" I step closer to her.

"I do. I do like him. He brings me sweets, and he takes me to the ballet, and he makes me shoes." She leans in and whispers like it's the most scandalous thing, "And he kisses me. In ways that drive me wild. That make me want more than kissing."

A groan works its way up my chest.

More.

I want that too.

"Say the word, and I'll give you anything you want."

"The word," she says, so deliciously that heat rushes over my skin, and I want to grab her hand, rush down the hall, and dart into that little alcove right behind *Starry Night.*

A quiet tucked-away corner.

No mystery is more interesting to me than the question of what it would be like to explore her body. How would she feel and taste? Would it be as life-changing as the first time we kissed?

I hear footsteps before I can tug her away and find out, and Gustave pops into the gallery. Have I lost track of time, or is he changing up the path and timing of his patrol through the rooms?

"Hey, Julien," he says, coming farther in when he sees me, which makes for a third option—that he was looking for me. And maybe Clio? "Want to hear something crazy?"

"Sure," I say nervously, because I don't have a clue how he'll react when he sees I'm not alone. But he doesn't acknowledge her, only me, even when she steps between us. So . . . Gustave can't see her?

She whispers, "This will be fun," so close to my ear that I only resist pulling her against me because kissing the empty air would be hard to explain.

Gustave fiddles with a bit of wire and some shiny red stones as he leans a shoulder against the wall, as if settling in for gossip. "I just talked to my buddy who runs the night shift at the Louvre. Says he saw a lemon fall out of a de Heem over in one of the galleries a few minutes ago. They were adjusting it for that Interiors exhibit or something."

Now he has my full attention. "Really?"

"Can you believe that?" Gustave shakes his head. "What a loon. Used to play rugby. Think he may have taken too many hits to the head back then."

"Hmm, yeah. That does sound crazy," I say. But what I really want to know is why lemons are dropping for this buddy of Gustave's. Could he be another human muse?

I try not to look at Clio's fingers plucking playfully at my T-shirt, try not to flinch when she taps my ticklish stomach. Have to stay still in front of Gustave. "What did he do with the lemon?"

"Threw it out," Gustave says, and my heart lurches. "Said it was stinking the whole joint up."

So, not another muse, then. Maybe there is no instruction manual, but that's just not what you do with art.

"Bizarre," I say absently. I'm thinking about my visit to the Louvre, the fire leaping into my hand, Bathsheba's drooping belly—and now, a lemon gone rancid. It's as if the art is throwing itself overboard, casting itself off the cliff of the canvases into the sea. But why is the art over there going full lemming while the Renoirs here are simply fading?

"You're telling me," Gustave says.

I can't think about the Renoirs without a pang of worry over Clio's painting. Worry over Clio. While

Gustave's attention is on the stuff in his hands, I look at her, but she's watching whatever he's doing, so now I have to look too.

"Can I ask . . .?" I point at the smooth copper wire and what looks like a fake ruby he's twisting it around.

Gustave frowns and holds it up. "I just can't figure out how to make this look right. I'd wanted to enter it in a subway art contest."

When I see the whole thing, I *see* the whole thing— where the wire should go, what twists and bends would make the piece look both edgy and clever.

"Maybe if you bend the wire through the ruby so it's like . . ." I demonstrate the angle I mean. Gustave looks at my hands, at the wire, at the rest of the miniature sculpture, and then something clicks for him—I can almost hear it. He does as I suggested, then lifts the piece and views it from different angles. "That does look good. Thanks, Julien." He chuckles and straightens up. "I think I'm going to call it Crazy like a Lemon." With a little wave, he turns to go back to his post near the front doors.

With him gone, I turn to Clio to ask her what she thinks about the lemon at the Louvre. But she's grinning at me—absolutely beaming—and words slip away from me.

But not from her.

"You're the muse," she says, wonder in her voice.

Her smile grows, spreading wider and etched with awe.

Not just that—happiness, excitement . . . and relief, like something long-expected has arrived.

You're the muse.

She's been waiting on *the muse*.

My world does another seismic shift. "You know about that?"

"That there would be a human muse someday?" She nods slowly, her eyes alight with happiness. "But I didn't know until you helped the guard just now that it would be you."

I run my hand through my hair, smiling ruefully. "It's new information to me. I don't entirely know what to make of it. But the whole thing doesn't seem as ridiculous when you say it."

She gasps. "There is nothing ridiculous about inspiring people to create things of beauty. Just think of a world without—"

"Slow down," I say, smiling at her passion for art. "I meant, 'human muse' sounds either pretentious or silly, except from you."

Clio makes it sound like something I want to be.

"Well, obviously," she says.

"What's obvious about it?"

She seems flustered for a moment, but it's gone so quickly I might have imagined it. "*Obviously* it seems much more reasonable coming from the woman from the painting."

I laugh, shaking my head. "Good point."

Gesturing to all the art I've interacted with, she admits, "Truthfully, I feel like a bit of a fool for not realizing it sooner." Her tone shifts to mischievous as she strolls closer.

"Do you now?" I match her playful turn.

One shoulder lifts in a shrug. "Well, I mean, how else would you be the only one to see me and the other paintings?"

"What about the guy Gustave mentioned? The lemon at the Louvre."

She shakes her head. "Forget the Louvre right now. Forget lemons." She trails a finger down my arm, sending heat to every point in my body, returning my thoughts to *more than kissing*, and only *more than kissing*. If a lemon fell from the sky or shot up through the earth to land in my hand, I'd toss it over my shoulder without a second thought.

"What lemons?" I ask, my eyes locked on her, as I take her hand, leading her to *Starry Night*, to the little nook away from the guards, away from everyone.

Where it can be just us.

Once we're there, her eyes swing behind us, checking for anyone, and then she smiles, all cat-that-got-the-cream. She backs up to the wall between two Monets—*The Artist's Garden at Giverny* on one side and *Regattas at Argenteuil* on the other. The way she leans her shoulders against the wall pushes her hips forward, hip bones jutting slightly beneath the gauzy fabric of her dress.

And she waits, expectantly, for me.

This is a dream. *She* is a dream. I have imagined this expectant, pulse-racing temptation since I first saw her on the wall at Remy's carnival of a home.

I've wanted her, all of her: lips, hands, mind, mouth, body.

Now I've gotten to know her, and my desire has intensified. Multiplied.

I step closer. "You know what you said a few minutes ago? About more than kissing?"

She nods, her lips parting slightly, and I can't look away from them. "Gee, I remember it perfectly."

"So sassy," I say with a wicked grin, cupping her cheek, then sliding that hand down to her shoulder, along her arm, to her waist.

Her eyes drop to my mouth. "Maybe I want kissing *and* more than kissing."

"At the same time?" I tease, my fingers toying with the fabric of her skirt as my hand travels lower to give her what she's asked for.

What my bold, confident, and sometimes enigmatic Clio wants.

More.

I crush my lips to hers, pressing my body against her.

Letting her know I want her too.

The second we collide, she gasps, a wonderfully needy sound that thrums through my entire being.

That drives me on.

I kiss her more deeply, and she answers by looping her hands around my back and grinding against me.

I heed the call too.

One hand holds her face. The other reaches the end of her dress, sliding under, traveling along her soft skin.

Her breath hitches the closer I get to the apex of her thighs.

My body heats, desire pounding through me as I cup

her, feeling her need, and she cries out, a desperate, gorgeous sound.

Then, she moans as I slide my fingers under the lace and against her, where she wants me.

I shudder.

She trembles.

I kiss her harder, a little deeper as my fingers explore all her lush wetness.

She moves with me, rocking her hips against my hand, seeking out more contact, more touch. And I listen to all her needs, all her wants, touching her the way she seems to crave.

We move and bend together.

We rock and moan.

But soon, kissing becomes too hard.

And our mouths fall away as I roam my lips across her chin, her jaw, my fingers playing with her, gliding over and in.

Soon, she's gasping, the sexiest murmurs in the world tumbling from her lips.

And my name too.

My God, the way she groans it as she's rocking against me, as her lips part, as her eyes squeeze shut, is the most sensual sound in the universe.

I stroke a little faster, crook my fingers just so, and when I see she's daringly close to shouting my name, God's name, a curse, I cover her mouth with mine, losing myself in her kisses, and she comes apart on my hand.

And nothing is better than this—the woman I am

falling so hard for reaching the heights of pleasure in the midst of the most beautiful art in the world.

Pleasure I gave her.

Pleasure I want to give her again and again.

Here, there, and on the other side of the gallery too.

Let the Monets watch. Let the Van Goghs gawk. Let all the Cézannes gaze at this woman and me as we tangle together in this museum in Paris after midnight.

Yes, I do have a Clio kink, and I definitely have an art kink.

Because I would really like to fuck her surrounded by all the masters.

* * *

After we clean up, we wander back to her frame, and she doesn't seem the least bit shy. Rather, she seems wildly delighted.

"So, that was decadent."

"Better than chocolate?"

She stops, running her finger along my bottom lip. "Better than an apricot tart."

"High praise indeed."

"The highest."

She takes a beat, her eyes locking with mine. "Can I do that to you?"

I laugh as my body screams *yes*. But practical me knows it's too risky. I bring her close, whispering in her ear, "I just want to make you feel good. There will be time for all sorts of other things."

She pulls away, arching a dubious brow. "I'm holding you to that."

"You can definitely hold me to it."

We reach her frame, and I can't resist another kiss.

We linger on each other with soft hints and mere whispers of kisses, until she says, "More," and crushes her hungry lips against mine in a feast of kissing.

At some point we break apart to breathe. "Tomorrow, I want you to come to my place," she says, so much mischief in her blue irises.

"The gardens?" I ask, processing what she's asking, a new possibility unfolding.

"Yes, and I'm going to hold you to it."

I groan in pleasure. A big art kink indeed.

I start counting down the hours.

15

I see a familiar face in my only tour the next day, and it's a welcome one this time. Emilie gives me a little wave and then a quick smile when I notice her in the group.

I wish I had seen her before we started. I want to ask if she's heard from the Paris Opera Ballet. It's so easy to imagine her on the stage. Even the way she moves around the gallery is graceful but powerful, as if a swan mingled with a leopard to make her.

When we stop at the Degas I've gotten to know, though, I do a double-take. How have I not noticed before that Emilie is a photocopy of Emmanuelle? She's older, but with the same delicate bones, the same black hair and milky skin.

"You look just like her," says a round woman standing next to Emilie, so I know I haven't imagined the likeness. "Maybe you're related."

The group turns their eyes on the flesh-and-blood girl, and Emilie's ears flame red.

"You never know," she says, glancing away.

The attention seems to make her uncomfortable, so I jump in and guide the group to the next painting, taking the scrutiny off of Emilie, catching her relieved and grateful smile.

When the tour ends and the group disperses, she lingers behind, as I'd hoped she would. I find her near the Van Gogh, tilting her head as she gazes at Dr. Gachet in his royal-blue coat.

"So?" I say, and she turns to smile shyly at me. "Are you dancing under the chandelier now?"

Her smile transforms into one that's broad and beaming. "And hanging out with the Phantom in the underground lake. But he hasn't crashed the chandelier yet."

"I knew you'd get in!" I grin, oddly proud of her, despite barely knowing her. "That's amazing. Congratulations!"

"Thank you." Then there's a pause, and Emilie seems to start and stop for a moment, before saying, "Would it be weird if I asked if you want to grab a coffee with me?"

"Weird to get coffee?"

"Weird for me to ask. The coffee is just coffee." She waves a hand vaguely. "Lucy is my only friend outside of ballet, and you know how she and Simon have been grafted onto one another."

I laugh, because that's accurate. "Sure. That would be great."

We leave and walk around the people lounging on the steps of the museum, stretched out in the warm August sun. I tense when I see Max on the sidewalk, but he's sketching a young couple, moving his pencil quickly across the paper. His hands are normal, supple.

Is normal Max a sign that thwarting Renoir's forgery efforts has banished his ghost to. . . wherever the spirits of artists go?

As Emilie and I weave past him, I say hello. It's like poking a bruise to see if it's healing. "How's it going, Max?"

"Going great," he answers, sounding like the Max I know. "Just found out I'm going to be teaching a class on caricature at an after-school program. Applied for the gig a few weeks ago. I'm stoked."

"That's great." And I mean it. The real Max is personable and will enjoy talking about what he loves, I'm sure.

He laughs. "Pretty soon, a whole generation of French youth will be drawing pointy chins and big noses."

I laugh too, relieved that Max has regained sole proprietorship of his own body.

Emilie and I pop into a café and order coffee.

"So, that Degas. You might not believe this, but you want to know why I got so red when that woman said what she did about me looking like the woman in the painting?"

"Red?" I ask, straight-faced. "I hadn't noticed."

She pretends to swat at me. The waiter brings our coffees, and Emilie stirs sugar into hers.

"Try me," I say. "You'd be surprised at the things I believe."

She hesitates than plunges, the words rushing out.

"I'm like the great-great-great something of some Degas dancer." Her nose wrinkles with an embarrassed grimace. "That's what my mother tells me, at least. It sounds crazy, doesn't it?"

"Emilie, that doesn't sound the least bit crazy." Or if it does, her crazy is nothing compared to mine.

"So, she was supposedly this amazing dancer. Her name was—"

"Emmanuelle." We say it in unison.

Emilie's mouth falls open in shock. "How did you know her name?"

I wave to dismiss my gaffe and improvise, "It must have been in the description in one of the catalogs."

That actually makes more sense than the truth.

"Sometimes I wish I weren't related to her," Emilie says with a sigh. She rests her chin on her hand, and I hear the faintest notes of music again, just like I did at the café in Montmartre.

"Why would you wish that?"

"It's too much pressure. I'll never live up to it."

The strains of music grow louder. Emilie's gaze is turned inward, so I glance around to see where the melody might be coming from. Thing is, I have a feeling, but I need to rule out mundane possibilities. "Do you hear that?"

"Hear what?" She looks around too.

"It sounds like flutes." I point to the ceiling speakers, even though the music surrounds Emilie, wreathing her in melody. "You haven't heard them at all?"

"No, but is the music pretty, at least?" She sounds amused.

I smile. "Very much so. But tell me why you think you won't live up to her?"

The music has become distinct now. The string section comes in, and the melody turns to three-four time. This waltz is familiar—iconic, even, recognizable without even knowing the ballet. The source isn't the café's sound system, but the down-in-the-dumps ballerina in front of me.

"Because I'm awful." Emilie sinks deeper into her propped fist. "I'm rehearsing right now for—"

"*The Sleeping Beauty,*" I finish.

Emilie sits up straight and gapes at me. "How did you do that *again*? How did you know?"

I shrug. "Just a guess."

It's like when I saw exactly how Gustave could finish his art piece, as clearly as if I had read a schematic. He only needed a final touch of inspiration. With Emilie, I hear music when she needs a boost of confidence.

I don't know how Remy's eternal Muses work, but this is how *I* work. Finally, something for my Human Muse User Manual.

Desperately, I wish I could text Clio and tell her my insight, right now, while I'm still giddy from it.

"A guess?" Emilie narrows her eyes then wags a finger at me. "Or perhaps you looked at our calendar and know that's the next ballet of the season."

"That must have been it. I'm sure I read it somewhere. I bet you'll even get a solo."

As soon as I say it, the music fades, like someone has closed the doors of the orchestra hall.

"I'm trying out for one." Emilie's shoulders have

relaxed, and so has her smile. "And thank you for saying that. I don't know why, but I always feel so much better about my dancing after I talk to you."

"I'm glad. You *should* feel good about your dancing."

"Will you come to the performance?"

"Name the time. I'm there."

She gives me a time and a date a few weeks from now, and we finish our coffee and say goodbye, both of us feeling good about the encounter.

But good feelings don't always last.

* * *

On my walk back to the museum, my phone pings with a text.

Remy: Julien, *mon ami*!

Julien: That's not at all a suspicious way to start a conversation.

Remy: *C'est vrai.* But promise to consider that I am but a lowly messenger for the powers that be.

Julien: What does that mean?

Remy: It means "Don't shoot the messenger." Here goes. The Muses want to know how everything is going with the *Woman Wandering in the Irises.*

Julien: Oh, really. The Muses want to know? Did you get an email, or do they communicate by skywriting?

Remy: Don't be absurd. They write a note and leave it in the basement.

Julien: Oh, well, of course. I'm heading in to work right now. That is a hint to get on with telling me the message.

Remy: Yes, of course. The woman in the painting—they want to know how she is.

Julien: Tell them she's fine.

Remy: Is she?

Julien: She's just great. Truly.

I make it up the stairs and wave to the guard at the reserved entrance. He lowers the rope and lets me through. The exchange gives my thoughts time to catch up, and I add another line, completely without sarcasm.

Julien: And tell them I do appreciate their concern.

Remy: I will.

I bound down the steps to the main floor, but then stop short when I smell that rose perfume, thick and heavy. I turn around and see Max walking to the door with that out-of-sync gait. I get a good look at his hands; they're curled up into the cuffs of a long-sleeved shirt. My chest tightens—that's not really Max at all.

What is Renoir up to now?

I suppose he could be up to nothing more sinister than gazing at his own masterpieces and reminiscing.

But I highly doubt it.

My sister is alone in the break room, head propped in her hands over a cup of tea. Even though a teabag still dangles over the rim of the cup, the drink has stopped steaming.

I reach behind me and close the break room door without her asking. "What's wrong?"

She pinches the bridge of her nose and slumps against the back of the chair. "It's Gabrielle," she says, mentioning the Renoir.

"The sun damage?"

"Yes. Her painting has it now too. On her shawl." I take the seat across from her in wordless sympathy, trying to keep calm, at least on the outside.

"And it's not just us now." Adelin's voice hitches with despair. "The *Young Girls at the Piano* is fading even more at the Louvre. And I heard from the Museum of Fine Arts in Boston today. *Dance at Bougival* is having problems too." Running a hand over her face, she says, "How is this happening? We didn't find any light coming in, and even if we did, Boston now makes three different locations. It's like the Renoirs are turning into ... *mall art.*"

Could the curse on Clio's painting be responsible?

Except that, while the problem might have worsened recently, the *Young Girls at the Piano* started to fade weeks ago, well before Clio's painting arrived here.

"What can I do to help?" I ask my sister as much as my boss.

"You have such a good eye, Julien. You noticed the problem with the *Young Girls at the Piano* long before anyone else. If you would go over all the Renoirs now— really fine-tooth comb them—that would give us a clearer picture of where we stand."

"Of course," I tell her. I round the table, and even though we're at work, I bend over and wrap my arms around her shoulders in a brotherly hug. "I'm so sorry you're having to deal with this."

She pats my forearm then gives it a squeeze. "I'm just sick about the damage to the art is all."

"I know. Me too." I squeeze her back and then straighten. "I'll get right on it—inspect those Renoirs like an auditor inspects a tax return."

At least that makes her chuckle.

With the museum's catalog pulled up on my phone, I start at the far end of the top floor and methodically work my way through the galleries. I know now why I can see the irregularities before anyone else.

On my inspection tour, I find trouble brewing on one more of our Renoirs. I send Adaline an email with the bad news that the masterpiece may soon join its fallen comrades, then let her know I'm going to head over to the Louvre and inspect the pieces over there.

I won't only be looking for sun damage though. I want to examine the warped paintings I saw the last time I was there, see if they're sicker.

I have to figure out what's going on before it hurts Clio.

16

It is August, so the Louvre is crowded everywhere and packed around the usual suspects—the Venus de Milo, works by Italian Renaissance old masters, and of course, the most popular resident of any museum anywhere, the *Mona Lisa*. It is always a zoo around her, with visitors holding their phones above the crowd to take pictures of the woman behind the glass, like it's some kind of Paris scavenger hunt.

Fortunately, none of the greatest hits are on my agenda. I head straight for the Interiors exhibit to check out the vanishing act pulled off by de Heem's lemon.

I locate the small frame quickly because I know what I'm looking for—it's a pint-size postcard of a painting that's easy to miss. And Gustave's buddy told a true tale—the painting is missing a lemon. Usually, it's perched near the edge of a table, the rind half peeled and the insides glistening tartly. It's as if it was never there at all.

I turn to a pair of travelers standing next to me—

two older women, American by their accents, possibly sisters by their matching brown hair and straight noses. "Excuse me. This may seem like a strange question, but do you see a lemon right there?"

I point to the spot where the lemon used to be, and one of the ladies laughs. "Is that a trick question? There's no lemon in that painting at all."

That's different since the last time I was here. Something has changed, making the alterations now visible to anyone. But still only I can see Clio—and it's the same when the other paintings come alive at the Musée d'Orsay.

But what has changed? Why can the visitors see the mutations of the art in the Louvre, and Adaline and the other curators see the fading of the Renoirs?

I hurry to the other galleries and reach the Ingres first. The drooping feathers in the odalisque's peacock fan aren't hanging out of the canvas anymore. Most are missing, like a rat tore them out, leaving behind a fan half the size. I locate the Titian next, with the woman looking at her reflection. What was a tiny fissure in her mirror is now an ugly crack down the middle.

The woman next to me is studying the painting thoughtfully, and I use the opportunity to say, as if it's a casual observation, "Funny, how she's looking at herself in a broken mirror, isn't it?"

Cocking her head, she considers it a moment more while I hold my breath. "It is. Like 'The Lady of Shalott,' but cracked up and down instead of side to side."

Bathsheba is next, and the change there is dramatic. Where her stomach had bulged out of the canvas before, now that belly is just gone, her stomach flatter, as if a plastic surgeon stopped by and gave the fleshy figure a nip tuck.

"That's one sexy biblical figure." The remark comes from a young German guy ogling the Rembrandt. "I don't remember her being such a babe, but she's got a rocking bod."

I run both my hands through my hair, pushing my palms hard against my scalp. Bathsheba has a rocking bod?

Regardless, I've discovered that other people can now see what I see, but they have no idea that they're gazing at art that's turning ill.

And I have no idea either how sick the art can get. Or whether I can do anything about it.

17

Simon is clearly James Bond. He's found where Max Broussard lives.

"You're 007," I say with an appreciative smile as we walk down a narrow stretch of sidewalk in Pigalle, an up-and-coming neighborhood, that's still quite ramshackle.

He blows on his fingernails. "My talent is boundless. And so is my affection for Lucy. Speaking of, she keeps asking me about Emilie."

Seeing where this is going, I try to deflect. "She's trying to set *you* up with her friend now?"

He rolls his eyes. "You know what I mean. Lucy wants us all to do something. The four of us. As two couples."

"Maybe she just doesn't want to hang out with you alone."

Simon reverses direction on the sidewalk. "On second thought, I don't have time to show you where Broussard lives."

"Kidding." I grab his arm and turn him back around, and we keep walking. Other than giving him a hard time, there's no reason to be cagey with Simon, so I test out the truth. "Thing is . . . there's kind of someone else I'm into."

"Really?" Simon raises an eyebrow as we cross an unevenly cobbled patch of street and turn onto an even narrower one. The dilapidated buildings around us tilt inward the slightest bit.

"Well?" Simon presses. "What's the story?"

My phone buzzes with a text—a quick look tells me it's from Sophie, who has been dogging Cass Middleton since we saw her a few days ago.

Sophie: Cass is up to something, going in and out of a church near her shop in the afternoons. Will stake her out tomorrow at this time and alert you, okay?

I tap back with a thumbs-up and tuck my phone into my pocket while I tell Simon, "It's complicated."

"Oh, well, don't tell me because my little pea brain can't handle it."

"It's just that it's still early."

"So how do you know her?" he asks.

"She hangs out at the museum."

"Have you talked to her? Asked her out?"

"Not exactly *out*."

"Do you need me to come by and do it for you?"

I can't decide whether to laugh or panic. "Ha. Hardly."

Finally, we reach our destination -- Max Broussard's home. The quiet side street squeezes between a graffiti-covered brick building on one side and what looks like a shabby sort of studio space on the other. Through the dirty windows of the building, I see the place is a mess, stacked with smocks and pottery wheels, kilns and sculptor's tools, sketch pads and pencils. "This is where he lives?"

"Nope. He lives there. In a connecting flat. Place can't be more than ten square meters. A total dive. Inherited it from his grandparents. His parents are gone too—died in a car crash. No family estate in Normandy to keep his priceless art in either." Simon points through the window at an easel holding a sketch pad with a drawing of a dog with floppy ears. "That's where he draws. This guy defines starving artist—living hand-to-mouth, barely making ends meet. No way does that bloke own a secret Renoir."

The big question, though, is why did Renoir choose this young artist to inhabit when Max isn't even a painter?

"And check this out." Simon unfolds a piece of paper from his back pocket and shows me a caricature of Lucy. It's cute—her green streaks look like wings in her hair. "Lucy makes a bang-up secret agent. She had him do her caricature across from the museum this morning so she could get him talking."

Across from the museum. Of *course*.

Location, location, location.

Renoir must have picked Max for his proximity to the Musée d'Orsay. Before Clio came, I'd never seen Max look like anyone but Max. Supposedly, Renoir was in love with the model for *Woman Wandering in the Irises*. Is this a messed-up stalking situation?

I peer through the window at the clutter in the studio, hunting for something, anything. On the floor by the easel are papers, sketches, comic book drawings of cats and dogs with oversize heads and snouts. But at the bottom of one of the pages, I can see a number and nearly illegible letters, as if written by an unsteady hand—19 Rue de . . . something. I make out the first three letters of the street name and realize it's the address for the shop with the Jack Russell in the window.

Zola and Celeste's gallery. The same one that verified Clio's painting for us before it came to our museum.

Chills race down my spine as we take off.

* * *

Simon and I race up the Metro steps and then make for the gallery. Inside, Zola is talking to a customer who's considering a pink painted canvas with a miniature metal skateboard sticking out of it. Gotta love modern art.

Zola smiles at us and holds up one finger to indicate she'll be done soon, and Simon and I walk around as she finishes.

A few seconds later, the bell over the door gives a

cheery ding as Zola shows the customer out and waves goodbye.

"And to what do I owe the pleasure of this visit?" she asks, sweeping over to first give me a kiss on each cheek, then Simon. "And from double-the-trouble gents, no less."

"We're tracing the path of someone," I say quickly, desperate for intel. "A little older than me, about this tall, dark hair, and . . ." I crunch up my hands to mimic Max's twisted fingers as Renoir. "Like that."

"Oh, yes. I remember him," Zola says, a gleam in her eyes. "He was wheeling an art crate in a little shopping cart because of his hands."

Tension winds through me. "Why was he here? What was in the crate?"

She motions for us to step closer. "He had what he claimed was a Renoir. He showed it to Celeste, swearing —we're talking adamant—that it was the original *Woman Wandering in the Irises*."

That can't be.

"What's hanging in the museum, then?" I ask, brow knit, worry digging into my bones.

"He had the gall to say the one at the Musée d'Orsay is a fake," she scoffs.

My jaw clenches. "That takes some nerve. There's no way that's true."

Zola leans against the counter. "Indeed. The man claimed that Renoir himself left the original to Broussard's family and specified that the painting never be shown, never be exhibited, never even be touched by anyone."

Never be touched . . .

There's something so tragic about those words applied to Clio. I can't imagine never having been able to touch her, hold her, kiss her . . .

Simon raises a hand, like he's in class. "But what's the point of painting something only to hide it away? And never look at it? Art is meant to be seen."

"What did Celeste say about his painting?" I jump in, offering a prayer that Celeste's eagle eye came through, spotted Ghost Renoir's fake for the fake it has to be.

Zola smiles slyly, like she's proud of her wife. "That it was a near-perfect replica, maybe one of the best she's seen, but it lacked Renoir's signature pigment."

Yes!

"What's that?" Simon asks. "Like a custom paint?"

"Renoir had a special pigment for his signature, so his own work would always be verifiable and unique," I explain, relieved that Celeste could tell easily.

Simon nods. "Got it. So that proves Broussard's painting is a copy?"

"Yes," Zola answers. "But interestingly, it's quite an old one."

That is interesting. "How old?" I ask, an idea taking shape.

"More than a hundred and thirty-five years old."

"As old as the original painting . . ."

My mind whirls. Remy didn't say how his great-great-grandmother actually got the painting in the first place. But I bet Suzanne Valadon made the copy to protect Clio. I bet she copied the portrait and swapped it out a hundred and thirty-five years ago, giving Renoir the fake, and keeping the original – the cursed painting with Clio in it – safe with her family over the years.

If Renoir thought he had successfully locked Clio away in a painting for the rest of time, he wouldn't look for her.

With a shudder I remember what Max said the first time he showed up on my tour—that some women are trouble and they shouldn't be let out.

Renoir wants Clio to stay trapped. Whatever magic keeps her in the painting can't be undone if she's in someone's attic. That's where he wants her. Hidden away.

That's it!

I want to fist-pump and shout, but I'm still in the gallery, and Zola and Simon are looking at me with concern, and I still have more questions because why would Renoir want to trap her? Why would he do this?

That's the next mystery for me to solve.

I thank Zola profusely, and Simon and I exit to the street.

As soon as we step outside, he says casually, "So, want to let me in on what's really going on?"

I turn to him. I'm not sure I could ask anyone but Simon this question, but we've been friends for a long time. "Do you believe in ghosts?"

"*Should* I believe in ghosts?" he asks as we set off walking.

I take him through my Ghost of a Great Artist Comes Back to Preserve His Legacy theory as we pass more antique shops and art galleries lining the street by the river. He nods thoughtfully as he follows along.

"And so Renoir's taken up cohabitation in this street artist Lucy and I have been tailing?" Simon asks when I'm done.

"Yes. And a bunch of Renoir's paintings are fading. Not just at the Musée d'Orsay, but everywhere. And somehow that's related to the *Woman Wandering in the Irises.*"

Simon shakes his head and claps me on the back. "It is truly never a dull moment with you, Garnier."

I stop walking. "Does that mean you don't believe me, or you do?"

"Does it matter? I'm your friend, and whatever you need me to do, I'm all in. Whether I believe in ghosts or not."

"All right. Whenever Remy figures out what's going on with Cass Middleton, you're coming with me then, okay?"

"As if I'd miss it."

"I'd better get back to the museum."

"To your complicated woman." His grin is knowing, and my sheepish shrug is an admission. It's not even a lie. I'm most definitely going to see my complicated, compelling Clio, who has invited me back to her place tonight.

18

Clio gestures to the gardens where she lives, a sly look in her pretty eyes. "Touch my painting."

I lift an eyebrow. "I thought you'd never ask."

She nibbles on the corner of her lips. "Right. I'm sure you didn't at all expect a little naughtiness."

I lean in, brushing a kiss to her sweet mouth. "I never expect. I always hope."

"Hope is good."

I pull back, rubbing my palms together. "All right. Where am I touching this fantastic, gorgeous, sexy, stunning, brilliant, beautiful work of art?"

"Flattery will get you everywhere," she says, a flirty tone in her voice. "Including in there." She tips her forehead to the painting.

"Exactly where I want to be," I say, running my fingertips down her arm, savoring the feel of her warm skin, the way she responds, the goosebumps that arise in my wake.

"This is what I want you to do. Touch the flowers

first. The irises. So you know you can go through the painting without flipping out."

"I'm not going to hurt the art?" I ask, shrinking away a bit, thinking of the other Renoirs. I don't want to add to the list of art work that's been damaged around me.

"You're a muse. You can't hurt a painting." Her voice softens, and she takes my hand between both of hers. "Your hands are no ordinary hands. Your eyes are not like the eyes of others. You see things other people can't see. You can touch things other people can't touch."

She uncurls my fingers one by one, kissing the tip of each one softly. I want to do so much more with her, like we did last night, and then more than that too. But I let myself exist in this one achingly magnificent moment, with her velvet-soft lips against my skin.

"Now," she instructs. "Reach inside."

I take a breath and stretch my hand out like I'm petting a nervous animal. The canvas feels crackly, the petals on the irises chipped.

"That's it. Keep going. You can't hurt it, Julien," she whispers in my ear, her voice pure poetry. "Close your eyes and just feel."

Clio makes me believe I can be better than I ever have been before. I listen to her and close my eyes. Everything is dark now, but I can touch. This time, the canvas yields as I press my fingers to it. The surface stretches and invites my hands in. Against the blurry black of my closed lids, I see a momentary flash of silver, and in my palm is the softest flutter of a petal, smooth and real. I open my eyes. I grasp, tenderly but firmly, a bouquet of irises.

My jaw drops. I blink several times, astonishment tripping through me.

"I told you so," Clio teases.

"I never doubted you," I say, meaning it.

She smiles. "Good. I like that you trust me." She gestures to the canvas. "Now put them back."

I do the reverse, much as I tuck things back into the paintings every night, and the flowers fold back into the frame.

"And now, perhaps you'd like to come on inside and see my house," she says. "Just don't take anything with you except the clothes on your back."

I hold out my hands wide, almost in surrender, like I'm showing her how much I do trust her.

I stare at her painting again. It seems odd without her in it. The space where she resides is empty, but not blank white. It's filled in by other colors, but as if the colors have spilled into the middle. I reach my hand through, and the midsection of the painting expands inward, creating a weird and warped sort of tunnel. There's a rushing sound far away, like wind is whipping open a secret passageway.

"After you," I say. "This is definitely a ladies-first situation."

She drops a quick kiss onto my cheek. "Such a gentleman."

She steps inside the painting, and even though this might be the most daring thing I've ever done, riskier than breaking into a shop, crazier than believing in ghosts of artists, and more mind-bending than talking to Degas' dancers, since I don't know how I'll return, I follow the woman I'm crazy for.

Because I trust her.

I step into the frame, stealing away from the museum and into another realm.

As I go, the canvas closes up, and I am on the other side.

19

I have been to Monet's garden before. An hour west of Paris, it's a popular destination for many visitors to France.

But this is like a high-definition version, somehow more vivid than reality, with orange dahlias that blaze like the sun and pink poppies the color of the inside of a seashell. All the flowers are in bloom. In front of me lies a blanket of pale-blue forget-me-nots. The hues here are more vibrant than any palette I've seen on the outside.

"We're not in Giverny anymore," I say in a daze, my eyes feasting as I take in the scene.

We are someplace else entirely. Someplace that doesn't exist for anyone else, anywhere else. Someplace that exists only beyond a painting. The flowers, the pond, and the trees are fully alive, but also slightly gauzy, slightly surreal. The scent is too, like a perfect gardenia.

"Do you like it?" she asks, eager and hopeful.

"God, I love it," I say, then whirl around, facing this brilliant beauty. I cup her cheeks, hold her face passionately, and meet her gaze. "This is a gift. You are a gift."

A faint blush spreads over her cheeks. "Thank you. Come. Unwrap more of it," she says, stepping away, beckoning me to follow.

I will follow her anywhere.

"Do you want to see the bridge that Monet painted over and over?" she asks.

"Hell yes."

Clio points. Hovering over the glassy blue surface of the pond is the green bridge from Monet's backyard. I take her hand, squeezing her fingers, as we walk over where purple tulips edge the water, past the water lilies, hazy and quivering. We duck under weeping willows that brush our backs, and when I stand up straight again, I step onto the Japanese bridge.

Everything is gorgeous.

Everything is perfect.

But it's also all she has.

My chest tightens like a noose, thinking of her trapped by beauty.

"Do you love it or hate it here, Clio?" I ask, because even though it's a strange and wondrous place, it's also her cell.

A sad smile crosses her lips. "Sometimes both, yes. I used to pretend there was a door at the end of this bridge. A plain, simple wooden door with an old-fashioned ring handle. Dark metal. You'd pull it open"—she demonstrates opening an invisible door, pulling easily —"and there. The other side." She stays frozen like that, looking at her imagined world. "Now I've finally been on the other side." She takes a long, lingering beat, punctuated by a sigh. *"Free."*

She turns back to me, and my heart aches for her for being stuck for so many years. More than a century. "And being with you, that's an escape too from the life I've been trapped in."

She lets her voice trail off as her lips zero in on mine. She leans in, pressing lightly at first, grazing my lips, and I let her lead, like she seems to want to. She could take me anywhere, and she has. I push my hands through her soft hair, letting the strands form a waterfall through my fingers. She leans into my touch like a cat, and kisses me back, slow and soft as if we could do this forever. This kind of long, unhurried, luxurious kiss. A kiss that turns you inside out with bliss.

But eventually we pull apart.

"Why don't you leave the painting for good? Can you escape from the painting? Leave the museum?" I ask, but even if she left, what would she have? Where would—or could—she go? It's as if she's traveled through time.

She gives a sad, plaintive smile. "I can. And it's simple. You don't need a crazy car chase or knife fight to free me. Nothing violent, nothing dangerous. It's simple because art is grace. Art is class. You can free me by holding open the door and letting me out."

My heart soars at the prospect. But not for long.

Because her tone is heavy.

There will be no freeing her easily.

"But . . .?"

"But that won't change the curse, and besides, I don't want to go."

I latch onto the last part of her answer. "Why?"

She strokes my cheek. "Do you want me to just keep saying it over and over? I told you last night. Because of you."

I laugh. "It doesn't really get old to hear." My eyes drift to the green slats of the bridge, and I want to feel them, their realness. I lie down with her there. The overhead sun warms me. "But tell me, why me?"

"We speak each other's language. We like the same things. We both love art. We love it to the wild depths of our souls."

I grin. "Why, yes, I do believe you understand me perfectly."

She touches my wrist as she talks, running a finger across my palm. "I think I do, and do you want to know why?" Her eyes twinkle with secrets about to come undone.

I prop myself up on one elbow, all eager and then some. "Yes. Tell me."

She trails her fingers up my arm now. "You want to know who I am?"

My bones vibrate with need. "Yes. I'm dying to know." This is all I want.

"Everything?"

"Yes!" I say desperately. "Tell me."

"Like, about my family? And where I'm from?"

I make a rolling gesture with my hands, letting her

know I'm eager and ready. "Tell me." I lace my fingers through hers. She squeezes back.

She props herself up on her elbow, mirroring me. "Here's a hint. I have eight sisters," she says, like she delights in delivering that detail. "Eight."

She says the number as if it's the answer to a riddle, and I have to figure out the question. I picture the digit as a swirling figure, two intertwined circles.

"Eight," I repeat.

"I'm like you," she continues, all flirty and sexy. "Only eternal."

It's as if there were a few notes playing in my head and then someone turned up the radio and the song is now blasting at full volume, and I know all the lyrics. "Do you have a sister named Calliope?" I ask in a hushed breath.

She nods happily, like she enjoys revealing this secret.

How did I miss this? Of course I know *a* Clio is one of the nine Muses, but then it never occurred to me that *my* Clio might be an actual Muse.

That's how I missed it.

I simply thought she was like any other woman with that name. Cognitive dissonance perhaps. The notion she might be Clio the Muse seemed too preposterous that I never considered it. I always assumed she was simply a woman from many years ago with that name.

"And do you have another sister named Thalia?" I ask.

A grin spreads across her face. "Yes. Though Thalia is more like a mom to me."

"You're a Muse. One of the nine Muses. You're one of the nine actual Muses?"

"One of the nine indeed," she says, pleased, like she's just given me a fantastic birthday present, and holy hell, this is another gift. This knowledge. This insight into her. Clio isn't just a young woman from Montmartre. She's so much more.

"Erato, Euterpe, Melpomene, Polyhymnia, Terpsichore, and . . ." I say, rattling off the names of the other Muses from myth, but I blank on the last one.

"Urania," she says with a wild grin. "Impressive that you know them. My family."

I shake my head in astonishment. "You're a Muse? Like, a real Muse? Not just, like, a human muse? But the Muses from forever and ever?"

She holds up her hand like she's swearing in court. "As I live and breathe, I'm a Muse. An eternal Muse. Thalia made me. She made all of us."

"Made you?"

"Well, we weren't just born from human mothers. We were made to be Muses."

The sky could fall, the earth could split open, this garden could tear in two, and I wouldn't notice. I am inside a painting with a Muse, and I know this moment must be a mirage, or maybe it is hazier than that—a reflection of a mirage, a dream within a hallucination. If I was amazed at paintings coming to life, if I was astonished to learn why I can see them, that's nothing compared to learning this. That the woman I've grown so fond of is a Muse.

She flicks her fingers, and a spray of silver dust lands

on me. "There you go," she says, showing off with delight.

I catch her hand and touch her bracelets. They should be wispy, since they're hairbreadth thin, but they are as solid as a bank vault. "Is this where you keep the silver dust?"

She laughs and shakes her head. "No. Our bracelets are our marks. They mark us as Muses. And I'm the Muse of painting."

"I thought Clio was traditionally the Muse of history?"

"I was, but when painting became big during the Renaissance, I switched."

"'Switched,'" I say, then laugh. "Like a midlife career change."

"Exactly."

"What do you do with that silver dust?"

"It's used for inspiration."

"Oh, sure. No biggie." I pretend to flick my fingers. "Hey, want to be inspired? Here's my silver dust."

She pushes my shoulder and laughs. "You're the one who drew shoes with it."

I sit up and drag a hand through my hair, questions bubbling inside me. "How on earth has one of the nine Muses been inside a painting since 1885?"

Her expression shifts to one of resignation, but there's a touch of anger there too. "Renoir trapped me," she says, her voice containing a hard edge. "That's why I didn't tell you right away who I am. The last person—the last human I saw—essentially put me in a cage. I have a tiny bit of a trust issue," she says, and holds her thumb and forefinger together to make light of the statement, but it's a heavy one nevertheless. Of course she'd have trust issues. "But I felt that you were different from the first time I met you. I wanted to make sure. I wanted to tell you when I knew I could trust you."

I reach for her hands, thread our fingers together, and squeeze. "You can trust me, Clio. I would never do anything to hurt you. I only want to help you. But why did he trap you?"

"We used to talk, Renoir and Monet and Valadon and I. I was the Muse for all of them, and we had many discussions about the nature of art. Renoir had firm beliefs that only great artists like himself should make art, be revered and admired. That we Muses should save our inspiration for the worthy—which, of course, included him. And I didn't agree."

"What did you say?"

"I told him—I stood there in the garden, and I said, 'I believe it's my destiny to guide art and artists to a more open age where anyone can make art and anyone can show it.' Things were different then, Julien. During his time, art was very closed off."

I nod. "I know. It's different now, with so many ways to experiment and exhibit it. There's public art and graffiti art and videos and cartoons and experimental music . . ."

"And that's what I always believed would happen. That anyone could create art, that anyone could consume it. And I told Renoir about human muses. That they would exist, and that they would do more of the work of inspiration. He did not like that idea whatso-ever. And so, he trapped me."

She says it clinically, but perhaps that's so she can make it through the horror of the tale.

"How?" I ask, cringing. "Did he stuff you into his canvas?"

"He took my powers of inspiration and twisted them. Muse dust is very limited but very powerful, and binding. He had been painting the gardens, and said he wanted to show me what he'd done so far, but when I looked at his canvas, he took me by the wrists and flicked my fingertips onto the painting. And I went into it. It's like a reversal, the way he used the dust on me. The last words I heard were 'Let's see if a human muse can free you someday.'"

Every part of me aches for her. For the bitterness, for the pain. For having everything she loved, every-thing she believed, turned against her.

"I'm so sorry that happened to you, Clio," I say, but how do you even begin to comfort someone who's been caged for so long, even if the bars are beautiful?

She holds out her hands as if to say *c'est la vie*. "I've gotten used to it, I suppose."

"So he did curse your painting. He cursed it with your own powers."

"It's ironic because every idea he rejected—human muses, art for everyone—his arrogance put all of that into motion."

"But here's the thing. He's still after the painting," I say. I hate telling her that Renoir is back, but I can't keep it from her. I tell her about the haunting of Max, and then what I learned today—that someone had swapped in a fake and taken her actual painting to the house in Montmartre, which would become Remy's. Where we would eventually meet. There's no point in hiding it. Whatever we're in, we're in it together.

"It's like he's trying to get you back. I mean, you're safe here at the museum. But why now? What is he so worried about?"

"I don't know. I was cut off from everything when he trapped me."

"Besides, if he was crazed enough to trap you, you'd think he'd have—" I stop talking, but she can add two and two.

"Destroyed the painting?"

I nod, wincing at that horrible idea. "Well, yeah."

"He wasn't violent. He was, oddly enough, a gentleman. And he would never do that to one of his creations. He loved his art more than anything in the world."

"Art can be a stupid, jealous thing."

"In a way, I kind of know how he felt. I used to love art more than anything. But then I started thinking more about the process, and it never made sense to me why it was only the nine of us Muses who could bring about true and great inspiration. It didn't feel right to me. And my beliefs started changing about making art, but also about what I wanted. The only problem is you can't really *want* as an eternal Muse. You just *do*. You just do the work."

"So let me free you, then." It's the least I can do for her. "I mean, that's what this curse or prophecy or whatever is about, right? A human muse will free you from your painting. You said all I had to do was open the doors of the museum and let you out."

She looks at me and lays a soft hand on my cheek. "If you did, I'd just have to go back. I'd have to work. The painting is what binds me to the museum, and the museum is what lets me come out at night. Once I leave the museum, I'll be bound again. Bound to be a Muse all the time." The weight of that burden darkens her voice. It's such cruel beauty, the way these traps contain her. "I used to love working all the time. But being in that painting for so many years, I'm not the same. I don't know what I want anymore." There is so much sadness in her voice.

I latch onto what she said about family before. "But your sisters—do you want to see them? Do they need you back?"

She shrugs, shooting me a little smile. "I'd like to see them at some point, but I'm rather enjoying where I am this second. Besides, my sisters have obviously filled in for me all those years. I didn't inspire Toulouse-Lautrec or Seurat. The later Cézannes aren't mine, and the later Monets aren't either, not the *Water Lilies*, not the *Rouen Cathedral*. Even your favorite Van Gogh was made without me. So my sisters must have taken over for me."

"Muse sick day," I joke.

"Extended leave of absence," she corrects.

"So, you're going to take a few more days off?" I ask, and I love this idea. I want as much of her as I can get.

"They got by this long without me. So I think I'll

play hooky a little longer," she says, her lips curving up in a grin. "That is, if you'll keep having me?"

"I'll have you any way I can. I'll give you whatever you want, Clio," I say, even though my heart is heavy inside because whatever we are will inevitably unwind. It will never be more than an escape into a garden that isn't real.

She brushes her lips against mine, and I melt into her.

We kiss with the sun warming us, lying on the green slats of Monet's surreal bridge. As I kiss her neck, I tell her all the places I want to kiss her more, the visits I'd make on the treasure map of her body. X marks this spot on her shoulder, then this delicious one on her wrist, then this divine location at the hollow of her throat, as she shudders and pulls me closer with each touch. I'm an intrepid explorer uncovering a new land and claiming it with kisses. Even if time is ticking on the other side of the painting.

But on this side, the moment feels endless.

The moment feels like everything.

And then it truly feels like another world when she wraps her arms around my neck and whispers in my ear, "I know what I want."

The words glide out, all sensual and sure.

I meet her gaze, my body stilling, a wild hope racing through me. "Tell me what that is."

She doesn't tell me. She shows me. She slides her hand down my chest, along my pecs, over my abs.

To the waistband of my jeans.

I swallow roughly, my throat going dry, my body buzzing from the delicious contact.

And then from her eager hand sliding lower. I catch her hand, capture it in mine, and bring it to my lips, kissing her palm. "Are you sure? Now?"

She shoots me a sharp stare. "I'm positive. Do you not want to?"

"I want to. More than anything. I just don't want to . . ."

"Break me?" she asks with an eyebrow arch.

"Well, you *are* magical. I've never . . . been with anyone like you."

"I should hope not," she says with a laugh.

I laugh too, loving that we can do that in this moment.

"Also, shouldn't you be worried I'll break you?" she teases.

I grab her head, tug her close, and bring my lips to her ear. "No. Just don't break my heart," I say softly.

She sets her palm on my chest. "I won't."

It feels like an unbreakable promise.

I pat the back of my jeans, take out my wallet to locate a condom, and she laughs.

"Eternal Muses can't conceive."

"Oh," I say, filing away that tidbit. "I'm clean. Safe."

"Good. Then put that away."

"With pleasure," I say, returning the protection to my wallet.

I shuck off my shirt as she fiddles with the buttons on her dress, and soon she tugs it over her head.

My heart stops.

Breath flees my body.

She's gorgeous. More beautiful than I imagined, and I have definitely imagined this.

A lot.

We reach for each other at the same time, all hands and lips and hunger. Exploring each other's bodies, mapping skin, traveling along curves and planes.

She's eager, so eager, judging from the way she kisses me, from the frenzied way her palms journey over my chest to my jeans.

I push them off, and here we are.

Two muses.

One human. One eternal.

About to make love in Monet's garden.

Inside a painting.

My life is so surreal.

She climbs over me.

Well now.

This view is even better.

It is incontrovertibly the best view ever as she slides on top of me. I loop my hands into her hair. "Come closer."

She bends down to me, her lips brushing mine so gently, so sweetly, I am sure I'm dreaming again, or I'm really flying. I don't know, and it doesn't matter, but she kisses me like a song, like moonlight, like a sonnet.

Then, I guide myself into her.

And we both gasp.

And moan.

And wrap ourselves tighter around each other.

The ends of her hair brush across my chest, and a groan escapes my lips as she moves on me, rocking and arching, and *holy art*.

Holy muse.

This is the most surreal experience of my life.

A Muse is riding me in a painting.

Only it's so much more than that.

She is full of yearning and fire and heat, and all I can think is if I were to die right now, if I were to be struck down for being with a Muse inside a painting, then really, all things considered, this wouldn't be a bad way to go.

Because nothing is better than this. Nothing could be better than this.

Especially when I shift us, move her under me, gaze down at the woman I adore.

Yes, this is so much more.

Because as I thrust into her, as she curls her legs around me, as we kiss and pant and move, this is more than an art kink.

This is making love, and falling in love, and falling into each other.

We are racing and frenzied, as bodies collide, and my muse, my woman, arches her back, parts her lips, and comes apart beneath me.

I follow her there, losing myself to bliss, to pleasure, and I'm sure to pain.

Because I just don't see a way for us to be together.

For her to ever be free.

I'm spent, and she is too, so we lie like that, in our oasis that can't last, that's about to be pierced by responsibilities and rules.

By all the things that bind us.

But I let the moment wash over me, breathing in this last bit of secret hideout-ness, breathing in *Clio*.

20

Hand in hand, Clio and I amble through the garden toward the blue irises where the painting opens up. If I walk any slower, I'll be at a standstill. But as much as I want to stay with this woman—this Muse—I'd prefer it not be inside a painting. Especially the Renoir, where we're at the mercy of Max-slash-Renoir and whatever blight is afflicting the other art.

No, I swore I'd protect Clio, and I can't do that from in here.

Along the way, we walk across the bridge. At the top of Monet's arched bridge, Clio nudges me with her shoulder. "What are you thinking?"

With our fingers still linked, I tug her close and wrap my other arm around her like we're dancing, à la Fred Astaire, sort of, until we get off-balance on the slope of the bridge and stumble against the railing, catching ourselves with our clasped hands. Clio throws back her head and laughs as I put my other hand on the railing too, playfully penning her in.

"I'm thinking," I say, "about how much I enjoyed being here with you."

Her laughter quiets to something more gentle, and she reaches up to smooth the furrow between my brows. "That doesn't seem like something to frown about."

I catch her hand and kiss her palm. "Only because I don't want to leave."

She sighs. "But you must."

I nod and hold her hand against my chest. "I have to go so that I can work out how to free you."

Clio looks as if she hardly dares to ask, "Do you think you know how?"

I kiss her softly parted lips. "Not yet," I murmur when I finally allow a hair's breadth between us. "But I will figure it out. And I know more now than I did. Maybe enough to ask the right questions."

Tipping her head back, she closes her eyes and breathes deep, as if basking in the painted light and savoring the last bit of our evening together. When she looks at me again, her smile is sweet and spicy, like she's thinking about everything that's happened since she brought me into her painting. "It feels like a whole different universe than it did before."

I tug her away from the bridge's railing for another embrace before we continue on. "Why, Clio, are you saying I rocked your world?"

She swats playfully at my shoulder and starts a cheeky reply—and then stops, mouth hanging slightly open as if she's seen something baffling. Only she's not looking at any one thing, but rather all around us.

"Julien . . . do you see this? I assumed 'a whole new world' was a figure of speech but . . ."

I see immediately what she means. From the apex of the arched bridge, we've stepped onto its mirror image. It might even be the same one, but the light is different, brighter and greener than Clio's garden.

I know where we are. I didn't think anything could surprise me now, and yet this latest twist has proven me wrong. Somehow, Clio and I have walked into another painting in the Musée d'Orsay.

This is *The Water Lily Pond: Green Harmony*. Same bridge, different painting, one of Monet's many versions of his Japanese bridge.

We follow where it leads and step off the planks and into the museum. Clio stares wide-eyed as if we've been transported to another planet instead of a different gallery in the Musée d'Orsay—a gallery nowhere near Clio's painting.

Finally, she looks at me as if hunting for an answer, but I'm looking at her for the same thing. Her bewilderment makes it even more of a shock—she's been living in her painted world for more than a century, and has been a Muse for much longer than that. If she's surprised, I'm flabbergasted.

"Did you know you could do that?" I ask her.

She shakes her head slowly. "I had no idea. And I've searched every corner of my painting. The bridge never went anywhere except across the pond."

"So, what happened?" I have to say it aloud, even though we must be thinking the same thing—the only thing that's changed in the century she's been trapped is ... me.

Her gaze flicks to the painting and back to me. "We touched the bridge together. Our hands, remember? You were distracting me at the time, but I think that must be when something changed."

"Or the bridges in the paintings connected right at that moment." I rub my chin as I speculate. "The moment when two muses touched it together?"

"It must be," she says, still wide-eyed with amazement.

A new voice enters the discussion from not far away. "Convenient, wouldn't you say?"

Clio and I both jump and turn to see Dr. Gachet, Van Gogh's doctor from his famous portrait. It's the first time I've seen him corporeal. He stands, hands behind his back as if studying Monet's painting rather than us.

"What's convenient?" I ask.

His voice is low and sonorous as he gestures idly to the water lilies. "That the Impressionists painted so many versions of that bridge."

I know that—Monet's garden was apparently a popular place to paint—but now my mind boggles at the implications. "They connect?" I ask Dr. Gachet. "The bridges all connect?"

He spreads his hands in front of him in a noncommittal way. "I merely offer an observation. After all, I'm not the one jumping in and out of paintings."

I can only stare as the doctor, in his royal-blue coat, wanders along the hall. In the corner, Olympia stands, the sheet from her painting draped around her, waving flirtatiously at him. I've never seen her moving about either, but now she and the doctor link hands and walk off.

Clio whispers, "I think Olympia and Dr. Gachet have a little something going on."

Some of the impish humor is back in her eyes, and I shake my head in dazed amazement. "Just another night at the museum," I say. "If muses and bridges can hook up, why not famous portraits?"

"I don't blame them one bit," Clio says, wrapping her arm around my waist.

I drape mine over her shoulders as we head toward her gallery, then I'm struck by a thought. "You know what? We have another one of the bridges on loan to the Hermitage as part of a Monet exhibit. We could go there sometime."

Clio stops and grabs my arm. "I would love to do that. Do you think we really could?"

Glancing back at the Monet before it's out of sight, I shrug. "You've been a Muse a lot longer than I have. What do you think?"

She stretches onto her toes, twines her arms around my neck, and kisses me like there's no tomorrow. Breathless, she pulls back enough to say, "I think we have a date."

I walk her back to her canvas, kissing her again before she reenters. I can't get enough of her, can't remember a time when it took so much willpower to let a woman out of my arms.

Once I manage it, I ask her something that's been lurking in the back of my mind, where I'd pushed it so as not to spoil our time together. It doesn't seem fair to bring it up and leave her worrying all night and day, so I couch the question carefully.

"Clio, about Renoir . . . if he managed to work a curse to keep you from inspiring ordinary people and starting this new age of artistic enlightenment, what lengths might he go to in order to stop it now?"

Her shrewd and level gaze says I haven't slipped anything past her. "Do I think that, having failed to get his hands on this painting by forgery, he might try outright theft?" Fists on her hips, she says, "After spending more than a century trapped in here, I'm inclined to think the worst of him."

As am I.

I can't resist one last kiss, because she's as lovely fired up and indignant as she is any other time.

And kissing her distracts me from the rest of my thoughts, the part I don't want to say. I'm worried about something more destructive than theft. Renoir might not be able to bring himself to destroy the painting of *Woman Wandering in the Irises*, but if a human muse is the key to this prophesy, well, I don't think he'll have any qualms about destroying me.

I have to get to the bottom of this for both our sakes.

* * *

Simon and I grab lunch in Saint-Germain-des-Prés the next afternoon and eat outside on the steps of the church, where my friend is happy to give his opinion.

"I don't know, mate. If it were me, I'd have offed you already."

He takes a carefree bite of his cheese sandwich, and I give him a look. "How is that helpful exactly?"

"Well, if a human muse is going to usher in the new renaissance for the common folk, those who want to stop it would get rid of you before you can team up with the other Muses. Ipso facto, elitist art snob wins."

"I figured out that part for myself. I mean, how does it help, you telling me that?"

"Seeing as how you head home well after dark every night since that painting turned up, and nobody's conked you over the head and dumped you in the Seine yet, that seems to suggest Renoir doesn't see you as the threat."

That leaves Clio as the target. I don't think Renoir has it in him to destroy his own work. But steal it? No question. Make sure it's lost forever? Certainly.

My phone pings with an incoming text.

Remy: How fast can you get over to the Marais? Seems one of our forgers has recently found religion.

* * *

Remy fits in well in the Marais, with its mix of trendy and vintage, chic and quirky. He greets Simon and me, and we set off toward the vintage place where Cass Middleton has set up shop, literally and figuratively.

"I already figured out that this was about Cass Middleton," I say as we pass her store. "Want to explain the rest?"

"You'll see."

At the corner, we turn into an alley full of boxes and trash cans beside the back doors of shops and restaurants. By counting the doors, I know which goes to Cass's shop, and directly across from it is an unexpected pair of arched doors. Remy yanks them open, and the three of us head down a stone path that ends at a church.

Remy leads us inside, where it's musty, cold, and quiet. A few candles flicker by the altar, and a pair of painted Madonnas watch over the nave from high above.

"We've been keeping tabs on Cass Middleton," Remy says. "Sophie has spotted her crossing the alley to this church with easels, stretched canvases, and paint supplies." There are no signs of a makeshift studio—not so much as a whiff of linseed oil.

"Are you sure this is where she was headed with them?"

"Yes. She's been going back and forth—was here this morning, in fact." He looks around as Simon and I do the same. "Maybe she's using another room or a basement?"

"Let's spread out and look," I say.

Simon heads for the altar, and when he's out of earshot, I ask Remy in a low voice, "Did you ever learn why Suzanne Valadon asked your family to keep *Woman Wandering in the Irises* safe?"

I'm almost certain I know, but confirmation would be nice.

Remy shakes his head, seeming to genuinely regret that he can't give me an answer. "Only that there was a woman trapped inside the painting until a human muse came along. The family henceforth had to keep it safe until then."

From the start, it's seemed like anyone involved has a piece of the puzzle, but no one has the whole story. Remy doesn't know there's an eternal Muse in *Woman Wandering in the Irises*. Clio doesn't know what happened to her painting after Renoir's last words, cursing her.

As for Renoir, I don't think he has all the answers either. His forged papers were convincing, but none of his stories have been. Maybe I can't figure out his plan because he's still figuring it out himself.

Remy and I fan out too, but there's not much to search. The church is tiny, and there's no sign of a way into another room or a basement. I throw up my hands in frustration. "Nothing. Now what?"

"Now," says Simon from where he's casually leaning against the altar, "I dazzle you with one of my random bits of knowledge." He taps the top of the altar. "A lot of these old alleyway churches have served as handy places to stash relics, refugees, riches. But sometimes . . ."

He braces his shoulder against the raised altar and shoves like a quarryman. The stone altar groans as it moves over a few inches to reveal a door in the floor.

"Voilà. You get a hidden staircase in front of everyone's eyes."

"Consider me dazzled," Remy says, his sculpted eyebrows climbing. I think he's more surprised by Simon than the door, but that's my Scottish friend all right—more than he seems.

Simon holds up a hand as if demurring applause. "It's nothing. Brilliance is all in a day's work for me." Then he takes the first step down, looking back at me. "You coming, mate?"

"Of course." I hurry over, and Remy follows, peering at the uneven stone steps and wrinkling his nose.

"I'll keep a lookout up here. I am extremely particular about basement upkeep."

I can't argue with that, so I thank him and follow Simon down a loop of stairs. I find the switch for a work light and pull it, illuminating a breathtaking and chilling sight.

Two easels. Two paintings in progress.

Renoir may be loathsome, but his work is astoundingly beautiful. And there's no denying this is *his* work.

On one canvas, the artist has begun the *Young Girls at the Piano*, and *The Boy with the Cat* is underway on the other easel. Those were the first two Renoirs to fade. Is he replacing his own work?

Simon pokes around the stacks of empty canvases against the wall. "This proves that the Middleton woman is forging paintings, right? What next? Do we call the metro police or go straight to Interpol?"

I'm sure Renoir's been here, inhabiting Max. But it must be Cass doing the actual painting. Renoir needs a master art forger to reproduce his masterpieces. The ghost can't simply paint them in a borrowed body—whenever he takes possession of Max, his fingers twist into an unusable shape, mimicking the deformity of Renoir's arthritis.

"I don't know," I answer Simon. "It's going to be hard to explain the spirit of Renoir coaching his forger."

"But I don't get *why*. He can't sell them, right?"

I picture Clio in the painted sunshine of Monet's garden, telling me how Renoir loved his art above everything else. How it means the world to him.

"Losing his art has got to be his worst nightmare," I say. "Maybe he has his reasons. If he can replace the works with exact replicas, he can preserve his legacy."

Simon points out, "They won't be exact replicas though. Not without the secret formula thingy in the signature."

That's true. And who knows if he can even create the signature pigment with modern supplies?

A door slams above us. Simon and I look up at the old musty ceiling at the same time. "Let's get out of here," I say, and I don't have to tell Simon twice.

We rush up the steps into the chapel, where there's no sign of Remy.

There's no sign of the fist that blindsides me either. Not until it smashes into my face hard enough to spin me around and drop me to the ground.

Pain tears through me, ripping through my body.

"Trespassing in a church? That's a step up from snooping around my shop," a woman's English accent taunts.

A yell comes next, and I flip over, still wincing, as Simon flies out from behind the altar and jumps Cass Middleton. She jabs an elbow into his solar plexus and then a fist to his groin.

"Oi!" Simon twists away from the brunt of it, but it still lays him out. Hell, it nearly paralyzes me in sympathy.

Where the hell is Remy? Before I can look around for him, Cass grabs the neck of my T-shirt and twists so tight that I struggle to breathe.

"You looking for your friend? He's all right. Tied him to the baptism font with his scarf." I can get a hit in on her now, if I get enough breath, but she backhands me so hard my brain rattles in my skull. Then she pins me to the ground with her foot on my chest.

"Now, listen up. I don't go for violence," she says without a shred of irony, "but I might make an exception for guys who keep sticking their nose in my business."

"*Might?*" I wheeze, keeping her attention on me and away from the movement I spot behind her.

"You think it can't get worse than this?" She steps harder on my chest to make her point.

I gasp for breath.

Then Remy taps her on the shoulder from behind. Cass whirls, and my *bon ami* throws a punch like a prizefighter. It knocks her back, to the stairs, where she rolls across the edge of the door down into the basement, with a few loud thumps

I crawl over to peer down. She's at the bottom of the

stone steps. I'm glad she's not dead, and more glad she's moaning too much to get right back up.

Remy joins me at the edge and, livid, shakes the tattered remains of his scarf at her. "This. Was. Hermès!"

21

That evening, Clio waits for me in the corner of the gallery, reading a book. It's a sight that makes my breath catch, because she's so beautiful and because of the book—I'm pretty sure I've seen it on a tabletop in a Cézanne.

"Is that from Cézanne's *Portrait of Gustave Geffroy*?" I ask.

"Don't worry. I'll return it later. But it's pretty good and has kept me—" She places a bookmark inside and looks up, breaking off her speech when she sees the cut on my cheek. "Oh, Julien!" Jumping up, she reaches for my face, but stops herself before she touches me. "What happened? Are you okay?"

"You should see the other guy," I joke lamely, even though the other guy is a woman and she stumbled out of the church several minutes after us.

That's what Simon told me since he hung around when the police showed up.

Besides, the only person I care about now is Clio.

She threads her fingers through my hair and kisses my forehead tenderly.

"Better now?"

"Not yet. I need another."

I feel her soft lips on my eyelids. "Does that help?"

"Only a little."

There's a flutter against my bruised cheek.

"More please."

She kisses my jaw where Cass first whacked me. Soon, her lips find mine. Hers taste like cherries, and I want to stop time. To stay with her right now.

"Clio," I say softly.

"What is it, Julien?"

"Nothing. I just like saying your name." I run my thumb across her lip as it stretches into a smile. No, a grin, and then she's grabbing my hand and pulling me along the gallery.

"Come with me. I have something to show you."

* * *

Minutes later, we're inside *Starry Night*, my favorite Van Gogh.

It's a dreamscape—lush blues drip over the water, and banana-yellow stars sparkle in the night sky. They cast long rays of moonlight, like gas lamps glimmering across the Rhône.

We step into one of the sailboats on the river.

"Lie back," Clio says, letting me rest my aching head in her lap.

"My headache feels better already," I say as we drift into the Rhône.

"Are you going to tell me what happened to you?" She's all sweet sympathy, but there's real concern beneath it. Maybe she's worked out what I did—that I might be in danger from Max. She's certainly smart enough to add things up, and I decide it's time to level with her the best I can, considering how much I don't know.

I give her the details of my afternoon excursion, but I also brief her on the fading Renoirs. I haven't wanted to worry her, but now that I know she's a Muse, there's no better person to help me figure it out.

Sighing sadly, I tell her, "It's as if all the colors are bleeding away. I can't figure it out. Maybe it's related to your curse, maybe not. It seems like Renoir is as worried as any of us."

"Of course," says Clio. "His art is what he prizes above all other things."

"Here's my thought—you said Muse dust is very powerful, potent enough to trap you. Could it also have been used to put a curse on Renoir's paintings?"

We float lazily over exaggerated ultramarine as she strokes my hair. "I suppose it's possible. But art magic is highly specific. It's for inspiration and creation. But it's also the only thing powerful enough to change art—transform kernels of ideas into fully realized masterpieces."

"Okay, hear me out on this, but I have an idea." I twist around to look up at her. "You don't owe him any favors, but maybe you can fix the Renoirs with your Muse dust."

She tilts her head, then nods. "I can try it. I'm not fond of him. Clearly." She shakes her head with a guilty sigh. "But despite everything, I do still love his paintings. Is that awful, to love the art of someone like that?"

"The paintings contain the beauty he saw, and that's what you love. That's what has outlived him."

"So when we leave this painting, we'll try."

I toss out another theory, one that's been tugging at my mind. "Do you think the other Muses could have cursed his art?"

Her mouth drops open in unmistakable horror. She holds up her hands. "Absolutely not. It goes against what we are. We love the art, not the artist. The job of an eternal Muse is to coax out the idea, and our magic and our love keep the art and literature and beauty alive through the years."

"So how does it work? Being a Muse?" I ask. The golden stars bathe the night around us in a warm glow as shimmery water laps the boat. The sound of the sweet waves is as gentle as Clio's hands in my hair.

"Do you know the opening of Homer's *Odyssey*?" She quotes the first line of the epic poem. "*Sing in me, Muse, and through me tell the story.*" She taps her chest. "My specialty is painting, as you know. From our home, we can go anywhere in the world. Poets, writers, painters, dancers, actors, musicians—we sense they need us, and we travel."

"That's fantastic, like inspiration on call. I want to

know more. Tell me who else you've inspired. Who are your favorites?"

"J. M. W. Turner. I loved helping him with his seascapes. I also adored working with Ingres. And Géricault—I'm especially proud of him for *The Raft of the Medusa*. He struggled so hard with that one, the depth of emotion in it. I put so much love into that painting to help him realize its potential." I love hearing her talk like this. She's even more enchanting than usual, especially as she runs her finger along the neck of my T-shirt. I relax into her touch. "Vermeer and Rembrandt too."

"If you inspire all these artists, you must be able to speak every language. So you can talk to them, right? That's why you speak perfect French, but you don't have the accent of someone who was born here."

"It's true. Are you impressed?"

"Everything about you impresses me," I say, and she rewards me by leaning in for a kiss. "So how do you say in Dutch, 'Oh, Mr. Rembrandt, I think you need a bit more brown in this self-portrait'?"

She answers immediately.

"You know I have no idea what you really said."

"I said exactly what you asked."

"How do you say in Italian, 'Leonardo, I think the *Mona Lisa* is lame'?"

She laughs and rattles off a quick Italian phrase.

"All right, I have a good one. How do you say in Spanish, 'Mr. Goya, your paintings are so beautiful they remind me of the most amazing woman I've ever met'?"

She blushes and lowers her face, then repeats Spanish words back to me.

Headache gone, I sit up in the boat so I'm facing her, my heart thundering in my head. "How do you say in English, 'I can't imagine being without her'?"

She looks at me, her eyes brimming with passion. "I feel the same."

I take her hand. Run my index finger along hers. Feel her skin warm to my touch. "Clio." I breathe her name into the painted world we're floating in. I cup her face in my hands, my palms on her cheeks, holding her soft and close as golden starlight streaks across the night. All my nerves fly into my throat as I ask the next question. "How do you say in French, 'Clio, I'm falling in love with you'?"

She loops her fingers through mine, lacing them tightly. "Julien, I'm falling in love with you too."

And then she takes my face in her hands, gentle and tender, and kisses me.

I am truly in another world.

More so when the kiss turns urgent.

Heated.

When hands slide up and under clothes, and breaths become needy and desperate. When my shirt is off, she stops, seeming nervous.

"What's wrong?"

"You're hurt. I don't want to hurt you more."

I laugh. "Trust me, being with you *only* makes me feel good."

"Are you sure?"

"I promise."

She runs her fingers gently down my chest, over my stomach. "No pain?"

"Only pleasure," I whisper.

"Only pleasure," she repeats softly against my lips.

Then we lie down, shifting side by side, hands exploring, touching, traveling.

Lips everywhere.

Mouths needing, seeking, finding.

And soon, we're a tangle of limbs and flesh.

And then, I am inside her, making love to a Muse, in a boat, in a painting.

Under all the stars in the most beautiful sky.

We are side by side, face to face, as she hooks her leg over my hip. Slowly, we move together, taking it easy, savoring every second.

Her eyes lock with mine as I go deep in her, and when her lips part and she leans her head back, all I can think is how much I need this, how much I need her, and how I have to find a way to save this woman.

Because I want this life with her inside a painting. All surreal and dreamlike.

But more than that, I want a real life, beyond the blue waters, past the starry night, far past the frame.

Into the world where I spend my days.

Because I want my nights with her to become days with her.

I want it all with Clio.

We lose ourselves in each other, in the sounds, in the touch, in the connection.

Once upon a time, many weeks ago, I fell for a work of art.

A painted image of a woman.

I didn't know her. I hadn't talked to her.

Now, I've fallen for the real woman behind the painting. I know her. I talk to her.

I touch her.

And I'm certain, too, that I won't be happy in a world without her.

22

After we leave *Starry Night*, we head to *Gabrielle with a Rose*, and Clio puts her hands on the painting, closing her eyes as she concentrates on repairing it. She smooths her palms over the shawl where the work is the most faded, and tries to coax the color back into the layers of paint.

Without success.

She might try until the sun rises, so I finally tug her away and see her to her painting, giving her a good morning kiss before she goes still.

On my way out, I pass *Gabrielle with a Rose* again, and I catch sight of *The Swing* hanging nearby. I step closer —a woman stands on a swing in a sun-dappled garden, and the dark-blue bows on the front of her dress are now gray-blue, and the whole gown looks faded from too many washings. I pause to touch it gently with my palm, the way Clio had smoothed Gabrielle's shawl, and I feel as if I'm saying goodbye to another friend.

When I reach the front doors, I wave to Gustave. "How did your sculpture in the subway art contest go?"

He grins broadly. "Fantastic! Can't thank you enough for helping me figure it out."

As I congratulate him, something Clio said hits me —about helping artists realize the potential in their work. I did that for Gustave. I keep hearing how I'm a human muse, but it's only in this moment that I *feel* like one.

And it feels pretty damn good.

His phone rings, and he glances at it. "My buddy at the Louvre," he says, offhand. "I wonder what bizarre story he has this time."

"I wonder," I echo, but with a pit in my stomach.

Gustave answers the call, waving goodbye. I return it but pretend to check my phone for an excuse to stand there and eavesdrop.

"Oh, sure, I believe you," Gustave says a few exchanges in. He catches me still there and rolls his eyes at whatever his friend is telling him. "Our seascapes spring leaks all the time."

I raise my brows in a silent question, as if it doesn't matter and my gut didn't just knot like a pretzel. Gustave tilts his phone away from his face and stage-whispers, "The big Géricault in room seventy-seven is dripping onto the floor, apparently. Told you he was a loon."

"Sure," I say. "A real nutter."

Worried my face will break, I turn toward the door, and Gustave turns back to his phone call. "Well, just mop it up. See you on Sunday for cards?"

I stagger outside, like I've been trounced all over again.

* * *

The Louvre doesn't open for another four excruciating hours. I go home and manage a bit of sleep, then wake so tired that I wonder why I bothered. A shower helps, and so does coffee, then I'm out of the flat and at the museum in time to be one of the first people in the door.

The Raft of the Medusa is an early eighteenth-century painting of survivors of a French shipwreck clinging to a raft in a storming sea. I take the marble steps to the upper floor two at a time, my mind on where I'm going, not where I am, and I nearly flatten a red-haired woman heading the opposite way. I say sorry, but she's already gone.

If people are running away, it's got to be worse than the drip Gustave's friend reported.

I turn the corner and freeze. It's like gawking at a train wreck—wanting to look away, wanting to see everything, wanting to help and knowing you can't. *The Raft of the Medusa* is gushing. Seawater pours out of the massive canvas from the rocky waves Géricault painted, the ones Clio helped him to create.

A custodian races by with a mop and a bucket, wholly inadequate. Next comes management—a man in a suit, barking instructions into a phone until he sees the flood and stops, jaw agape, no clue what to do. When an assistant runs in, slips, and belly-surfs across the gallery, the suit goes back to yelling, and the custodian gets to mopping futilely.

"Close this gallery. Close this gallery now!"

No one notices me duck through the crowd trying to get a look at the chaos. I find the Ingres in the next gallery and recoil at the sight. The blue cushions have folded over the concubine, and all that's left of her is one eye staring out desperately as the cushions squeeze and strangle her.

The candle in the La Tour has become a red-hot flame, setting the whole canvas ablaze. I reach the Titian just as the mirror tips out of the canvas and plummets to the floor with a deafening crash and a spray of shards. I find Rembrandt's *Bathsheba at Her Bath* shriveled up into tiny hardened pieces, like pork rinds, on the floor.

I text Remy as I join the stream of visitors exiting the Louvre. It's short and not so sweet.

Julien: I need to talk to the Muses. Now.

23

Sophie opens the iron gate to the courtyard at the Montmartre house as if she's been waiting for me. "I heard about the Louvre," she says.

"That's why I'm here. Remy says the Muses write notes. Maybe they'll write me a to-do list for this disaster."

We head inside and down the hall lined with art, the Jasper Johns and Monet's bridge, then into the media room and down the dark, spiraling stairs. Meeting me halfway are the bell-like voices I heard the night of Remy's party. There's something of Clio's pure, sweet voice in the sound. It pierces me in a new way, imagining her on these stairs, coming and going with her sisters.

Remy waits at the bottom, waving a piece of paper. "Thalia left a note for you, Julien!"

Not the employee handbook, sadly. It's only one sheet of thick embossed stationery with a line of hand-written script.

Julien—I'm working at La Belle Vie today. Fastest way to get there is to take the third door on the right. —T

I look at Remy. "Is this a summons?"

He shrugs that Gallic shrug. "You said you wanted to talk to them."

"Have *you* met her before?"

He smiles, which eases my nerves some. "She has crazy red hair, and she smells like pomegranates."

I look for a door, on the right or otherwise, and the closest thing to it is the rectangular outline on the floor, edged by the silver Muse dust. I nod to it. "Do we go through that?"

Remy shakes his head. "*You* go through that. Sophie and I stay here."

"It's for Muses only," says Sophie. "Only they—and you—can open it."

I look from sister to brother to the door. So, if anything happens on the other side, there'll be no one to let me out.

But there's no time to worry about that. Art is dying, collapsing like a sandcastle at high tide.

"I swear," I say as I crouch to touch the floor, "if I get stuck underground in Paris like the Phantom of the Opera, my ghost will haunt you both forever."

Remy laughs. "That won't be the strangest thing to happen in this house."

"Good point."

I kneel outside the shimmering outline. I could ask Remy or Sophie what the Muses do, but I can feel my way through this on my own. I spread my hands over the slab like I did over Clio's canvas last night and then place my palms on the stone, expecting resistance. But the stone slides over like a door at a department store. Instead of tumbling into a magical underground world of endlessly blue sky and sunlit green hills, I catch myself before I fall into the catacombs.

I don't understand the fascination with the Paris underground. It's creepy and airless, and I orient myself as my eyes adjust to the dark. Third door on the right, and I can't see my hand in front of my face. Taking out my phone, I thumb on the flashlight and find the door quickly, pulling it open by the old rusty handle. A staircase leads up to another door, which puts me in the back room of La Belle Vie, a famous perfume shop on the Rue de Rivoli. It's full of old-fashioned bottles with puffy atomizers, all hand-painted with delicate flowers and vines. They're works of art, beauty for its own sake, and it's somehow not surprising to find a Muse working here while the place is closed.

She's bent over what looks like a handwritten musical score spread out on the counter—a woman with loose flaming-red hair . . . and laboratory goggles. I watch for a moment as she pores over the pages then, with surgical precision, picks up something with a pair of tweezers and examines it. She flicks some silvery dust onto it, shakes off any extra, and replaces it on the score.

When she's done, I clear my throat. She jumps, whirls around, and then laughs at herself as she pushes the magnifying goggles on top of her head.

"Oh! Sorry about that." She offers me her hand—like Clio, she has a thin silver bracelet on each wrist. With her high cheekbones, she's delicately lovely, but her eyes look tired. "I'm Thalia, as you may have guessed. The owners of this shop are music lovers, and it makes for a quiet place to concentrate on coaxing out stubborn semiquavers. They can be so fiddly, you know."

"Right?" I say, as if I hear that all the time. "I was just saying that the other day."

It takes a moment for my humor to reach her, and then she laughs again. "I knew I'd be working on this symphony for a while, so thank you for meeting me here."

"Thanks for seeing me." I realize she's squeezing me in as she multitasks. Clio did say life as a Muse was all work. "So, is that from one of your composers?" I nod at the score.

"Sort of. It's a lost symphony, and Mahler isn't available to tweak it himself, so here I am." She waves away the extraordinary fact of a newly discovered symphony like it's yesterday's laundry. "I do some inspiration work myself, but lately my tasks are centered more on troubleshooting."

It's the perfect opportunity to cut to the chase. I don't just need help, I need information. And if a human muse is such a big deal, then it seems like I should rate some answers.

"Since you mention troubleshooting," I begin, and a tiny flinch from Thalia tells me something I should have realized. "You know what's going on at the Louvre, don't you?" But it's not a question. "How can you fiddle around with semiquavers or whatever when the art is coming apart at the seams? How can you not do something to stop it?"

"Do you think I didn't try?" Thalia asks sharply in what sounds like frustration, maybe directed at herself. "I was at the Louvre the second it opened. I laid my hands on all the damaged paintings." She pinches the bridge of her nose and ducks her head, and her hair falls in a curtain around her face. This moment and another —the mane of red hair I saw on the museum steps hours ago—snap together.

"I saw you there." I feel foolish for not realizing it straightaway, but I don't feel guilty for questioning her. "At the Louvre this morning."

"I tried to fix it, Julien. I was the first one through the door when the museum opened."

It's surreal that a Muse has to go through the front doors like everyone else. I look at her, leaning against the counter, looking bone-weary and sad and . . . human, even though I know she's not.

Thalia's shoulders slump. "I sent Calliope over to the National Gallery in London too. They're having the same problem with their Turners."

"The flooding?" All those beautiful J. M. W. Turners seascapes full of dappled sunlight on the water.

"All over the floors, Calliope said."

"Then what can we do?" I ask. "Because a mop and bucket aren't going to cut it."

"Julien," Thalia says, intense but calm. "You need to put your human brain to work on it. That's why we so desperately need people like you—you can think in ways that we Muses can't. Your mortality—your humanity—gives you insight and ideas that escape us."

"All I've been doing is improvising, Thalia." Suddenly I'm voicing a frustration that has been simmering for days, waiting for me to put it into words. "What good is being a human muse or whatever if I don't know how to fix this painting meltdown or the fading Renoirs? I'm banging around in the dark. How can I save any of the art like that? How can I keep Clio safe if you don't give me answers?"

"That's what I'm saying, Julien! I don't have the answers to this one."

This one.

The emphasis is tiny but meaningful.

"What about the Renoirs?" I ask on a hunch. "Everything started with the fading Renoirs. If he could trap Clio in the painting, could someone use the Muse dust to curse his other work . . .?"

There it is again—the tic in her jaw, the flinch between her brows, the drift of her gaze away from mine.

Oh . . .

I see now.

Not how or why.

Who and what.

My body goes cold.

My skin prickles.

My blood chills.

No. Just no. This can't be.

I swallow roughly, trying to understand, wishing I didn't just unlock the mystery.

But I fear I did.

"*You?* You cursed Renoir's paintings?" I don't want to be right, because this feels so wrong. So twisted against its purpose. "You cursed his *art*, Thalia. And you're a Muse."

Her eyes are wet but hard when they meet mine. "You have to understand, Julien. I love Clio. I love all my sisters. We are all we have—everything else goes into nurturing art and expression. And when he took Clio away . . ." She inhales a deep breath of righteousness that expands her chest and straightens her shoulders. When she speaks again, her words are focused and sharp-edged. "He robbed me of my sister. He robbed the world of all the art she could have inspired."

I have no room to talk. If anyone had taken Clio from me, I would be just as furious, and I don't know what drastic step I might have taken.

"Tell me what happened," I say. "After Clio was trapped, then what?"

If Thalia can fill in the gap in the story, maybe I'll find a clue how to repair, or at least stop, the damage.

She nods, the movement controlled and crisp. "Suzanne Valadon switched a forgery for the real *Woman Wandering in the Irises* and brought the painting to me. I tried everything I could think of to reverse what he'd done, used every tool in my kit. I took the canvas to museums around the world and hid inside until night fell to see if the magic there would free her. But the Muse dust is powerful, and he'd trapped her until a human muse came around. It was binding, and there was nothing I could do."

As she recounts the story, her eyes fill with fury, with the kind of anger that must have engulfed her then. "So, I did the thing I never dreamed that I, or any Muse, would do. I cursed every last painting of his but hers."

I feel almost guilty for how relieved I am at that, with everything else imploding. "Why now though?" I ask. "Why not ruin the paintings back then?"

Thalia leans against the counter, looking exhausted. "I wanted to take what he loved most, so I cursed his art. And I wanted it to hurt, so I cursed it to fade away . . . but not until a human muse appeared. Just as the wave of inspiration spreads, his legacy would fade away."

That's . . . genius.

I'm horrified about the art, and it's impossible to get past that. But if someone hurt Clio, I'd be just as wrathful, and as far as vengeance goes, Thalia's is inspired.

But then, she is a Muse.

If only this wasn't a perfect example of the law of unintended consequences. "The Renoirs started fading right after I interacted with the art—after I tapped into the muse part of me." She nods in confirmation. "Does he know about the curse? Why his paintings are fading?"

Thalia shakes her head. "He's never believed in a human muse, because he's never believed art and beauty can be created by anyone not touched by an eternal Muse. He thinks that to create great works of art you have to be special."

I connect more dots. Renoir knows his art is fading —that's why he's having Cass Middleton recreate the ruined pieces—but he doesn't know why. If he blames the damage to his paintings on Clio, or rather, the display of her painting, who knows what he might do to her still. Renoir wouldn't destroy his own work, but he could have Max cut her out of her frame, roll her up, hide her in a closet somewhere, and think his problems are over.

I suddenly feel as tired as Thalia looks. "Look, all I care about is saving the art and protecting Clio."

She cuts me off. "How is she? Why hasn't she come back yet? Are you going to let her out of the museum?"

Am *I* going to *let* her out?

Has Thalia not met her sister Muse?

"That's up to Clio," I say. The thought of her leaving is a twisting pain in my heart, but it's not up to me.

Someday, maybe soon, Clio will want to get back to her life as a Muse. The best I can hope for is that we can meet between her duties. A stolen kiss here, a brief moment there. I'll take whatever she can spare me and be grateful to have that much.

"You love her," Thalia says, surprising me. I don't know what gave me away, but she's not asking. It's a statement and an expression of wonder.

"Yes," I say with certainty.

"And she is in love with you?"

"Yes." I don't doubt that either. Not after last night.

"What is it like? That kind of love?" Thalia asks, as if she's never even considered it before.

How am I supposed to answer that? Poets and song-smiths have been trying forever. It's feeling as if the stars exist only to shine on the two of you. Feeling as if time stops and your whole heart is full.

Feeling like the impossible has become possible.

My eyes fall on the score spread out on the counter, and I say, "It's like finding a lost symphony."

Thalia smiles. "That sounds wonderful."

"It is," I say with absolute certainty.

It's amazing, and I would stop time to enjoy it forever, but I can't, and there is work to do.

"So, the curse. From what I can tell, it seems to have spread from the Renoirs to affect the other paintings around it, and we need to do something to reverse it. Last night, Clio tried to fix Renoir's painting of *Gabrielle with a Rose*, but . . ." I spread my hands, empty of results. "You've tried, and I assume Calliope tried in London. Nothing seems to work."

Thalia looks at me. Her eyes sharpen. Her tone is crisp but curious. "Well, have *you* tried?"

24

I stand in front of the painting I touched this morning and consider asking one of the Musée's visitors to pinch me. *The Swing* looks perfect.

Absolutely perfect. The woman's white dress is luminescent again, the blue bows radiant. I did that. While I was out all day, the magic went to work.

Why my touch and not Clio's or Thalia's or one of the other eternal Muses?

I answer my own question almost before I finish it. A human muse set the curse into action—ignited it in a way. Logic dictates that a human muse can reel it back in.

Since I can't very well run around the gallery touching all the Renoirs in front of the visitors, I'll have to take care of the others tonight.

But then I see that *Gabrielle with a Rose* has been taken down and a small card placed beside the empty space: *Removed for conservation.*

That gives me a place to start.

I head for the lowest level of the museum, far below ground. If *Gabrielle with a Rose* was taken down this morning, it shouldn't be too hard to find the painting in the storage room. It'll be near the front—especially since the restorers will be in to look at it. Right now, though, the long hall leading there is deserted. I detour to wash my hands—because it would be a shame to cure magical damage and cause the ordinary kind—and then unlock the door to the storage room via the keypad.

Only a portion of the museum's collection is on display at any given time. The ones that aren't on loan spend their sabbatical here, shelved on specialized racks, the lights kept dim and the temperature cool. I find *Gabrielle with a Rose* easily, carefully slide the frame out, and rest it against a nearby wall.

I'll have to be quick—anyone with the code can come in, and I won't be able to hear them approaching. I start where the damage is the worst, spreading my hands and pressing my palm gently against the canvas. I try to remember how long I touched *The Swing*. It wasn't very long at all. So, I lift my hands away and wait.

Nothing happens. I stand, walk through the racks to stretch my legs, and try not to check my watch every thirty seconds. *The Swing* didn't return to its proper state immediately, and the damage to it was much less extensive than that done to *Gabrielle with a Rose*.

Instead of pacing, I head back up to the staff offices and tap on Adaline's door. She's on the phone, but she motions for me to come in.

"Yes," she says to the caller. "We're as baffled as you

are." Adaline rubs her temple as she wraps up the mostly one-sided conversation. When she finally hangs up, she sighs. "That was the Met. The sleeping maid in their Vermeer snores, apparently. Trying to move it made things worse, so they've left all the art in place and roped it off from visitors."

I nod. "That's only sensible."

I don't realize how ridiculous that sounds until Adaline says, "Julien," like I've suggested tea on Mars this afternoon. "*None* of this is sensible."

We stare at each other for a long loaded moment.

Adaline cracks first.

A snort.

A smothered snicker.

We give in to mad, sleep-deprived hilarity so loud I have to shut the door so the staff doesn't think we're lunatics or monsters. Once we get ahold of ourselves, Adaline looks better for the release of endorphins, and I feel a bit better too.

She rubs her hand over her face. "You look like crap."

"You're one to talk," I say, since we're pulling no punches.

"Yes, but this is my job."

"It's mine too," I say, not meaning the internship.

"At least get out of here and get some fresh air and some lunch."

I look at my watch. I need to give *Gabrielle with a Rose* more time to heal, and now that Adaline's mentioned food, I'm ravenous.

"You want me to bring you anything?"

She waves me away. "Go on. We'll touch base later." Then she turns to her email, and I turn toward the door.

I stop, though, to ask, "How many museums does this make?"

"The Louvre, the National Gallery in London, the Hermitage in Saint Petersburg, and now the Met."

If my remedy works can I travel to museums all over the world and convince them to let me grope their paintings?

* * *

I text Simon, and we meet at a café down the street, where I order French fries and a croque monsieur with chicken instead of ham, and another one to take back to Adaline. If she doesn't want it, I'll have no trouble eating it.

Simon raises an eyebrow. "Hungry?"

"A bit," I understate, then drink my less-dreadful-than-usual French coffee. "This muse thing really is exhausting."

He shakes his head. "You know you sound mental, right? I mean, I believe you, because I've seen the news today. But it still sounds mad."

"Come to the museum with me tonight, then, and see for yourself."

With a gasp, Simon puts his hand on his heart like he might swoon. "The holiest of holies? You're too good to me, Julien."

"Now, that is certainly the truth."

My phone rings, and it's Adaline. I take a deep breath and mentally cross my fingers before I answer.

"Oh my God, Julien!" she says before I can get in a word. "It's *Gabrielle with a Rose.* She's perfect. Just perfect!"

Yes! I pump my fist as she expounds upon how *absolutely perfect* the painting is now.

"And that's not all. The curator in Boston called, and *Dance at Bougival* is getting its color back. I can't even . . . I don't even know . . ."

It sounds like the curse is retreating the way it spread, which is going to save me a lot of trouble—no need to conduct a painting restoration world tour.

Adaline rattles on in blissful relief and confusion for a bit, then rings off. I unwrap the second sandwich and dig in.

"All right," says Simon. "Now I have to see this. What time tonight?"

* * *

As the sun drops below the horizon, Gustave opens the front door for Simon and me. We have a bit of a hike to reach the galleries on the far side of the building, where the paintings I need to repair hang. Clio's painting is nearby, and I cannot wait to tell her the news.

Footsteps echo across the floor. I know that sound, and it turns my marrow cold.

I sprint forward, adjusting the strap of my messenger bag as it smacks against my back.

A muffled cry comes from Clio's gallery. I turn the

corner and see Max scraping off the paint of the signature.

Clio's no longer in the picture.

A low moan, laced with pain, draws my horrified gaze to where Clio lies crumpled on the floor as if she fell from her artwork. Blood spreads across her dress, painting her midsection scarlet.

Horror rips through me as the woman I love bleeds.

25

I grab Max first, tearing him away from the painting, and slam him to the ground.

"Hold him down," I tell Simon, and he does.

I rush to Clio and reach for her. "Clio, are you okay?"

She shakes her head, clutching her stomach. "It hurts. Oh God. It hurts so much."

She moans like a wounded cat, and Simon stares. He can't see her, but he can hear her, and his eyes are wide. But his hold on Max doesn't waver.

"I was coming out to see you," Clio says. "It happened so fast . . ." Pain contorts her gorgeous features.

I look over at Max. "How did you get in here?"

Max jerks his head away like a petulant child, refusing to answer. Simon twists the collar of Max's shirt. "He asked you a question. How. Did. You. Get. In. Here?"

"Stairwell," Max chokes out.

"You were in the stairwell all day?" Simon asks. "Hiding out till the museum closed?"

Max manages a quick nod.

"And to think I was just about to save all your paintings, Mr. Renoir," I say. With a grotesque kind of happiness, his eyes widen and realization dawns.

I turn to Clio, my pulse hammering with fear. She's been cut across the stomach. I take off my shirt and press it to her wounds, stemming the flow of blood.

She cries out.

"It's going to be okay, I promise," I say, but it feels empty because I don't know what to do next. "Should I try some of the Muse dust?"

"It won't work," she says.

Then what? It's not as if I can whisk her off to the emergency room to see a doctor.

Wait . . .

A doctor.

There is a doctor in the house.

Excitement trips through me at the possibility, the chance. My pulse spikes as I blurt out, "Clio, I'm going to lay you down for a second so I can get Dr. Gachet, okay?"

But her eyes are closed, and she barely acknowledges me before I lower her head gently to the floor, with Simon watching me, bewildered. "Don't let Max move," I tell him, and race to Dr. Gachet's frame on the second floor. There, I wipe the blood on my hands off on my jeans before I knock on the frame. "Dr. Gachet!"

He yawns, and his mouth stretches through first. "Yes?"

"Come out," I tell him quickly, my heart racing. "I need a doctor."

"Of course," he says. The rest of him, in his shimmery, shiny royal-blue coat, squeezes out of the painting, and I bring him down to the first floor.

Clio is curled on the ground, twisted in on herself. Blood trails between her fingers where she has them pressed over her midsection. Dr. Gachet wastes no time bending to examine her wound. Olympia takes notice too, and jumps out of her frame, hovering nearby, watching.

Dr. Gachet turns to me. "She needs to be stitched up."

I shake my head, grabbing and discarding ideas at the speed of thought. "We don't have a single painting of a hospital to go into. No medical equipment that I can grab."

"Julien," says Dr. Gachet, calm and patient. "This is real blood, not paint. She's not like us. She needs real stitches."

"What do *you* need, then? To fix her? Tell me, and I'll get it," I say in a rush.

He lists the equipment that will help him help her. Scissors, thread, a needle, and a little painkiller would be ideal.

I run my hands through my hair. Scissors I can grab from an office, but a needle and painkiller? I'd have to go home, or to a drugstore. "There's no way I can get all that in time."

"Julien."

It's the tiniest whisper. I kneel at Clio's side and ask softly, "What is it?"

"Draw them," she says. "Draw them for me."

Yes!

With blood-covered fingers, she flicks a bit of silver dust into my left palm while I fumble inside my bag for my notebook. I throw it open and listen as Dr. Gachet describes in detail the instruments he'll need. I draw like a surgeon, fast and precise, then trace the lines with the dust. In seconds, the flat white of the paper takes on shape, turning tangible under my touch. The tools I slide to Dr. Gachet to begin his work, and the painkiller I give to Clio.

"Holy crap." Simon sits on Max and watches me while his jaw hangs open. He's pointing at the scissors Dr. Gachet holds. Simon may not be able to see Dr. Gachet or Clio, but he can see a needle stitching up an invisible wound.

"Yeah," I say ruefully. "This is what I meant by the situation being complicated."

"You are the master of understatement, mate."

I turn back to Clio. She reaches feebly for my hand, wraps her fingers around mine, and winces. "The medicine will kick in soon. Just squeeze tighter till it does."

"It's coming along. Hang in there," Dr. Gachet says, his bedside manner calm and reassuring as he makes neat stitches to bring the edges of Clio's skin together.

Finally, her tight grip loosens, and her knitted eyebrows relax as the medicine takes hold.

Dr. Gachet finishes, making a knot. "There. She'll need rest, but she's going to be okay."

I take my shirt and pull it on, bloodstained and filthy. I turn to Olympia, who's crept a little closer. "Can you watch over her for a bit?"

"Of course, love," she says, kneeling to stroke Clio's hair.

I give Clio a kiss on the forehead. "I'll be back soon, I promise."

"I know," she says, and her eyes flutter closed.

Now it's time to deal with Max. "Let's take him to another room," I tell Simon.

He yanks Max upright and drags him to the next gallery, where I face him, eye to eye. "Do you get it yet? No matter how many paintings you remake, you can't protect your legacy by replacing all of your originals with replicas."

"I just wanted the pigment to make my paintings." He sounds shaken. "I didn't mean to hurt her."

I seethe. Grit my teeth. Then speak. "But you did hurt her. You hurt her then, and you hurt her now. Is that what great art is? Hurting others? Is that who you are? Is that why you're back?"

With a touch of defiance, he lifts his chin. But his voice wavers, a note of contrition coming through as he says, "No."

"You have to stop then," I say, holding my ground. "You're causing more damage. You're creating nothing but pain. That can't be your legacy."

He heaves a sigh, but then nods again.

"And it's not just your paintings that are ruined. Have you been to the Louvre? Just look around. All that art is dying because of you."

He winces, like now he's in pain. Finally, I think I'm getting through.

I point to *The Swing*. "That was fading this morning, and now it's not. I fixed *Gabrielle with a Rose* too. I'm not even a great artist or an eternal Muse, but I'm the only one who can fix your paintings. Face it—art isn't just for the elite. Art belongs to everyone. Get over it."

Renoir's eyes flick from painting to painting and then to me, his pupils flaring with desperation. "You can fix them?"

"Yes," I grit out.

"Will you fix my paintings? Will you save them?"

"Yes," I say, exasperated. "Despite what you did to Clio, I'll save your work. Your legacy will go on, I promise. Under one condition."

"Name it," he says, and he's begging now.

"You need to leave us alone, leave *Max* alone, and get rid of your fake paintings."

"I will." He mutters a strangled "I'm sorry."

"Save your apology for the one who deserves it."

Simon and I drag him back to Clio's gallery, where she's resting on a bench, Dr. Gachet and Olympia on either side of her. Simon is gripping Max's hands so they're behind his back, but when he gets close enough, he bends down and speaks in a low, remorseful voice.

He doesn't say sorry though.

But he says something that perhaps matters more.

"Thank you. For inspiring me."

* * *

Gustave nearly falls over when he sees Simon and me escorting Max out the front doors. I promise to explain later. Maybe by then I'll have thought of something to say.

We hail a cab to take us to the Marais, then the three of us climb into the back seat, Max in the middle. We ride in silence for a bit, and then Simon says, "So. You're dating a painting?"

I correct him. "I'm 'dating' a Muse who is stuck inside a painting."

"Oh, okay, then. That's not nearly as weird." After a moment, he asks, "Do you love her?"

"I do." The reply comes easily, naturally. "I do love her."

Simon nods. "Good. I'm glad about that."

＊ ＊ ＊

At the tiny church where Renoir has set up his studio, I take the knife he used at the museum from my pocket and hand it to him. Then I wait while he slashes through all the forgeries Cass has made for him. Big, unrepairable X's.

When he's done, he looks at me, flexing his knotted fingers. "You promised to fix my art."

"Yes, I did. And I will. But you should go."

He nods, then stretches his fingers straight. There's a gust of wind, and it carries the trailing telltale scent of rose perfume. I'll never smell roses the same way again.

Max—the real Max—shakes his head as if he just

woke from a strange dream, then looks around, dumb-founded.

"Hey, bud." Simon claps him on the shoulder. "You've been sleepwalking. Let me take you back to your pad."

Thank you, I mouth to Simon before they go.

* * *

After a stop to buy an "I LOVE PARIS" T-shirt to replace my ruined shirt and a sandwich at the first vendor I find, I return to the Musée d'Orsay and get started healing the Renoirs like I promised. By the time I finish the first two, the rest have started to restore themselves. So, the curse retreats the way it advanced. Like dominoes falling, all I have to do is touch a few and the rest follow.

I am calm in a way I haven't been since the first night the art came alive for me. Now all I have to do is wait to see how the cure affects all the other paintings.

How it spreads to them.

How it saves them.

Because it will.

Everything is going to be fine. Everything is going to be better. I inhale deeply, relieve Dr. Gachet and Olympia of their bedside watch, and take Clio to the South of France.

26

We escape into a beach inside a Cézanne.

Soft waves lap our feet. Warm sand pillows our heads. It's the perfect place for rest and relaxation, which is just what the doctor ordered for Clio. I am all too happy to be her companion on a quick trip to the painted seashore in Marseille.

"Just think right now of all the sick paintings that are starting to feel better. Because of your touch," Clio says as she squeezes my hand happily. Her other hand rests on her wounded stomach. Her face is still pale, but she's had some water and some of the sandwich I'd picked up for her.

"I'm going to hang up a shingle that says 'ART DOCTOR FOR HIRE, AT YOUR SERVICE.'" I tuck my hands behind my head and let the warm sun of the Mediterranean beat down on my face. "By the time we return, the reports will be pouring in from all the other museums."

"I can't wait to hear the good news," she says. Then

she shifts gears. "What else did Thalia say when you saw her this morning? Did she ask about me?"

"Yes."

"Did she want to know when I was coming back?"

"It's like you can read her mind," I joke.

"What did you tell her?"

I prop myself up on my elbow and run a finger along her bare arm. "Clio, when you go back is entirely up to you."

"Do you think I should?"

"If you want to."

"But will I still see you?"

I laugh. "I'll see you as much as I possibly can. Meeting Thalia just once makes me appreciate how busy you all must be."

"Maybe I can convince Thalia to let me work less."

"Part-time Muse?"

"Why not? Maybe when there are more human muses, it will lighten the load on the eternal Muses so we can do things besides work." Her voice is wistful. Longing. "I could meet you between assignments. See you here and there. Would that drive you crazy?"

"Totally. But I'd do it happily. Clio, if I could see you for five minutes a day, I would. If I could see you for five minutes a week, I'd sign up for that too. All I want is for this not to end."

"Good. Because I think I can convince her. After all, I *have* been trapped for more than a century," Clio says, and bats her eyes then pushes out her bottom lip so it quivers. "How's that?"

"Just add a sniffle to the mix, and she won't be able to resist," I say.

"Maybe a crocodile tear or two?"

"Go for it. I'll bet you can work her guilt to your advantage for a good long while." I'm teasing, even though it's true. Then I shift gears. "When do you think you'll leave?"

"I want to rest up for another day or so. It still hurts," she says, gently pressing her hand to her belly. "But then I guess I'll go."

She sounds so sad, and her voice breaks again. "But we'll see each other," she adds, and she bends to me, her lips touching mine so gently, so sweetly. The ends of her hair brush my chest, and an intoxicated sigh that becomes her name escapes my lips.

"We have to see each other, Julien. I want more of this world. I want more of you," she says, and I wrap my arms around her and hold her, inside our faraway painted land.

We fall asleep on the beach, and I dream of nothing but all the possibilities of her.

I blink. There's sand in my eye. I blink again and scrunch up my nose, because now my eyes are starting to water. I sit up. So does Clio. The sand is blowing, like a breeze is sweeping along the seashore. The wind picks up quickly, and soon it's hardly a warm breeze, or a welcoming one. Within seconds, it's a thrashing wind, and Clio's hair whips across her face. She grasps at strands that lash her, and I fumble for her hand to pull her up. The water from the sea pounds the shore. We run toward the green fields near the edge of the canvas, but the sand swirls and buries the path. The painted grass turns brown and crackly.

The waves pursue us, snapping at our feet. With each step, the ground is looser, crumbling under our feet. "We're almost out," I say.

I stick a hand through the paint and out the other side, and then Clio and I slide onto the museum floor. We slip on something, and I stare in disbelief at the wet sand on the museum floor.

Clio coughs and sputters. The beach avalanche has stopped, and the beautiful Cézanne has sloughed off its insides. The rest of the galleries seem quiet, but it's like waiting for the thunder that's sure to follow a bolt of lightning.

This wasn't supposed to happen. I dosed the Renoirs. Why didn't the cure spread?

"We have to check on the others," I say. Even with her wounded midsection, Clio hurries with me on a mad hunt through the galleries, surveying all the paintings on the walls, from the far ends of the first floor to the hidden nooks on the second floor.

Everything else is fine, except for a Degas of an orchestra, where the music has become warped and the notes scratchy.

Clio covers her ears for a second. "Oh, that's not how it sounded when he made that painting."

"That's right. Degas was one of yours." Something clicks, and I stop, swiveling to face her with a hard look. "I need to check something." The plaque beside the painting lists 1870 as the date it was made.

This hunch involves math.

This painting and the Cézanne that just spat us out were made before 1885. But the Van Goghs, the Matisses, the Toulouse-Lautrecs came after, and they're unharmed.

The year 1885 is when Clio was cursed into the painting. That's the dividing line. Before Clio. After Clio.

I place my hands on her shoulders. "I think I know what's going on. It's all the art that you inspired that's having trouble. Everything modern is fine, the later Cézannes are fine. But we were in an earlier one, from when you worked with him." And I know something too—this is a brand-new problem. This has little to do with Renoir. This is all because of Clio. "The art you inspired is starting to crumble."

I pace, feeling stupid for making assumptions. "I think . . ." God, this is hard to say. It's like ripping off a piece of flesh. It's like tearing out a part of me. "I think that the art misses you." I don't, can't, voice the rest. The art needs her to keep being its Muse.

Clio rubs her temples the same way Adaline did.

"When did it start? Not the fading of the Renoirs, but the art falling apart? When was that?" Her tone is desperate. "I need to know. You have to tell me."

I think of the dancers twirling in the halls, of *Olympia*'s cat coming out to play. But that was just art coming to life. I flash to the first time I saw trouble brewing—the flame, and the feathers, and the transforming of Bathsheba. "A couple of days after Remy's party. Why?"

Hand pressed to her side, Clio darts into the main hallway, breathing hard. "The sun is rising. I have to go."

"Right, right. I know." I follow her quickly. "Let's set you free from the painting."

She shakes her head. "No. I can't go yet."

"Clio . . . you have a good reason to rest. Thalia will let you take it easy on your Muse jobs."

Her lip quivers. Her face looks pinched. "I don't think that's the problem with the art."

"Then what is it?"

Her eyes shine with the threat of tears. "It's daylight. I have to go back or—" She runs to her canvas and slides back inside, cut in her stomach and all.

I call out to her, but she's gone.

And I have no idea why the art she inspired is crumbling, but I suspect she does.

And I suspect, too, that she doesn't like the answer.

Which means I probably won't either.

27

We are not alone.

Around the world, artwork is spitting up.

Vomiting its insides.

A whole new spate of problems.

I clean up under the Cézanne, bagging the sand and leaving it below the frame, as the other museums around the world have done.

I spend my time tracking the art as it falls. A Goya in Saint Petersburg, a handful of Vermeers in the Met, a Morisot at the Art Institute of Chicago. The Renoirs are now all undamaged, that debt settled, but something far more dangerous has infected the other art.

I scroll through my email alerts even as I grab a late-afternoon coffee to go. At least one thing doesn't have to do with the art implosion. There's a note from Emilie, with an attachment.

Hi Julien,

I've been following all these crazy museum reports. How bizarre. I have faith you'll sort it out though.

If you're not too busy doing that, I got a solo in The Sleeping Beauty *(it's fine if you say "I told you so"), and you mentioned you might like to see the ballet. I have two tickets reserved for you and your girlfriend. You can get them at the link I attached.*

Best of luck and see you soon (I hope!),
Emilie

My *girlfriend*. In the midst of everything, that word still makes me happy. The thought that Clio will be free by the date of the performance even makes me happy enough to smile.

* * *

When night comes, Clio escapes from her painting looking ashen and weary.

"I know what's going on with the art. I figured it out," she says in a dead voice. She slumps against the wall and drops her head into her hands. "It is all my fault."

I sink down beside her, shaking my head, wanting to reassure her. "Clio, it's not your fault. Even Thalia didn't make the connection." I rub her back, encouraging her.

"It's going to be fine. The art you inspired needs you back, so we'll get you back."

"That's not it, Julien. That's not it at all." Clio lifts her face and looks at me. Her eyes are rimmed with pain. Her face is stricken. She lowers her voice to a confessional tone, like she's admitting a terrible crime. She whispers, "I caused it."

"No, you didn't," I say, denying it for her.

She nods. "I did." She winces, draws a breath, then seems to steel herself. "They're dying because I love you more than them."

What?

I sputter. I blink.

I can't believe that. I refuse to believe that. She has to be wrong.

I start to protest, but words are like sawdust in my mouth. "No" is all I can manage.

She takes my hand, squeezing it. "Yes." She sounds forlorn. She sounds like she lost a symphony. "It has to be the reason. No Muse has ever been in love before. We only love art, or literature, or music. We love each other, and the art form we're inspiring. Our magic is for inspiration, and our love is for preservation. That's it; nothing more. When I started caring about you, all the art I inspired, all the art I loved, got sick. It can't be any other way, Julien."

"People can love more than one thing, Clio." I sound more desperate than logical. I *feel* desperate. This can't be the answer. "Emotion isn't a finite commodity."

"For *people*, Julien."

I stare at her, struck silent.

"I thought about it all day. The Géricault—that was the first to die," she says, and puts a hand on her heart. "That painting was so hard for him. Remember how I told you that? How I had to give it so much of my love to bring it into being, and to keep it alive? The Ingres at the Louvre too. And Rembrandt. I've loved them all," she says, recounting the works she nurtured, her passion for the art permeating her voice. "All I've ever done is put my love into paintings. Then you came along, and I started wanting you instead."

Her words warm my heart, but I can't be distracted by these feelings. I have to convince her of the wrongness of what she's saying. "That's not true. The art started changing before you came to the museum," I point out. "You were still at Remy's house. The day after his party, I went to the Louvre and first saw the changes. The timing doesn't line up for your theory to be true."

She shakes her head with heavy sadness. "I wish that were so. But I fell for you before I even came here to the Musée d'Orsay, Julien. It was the night you talked to me for the first time. Remember? I tried to break out then because I wanted to see you. So, you see, as soon as I felt the first inkling of something for you, the paintings began to change. The deeper I fell for you, the sicker the art got."

I grab onto that one light spot in the darkness dropping onto me. "The first time I talked to you, huh?"

She smiles. "Yes. You're so easy to like. Falling for you is the most wonderful thing I have ever done."

She looks radiant, like she's glowing because of me,

because of our love, and I can't resist touching her. I grab her and kiss her hard on the mouth, holding her face. Reveling in the feel of her. In the way she responds. In how we connect.

Her body aligns with mine, sensual and snug, her breasts pressed to my chest, her hips to my hips.

We kiss long and deep and hard.

We kiss like it might be the last time.

And though I despise that thought, I love every second of her touch.

Of these lips, this face, this heat, this life.

She kisses me with so much passion, I know she must be right. If I were a painting that had experienced love like this and then the love went away, turned elsewhere, I'd shrivel up and explode too.

But I'm not a painting. I'm a man who can hold himself together so that the woman I love can do what she needs to do.

"So how do we fix it?" I ask at last.

"I have to do it," she says in a careful, measured voice. "Let me try it here first. Where is the Cézanne from last night?"

"Where we left it."

We walk a few rooms over to the Cézanne. The bag of sand is nestled at the foot of the frame. The canvas is a messy stew of mottled oils.

"So, first, I'll just touch it," she says, and places her palms on the remains. Nothing happens. "Now, I'll concentrate on putting the love back into it." She lays her hands on the canvas once more, closing her eyes. Her lips part, and she looks so beautiful, the way she looked when she first told me she was in love with me. It makes me ache, and it makes me want her at the same awful time.

As she stands like that, the sand from the bag swirls around her on a gentle wind, then dances back into the frame, where it returns to paint and the colors become grass and sea and trees again, reforming a ravaged landscape into the luscious one Cézanne created.

I have seen so many amazing things. I've had my mind blown many times, but watching the art being repaired, like time-lapse photography running backward, has to be at the top.

When Clio opens her eyes, she looks the slightest bit different. It's hard to pinpoint how, but she looks a bit less like Clio and more like Thalia. Not in her features, but in her demeanor. As if she's been sharpened.

"There you go," I say, gesturing to the painting, restored to exactly the way it was before. "As good as new. Voilà."

I smile like she hasn't changed at all in the process.

We can do this. *She* can do this.

This is what has to happen, no matter how heavy the air or how hard my lungs have to work to breathe through the tightness that grips me.

When I look into her eyes, I know what she's going to say will slaughter my heart.

She squares her shoulders. Draws a deep breath. "The thing is, it's not enough for me to love the art. I have to put the love I feel for you into the paintings." She takes a beat, then deals the punishing blow. "To save the art, I have to stop loving you."

28

She is the poison, and she is the cure.

"It's like a debt," she says in an even voice. She taps her chest. "One I have to repay."

She sounds resigned, but resolute.

Meanwhile, I feel like I've been pummeled. Cut off at the knees.

I always knew that Clio and I had met in a strange and wonderful otherness that couldn't last forever. I thought we'd simply have to part, and that would have been hard enough. But this is worse, far worse.

Loving her unrequited.

Loving a woman who no longer loves me.

Tears streak down her cheeks, and even though I feel so heavy I could sink to the ocean floor, I wrap her in my arms so she can muffle her sadness against my shirt. I want to take her pain away. Even though I know I'll be wearing all her pain soon.

"I'm sorry," she says. "I'm so sorry. That only took a tiny bit away." She touches my cheek, so soft and tender that I have to close my eyes just to contain all the feelings that threaten to burst out of my heart. "I'm still crazy about you now, Julien."

Now. But soon, not at all.

"So I guess I should let you out the door. To do the repairs." My voice is empty.

"No. As long as I'm part of the painting, no one can see me except you. But once I leave the museum, I'm no longer bound, and anyone can see me then. Which makes doors and security guards a problem."

She keeps talking, thinking out loud. "I need time to focus, and to put my hands on the art. I'll have to be there when no one else is." I know what she's about to say, and I want to stop her, but I can't. "To repair the art, I need your help."

It's a sucker punch.

And I'm winded, doubled over.

"Because with me, you can go at night and travel through the paintings." My voice is flat. I'll help her, but I can't make myself excited about losing her love. "We can cross Monet's bridges when we touch them at the same time."

"Exactly. Most of the museums we need have Monets with bridges, don't they? He made all those paintings after I was trapped, so we know they'll be intact. We can travel through them almost instantly."

She's put those details together fast. She's brilliant, and breaking into a museum through a painting should be the coolest thing I've ever done, but it means I'll have to witness my own execution. I'll have to watch her fall out of love with me.

"Let's go now," I say, walking to the nearest bridge painting. I want to get this over with. The longer I have to think about it, the harder it will be.

Clio shakes her head. "There's a problem with now."

"What's that?"

"The Louvre doesn't have any Monets, or any other Impressionist paintings of the bridge. We can't get in that way. And I think we need to start where the problem started."

There is logic to that, but I don't feel logical. I want to rip off the Band-Aid.

As if she can read my thoughts, she wipes a hand across her face to dry her tears and steels herself. "Look, this is my problem. I can do it myself during the day after you free me. It's riskier but not impossible."

"Clio . . ." Now I feel like an asshole.

Probably because I'm being an asshole.

She shakes her head. "I should never have asked you. It's not fair."

"That's true," I say, and she blinks in surprise. "It sucks in every way imaginable. But I'm in this with you, and we have to fix it together. I want to protect you, and I will. The trouble is anyone can see me anytime. We have to come up with a way that I won't be spotted on security cameras roaming about foreign museums in the middle of the night."

"I actually have a few ideas," she says with a grin. "But what about the Louvre?" She looks over at the nearest Monet. "Can we somehow get one of these Japanese bridges into the Louvre?"

"Seriously?"

"Yes, seriously," she says. "Maybe . . . one from a private collection?"

"Sure. All my friends have a Monet or two lying around—"

Hang on.

Hang the hell on.

I grin, and this is the first time I've felt anything good since she told me the news.

I picture dusky-blue light on the slatted bridge, and I look at Clio and smile. "As a matter of fact . . . I do know someone."

We spend the rest of the night making a plan that would shame Ethan Hunt and his *Mission: Impossible* team. We study the layouts of the museums, mapping where the Monets are relative to the damaged paintings and plotting the fastest way to get from one to the other. I'm sure that's not what the museums intended their interactive maps to be used for, but we end up with a plan.

The Louvre will be the toughest. It's huge and has the most paintings that need attention, and our solution for getting in is complex, which means more points where it could go wrong. Anything that starts in a restroom is bound to be dicey.

The final thing we need—other than the loan of a Monet—is the phone number of Gustave's buddy on the night shift at the Louvre. We manage that by the grace of Clio's pickpocketing skill and dumb luck that Gustave doesn't have a passcode on his cell phone.

Number jotted down and phone returned, we've done all we can tonight.

Before she goes into her painting, Clio heals the warped Degas, and the orchestra stops playing out of tune. I'm afraid to look at her, afraid she won't care for me anymore, but she gives me one more kiss good night, and I savor it for what it is.

The last of its kind.

Museum security is nothing like the movies, where master thieves rappel in through skylights and hack surveillance cameras. And forget ridiculously complicated webs of infrared beams.

Most museums have alarms and monitors not much different than those in houses these days, plus a couple of yawning guards patrolling the galleries after dark. But the real deterrent is that it's virtually impossible to fence a museum piece anywhere, so robberies aren't worth the risk.

That said, I'd rather not be spotted by camera lenses or human eyes, and while we can travel between paintings of Monet's bridge, I can't take anything through the canvases but the clothes I'm wearing—no cheating with pockets. So, to be able to draw handy things into existence, I'll need the help of an advance party. Which is where my friends come in.

We meet up in a café that day, and, using the maps and layouts of each museum, I explain what I'll need in each city. The rest is the basic who, why, and where of the mission. I leave out the part about Clio falling out of love with me. I don't want pity. More than that, I don't want to hear myself say it.

Simon's buddy Patrick can help in London, where the Turner seascapes pour out of their frames at each high tide. Lucy used to live in Chicago, and a friend there owes her a favor. She snaps a pic of the diagram that shows where the pencil and paper need to be in the Art Institute, and texts it to her contact.

Remy, of course, knows tons of people in New York who can pop into the Met, but we're out of luck in Saint Petersburg, so Clio and I will have to get creative.

We call it a "scavenger hunt," and recruiting remote help is surprisingly easy. Talking Remy into loaning us his Monet isn't even that hard—the challenge is keeping him from hysterics when I explain what I need to do with it.

Outside the pyramid at the Louvre, I almost don't recognize Remy in jeans and a brown T-shirt. Sophie describes her own outfit as "unobtrusively understated." What they're about to do is totally legal, but it pushes the line from eccentric to odd enough that if anyone notices, it will throw a wrench in the whole plan.

Remy clamps his messenger bag between his arm and his side, but not *too* tightly. "It's like carrying around a freaking diamond. No—thousands of diamonds." He puts his fingers to the side of his neck, then grabs my hand and presses my fingers somewhere sort of around his pulse point. "Feel this. My heart is beating ten thousand times a minute."

I pat his shoulder with a small laugh. "You'll live. You want to go over it again? The Monet canvas is inside the bag, right?"

He nods. Walking himself through the steps does seem to settle him a little. "We took it out of the frame and off the stretcher bars," he says, referring to the wooden bars that keep canvases taut inside their frames. "Then we put it into a padded envelope and caught a taxi, because there was no way I was taking a Monet on the Metro."

"Correction. *I* took it off the stretchers. Your hands were shaking too much to do that," Sophie points out.

Remy holds up a now steady palm to his sister. "Whatever."

I continue to review the plan. "Security will scan your bag like any other bag. There's nothing to set off an alert, but even if they decide to look through it, there's no law that says you can't take a work of art you own out for a stroll."

"Plus," says Sophie, "who is going to believe that it's the original? Because that would be crazy, carrying around an original Monet in a mailing envelope."

"Right. Right." Remy nods as if the repetitive motion will calm his nerves. "Then we go to the ladies' room on the second floor."

"The small one by the far stairwell," I confirm. "The one least likely to be patrolled."

"I have the double-sided tape in my purse," Sophie says, as always up for anything. "I take the canvas from the envelope and hang it under the sink where no one will see it. Then we leave the padded envelope behind in the bathroom."

"Piece of cake," I say, and clap them both on the back. "I have complete faith in you both. Now, get in there quick, before they close."

Remy salutes me, and Sophie grabs his elbow, and they head inside through the pyramid entrance. I can't take the chance of being seen there by someone I know.

So I wait and I pace, and twenty minutes later, they rush out, breathless and elated.

"We did it!" Sophie declares, then tells me how she hung their prized Monet. It's now out of sight, taped to the wooden underside of the sink counter. "It's not as bad as it sounds. I secured it on the very outer edge of the canvas, painted side down to further hide it, not risking a brushstroke of Monet's."

"Excellent."

Now all I have to do is hope that no one goes into that bathroom for the next several hours.

29

I don't have any carry-on luggage. This trip doesn't allow it, since we can't take anything into a painting. All we need are our hands and wits. I hope they're mightier than the sword, or the nightstick, I should say.

"Ready?"

"I just need to do one more thing. Come with me," Clio says, and walks across the main floor. I follow her, and we stop at a Toulouse-Lautrec. She tilts her head and offers a faint smile tinged with regret. "A proper goodbye?"

That is something I can't resist. I take her hand, and the museum is gone, wiped away by the sounds of the cancan, a dance that originated at a cabaret with windmills at the top of Montmartre. How I wish I were truly dancing with her in Montmartre. But this is as close as we'll ever come. We've fallen into the festivities as only Toulouse-Lautrec could imagine them, surrounded by turn-of-the-century-dressed men and women with high-laced boots and ruffled skirts who don't notice that we've crashed their painted party. Music plays from a band on the stage, drinks are shared freely, and revelers are everywhere. It's always a fête at the Moulin Rouge, but it is bittersweet tonight.

She holds her hands out. "May I have this dance?"

"But of course," I say with a smile, trying my best to keep the sadness at bay.

"This is what I want you to remember of me, not what happens next. This is what I'll remember. The before," she says, and her eyes are so tough and so earnest at the same time. I know she wants to believe what she's saying. I know right now she suspects she'll never forget this. But she won't feel it again. I will be just another memory, the same as all her other memories. Nothing special—just the week she ditched work. What made it so compelling? She'll wonder that days and weeks from now, barely able to recall the depths of our emotions.

Sick with the knowledge of what's about to happen, I wrap my arms tight around her as she leans into me, and I take my here and now. I do my damnedest to forget the destruction aimed at my heart. Instead, I layer kisses on her neck, and I taste her lips once more. I kiss her with everything I have, knowing it's our last. She kisses me back almost the same way. With almost the same passion. Almost the same wish to get lost in this final kiss. The dancers kicking their legs high in the air onstage might as well be in Peru. This is all there is. This is all I want. "I will never forget you."

"You saved me, you know. You saved me from being trapped. You're the reason I can be free from that painting," she says, and with her words, my heart is both caving and pounding. "I want you to know how much I wish there were another way. I love you, Julien. More than art."

That, in a nutshell, is the problem.

I fold her into my arms, and we dance for a few minutes inside the Toulouse-Lautrec, aware the whole time of the ticking bomb on the other side. But I let this moment stretch into itself.

I wish I could say I don't care if I ever return to the real world.

But I can't say that.

The enemy was never really Renoir. The real enemy has always been the impossibility of us.

I kiss her once more, a last kiss that has to last for all time.

30

The church bells across the river strike midnight. We're starting now so we can reach all the museums while it's still night in their time zones. I leave my messenger bag and phone under a bench, a home base here in the Musée d'Orsay. A few feet away is the Japanese bridge Monet painted. I step inside it with Clio, and we place our clasped hands together on the railing.

"To the Louvre," she says, and we step forward, our feet landing on another bridge, this one in Remy's painting.

I jam my palms out but still smack the tiled floor of the ladies' room hard with my hands. Clio falls out next, banging her forehead on a metal pipe.

Ouch, she mouths.

"You okay?"

She nods and rolls out from under the sink. She stumbles as she stands, getting tangled in her long dress. I reach out for her hand so she won't trip. She steadies herself, and I crawl out next. I smile at my partner in crime, or rather, my partner in uncrime. "It worked," I whisper, relieved that the painting's been safe from people and water since closing time.

"It's showtime," I say, and hold open the door for Clio. She heads for the Géricault, and the halls are eerily silent.

I have work to do too. I'd picked this entry point so I'd have a place to hide while I took care of Remy's painting. Hunching under the sink, I carefully remove the tape from the canvas then find the padded envelope Sophie hid between the trash can and its liner.

I check the time—Clio should have healed *The Raft of the Medusa* and be onto the Rembrandt now. So when I hear someone coming, I know it can't be her. I slip into a stall, close the door, and hop up onto the toilet seat, holding the Monet and the envelope. The door opens, and through the crack in the stall door, I see a security guard leaning into the mirror to search for something between her teeth.

"There you are!"

I'm tense enough that I almost jump and fall off the toilet. But she's talking about whatever she removed from her teeth and rinsed down the sink.

She opens the door to leave when her radio crackles.

"Problem at the *Mona Lisa*," the garbled voice says.

I hold my breath. *Please be safe, Clio.*

The guard brings the radio to her mouth. "What's the problem?"

"I think she's drunk."

The guard scoffs. "Really?"

"She's telling a dirty joke, I think."

"You think?"

"My Italian is rusty."

"I'm on my way," the guard barks into the radio. The door swings shut, and she's gone.

I exhale, and then it hits me—the Mona Lisa is doing what? Suddenly, I like the overrated painting a little better. Creeping out of the stall and putting my ear to the door, I listen, but *my* Italian is more than rusty.

The joke stops, and a minute later, Clio opens the door, breathing hard. "I had to fix the *Mona Lisa* too," she says.

"That's what's behind the famous smile?" I ask as I position the padded envelope with the Monet on top of it on the tiles near the door. "A tipsy Mona Lisa telling a dirty joke?"

"More like the satisfaction at her dinner guests' shocked faces." Clio flashes a smile of her own. "She was ordinarily such a *gracious* hostess."

We're laughing as we step into the Monet and return to the Musée d'Orsay.

We're also still holding hands, grinning at our success as we arrive back in the familiar blue-walled gallery. Clio's touch is almost enough to make me think there might be room in her heart for both art and me. But already she's not quite holding my hand the way she used to, she's not touching the inside of my palm with a finger or tracing lines on my wrist. I'm more like a guy she likes, not the guy she loves.

I call Remy. He answers his phone before it has time to ring. "Please have good news."

"The paintings at the Louvre are done. Call the

number I gave you for the security guard and tell him you left your Monet in the ladies' room this evening. He can't miss it; it's right by the door. And it won't be the weirdest thing he's seen this week."

Remy sighs in profound relief. "Thank you."

"Thank *you*. We could not have done this without it."

He rings off to call Gustave's friend at the Louvre.

I turn to Clio. "How was the art? What did it look like?"

"Titian's mirror repaired itself. Bathsheba reshaped. The flame in the La Tour relit, and it's flickering in paint now," Clio says, and she's so animated and excited to tell me about the reformed art.

"And the Géricault?"

"It was as if the water crashed backward and the waves rolled right into the frame. Then the canvas sort of slurped it all up. It looks just like the day it was made."

"It's amazing," I say. "Russia now?"

"To Saint Petersburg we go."

Clio might not be visible to anyone but me, but she's audible to everyone. Including a guard who happens to be one room over from the Monet exhibit at the Hermitage. To complicate matters, the museum hasn't updated its website lately, because the layout we saw of this gallery is just a tad wrong.

The guard jerks his head when Clio's footsteps clip past him on the way to the Goya. But when he swivels around and sees me, I must appear—though it would be impossible—to be the source of the footsteps. At the very least, I'm an intruder. I'm about to jump into the closest Monet, the one I picked in advance for protection, but all the Monets near me are his earlier works that Clio inspired—thanks for nothing, Hermitage website—and I'm not about to take shelter in a painting that could collapse in on itself.

I scan the room quickly as the guard calls out to me in Russian.

I don't know what he's saying, but he's not happy. He moves toward me. I spot a later Monet, one of the *Haystacks*. It's a few feet from me. I step toward it as the guard comes closer. I reach my hands inside the painting and take out the haystack. It's big, but it's not heavy. I hold it in front of me as a shield. I don't think he can see the haystack, since he's not a muse. But like *Olympia*'s cat and Cézanne's peach, the haystack is real, and it occupies space.

More Russian words fall from his lips. I shrug my shoulders but stay silent. Accents won't disguise me. The guard is now mere feet from me, and he tries to grab me, but the thick bale of straw is a prickly buffer between us. He keeps lunging and keeps getting bounced back by the invisible haystack. Finally, he fumbles for the radio on his belt and calls for backup. He goes for his phone next and snaps a picture of me, of the Teflon guy he can't touch.

C'mon, Clio. It's only one painting.

I hear heavy running footsteps bringing another guard, who fires off more Russian orders at me.

Seconds later, Clio's racing through the halls, and both guards turn their heads at the noise. When she slides into the gallery, she sizes up the situation with a glance. She knocks off the second guard's cap, and when he swivels around, Clio comes up behind the first guard and says something in Russian. His eyes widen, and he looks down at his pants, his face reddening. It gives Clio a chance to grab my hand, so I drop the haystack, then we run like hell to the bridge.

"What about the haystack?" I ask as soon as our feet touch safe ground.

"I'll go tomorrow morning and put it back. It'll take two seconds, but that was more time than we had just then," she says.

"Right. How was the Goya?"

"Oh, it was beautiful." She lays a hand on her heart. "I was so happy to see it again."

Happy. I wince.

"But I still like you," she says, and she sounds like herself, or as much of herself as there still is. She's got that shy and sweet look about her, and part of me thinks she may even dive in for one more kiss. But she doesn't.

"What did you say to that guard in Russian?"

"I told him his fly was down."

I laugh, and she smiles, and we're still in this together.

"Hey, Clio. As a favor, could you try to be just a little quieter when you run down the halls? I'd kind of like to not run into another security guard if I can."

"Maybe you should draw me some padded socks,"

she says with a wink, and I enjoy what I suspect might be our last inside joke.

The Impressionist room at the National Gallery in London is blissfully quiet. So is Clio as she taps the Muse dust into my hand. I close my fist around it then put the loose dust in my front pocket. Meanwhile, Clio heads—with careful, silent steps—away from the Monets and on to the Turners, a few rooms away.

I spy the bench I'd picked out and reach underneath. Yes! Simon's friend Patrick came through. I untape the sheet of paper and pencil, lie flat on my stomach, and sketch quickly. The drawing is a contingency plan, so I tuck it under the bench and, with thirteen minutes left to wait, pop into a painting of Monet's water lilies, out of sight of any passing guard.

I'm soaked to my knees the second I enter the painting, but it's peaceful here at Monet's pond, and so I slosh to the bank and sit, careful not to let my jeans pockets get wet. There are more than half a dozen damaged Turners here in the National Gallery, so fixing them will take time.

But it will also take more than that. Clio will pour her love into the Turners and they'll be right again, and my world will be wrong—I can't imagine she'll feel much of anything for me after repairing that many paintings.

When I leave the painting ten minutes later, I leave the water behind too, coming out completely dry.

The room is still quiet, so I pace and wait. I should have stayed in the painting a little longer.

I drop onto the bench too hard and push it an inch or two. That's all, but in the quiet, I might as well have blown a trumpet.

Cursing my impatience for making me careless, I pluck the drawing from under the bench and sprinkle it with a pinch of the Muses' dust from my pocket.

Two sets of footsteps move with purpose toward the Monet room. One set is Clio's, and she rounds the corner into the Impressionist room.

"Guard coming!" She mouths.

"Did you get it done?" I ask the same way, relieved when she nods.

Jerking my head toward our exit painting, I trace my drawing with silvery fingertips, cupping my hand around the bird that comes to life. I release it near the door and hear the flurry of wings and the startled guard saying, "Bloody hell!" Just as we go, I get a snatch of him calling wildlife rescue.

Clio and I walk toward the bridge inside the painting, and she tells me about the magnificent sight of the waters and the sunsets being remade, of how the light streaked across the paint in just the way Turner had always envisioned. As I listen to her, it occurs to me that in some ways she's not that different. She isn't cold or callous. She's still warm and glowing, but she only has eyes for the art now. She is slipping away from the woman she was with me and reverting back to the Muse she was made to be. I want to share this moment with her, to rejoice in the saving of the art, but each reborn painting crushes me a little more.

She almost forgets to reach for my hand when we walk onto the bridge on the way to the Met. I feel as if the ground is starting to sway as she changes.

"Oops, sorry," she says, like it's no big deal, and it isn't to her, because she no longer has the desire to hold my hand.

* * *

For no good reason, I opt to bide my time in a church. Tired of water lilies, I guess. The real Rouen Cathedral in Normandy was bombed during World War II, but here it's still perfect. I thought it would be peaceful waiting for Clio there, and it is.

Much too peaceful, and my thoughts are too loud.

My feelings churn from angst to resignation to anger at the unfairness of having to participate in the excision of Clio's love from my life.

I leave the painting before I *really* start to wallow in misery.

My feet are barely on the floor when there's a cry from another room.

Clio.

I bolt down the hall and then turn into a room full of modern art, spinning around when I realize it's not the direction where the noise came from.

There's a shadow by the entry, a not-Clio shadow, and my heart stops.

I quickly survey the room and dive into the nearest

painting. My jaw drops when I reach the other side of the drip marks, and I think I may laugh harder than I've ever laughed in my life. Jackson Pollock always said his abstract art was about the art and the paint itself, nothing more.

Pollock lied.

I'm inside a gigantic refrigerator. There's a jar of pickles, a container of mustard, and some yogurt that is probably way past its expiration date.

This is what art historians and modernists have been ruminating on for years?

I'm here to say Jackson Pollock painted appliances.

I leave, and thankfully the shadow from before is gone, as I double back to our exit. Clio is waiting for me by the bench. I can tell she's been crying, but she looks worried now, and when she sees me, she motions for me to run. I do, as quietly as I can, and she surprises me by grabbing my hand and pulling me under the bench, shifting so I'm on top of her. The front of the bench shields us from view, but this is the cruelest torture. I'm pressed against her, and I can feel her heart beating against mine. I want to smother her in kisses, but she's simply my accomplice now, nothing more.

She presses a finger against her lips. Footsteps pass dangerously close to us. I don't breathe until they leave the room. Then she rolls out from under me, and we head for our final destination.

"Why were you crying back there?" I ask once we're safely on the bridge.

"It was the Vermeers."

"Well, are they okay? Did you fix them?"

"Yes, they look so beautiful now." Her voice breaks. "I was overcome."

* * *

Chicago is our final stop.

The sick Morisot is only a few rooms away, and I'm so pummeled by witnessing Clio losing her love for me that I barely care if I get caught. Worst-case scenario, she can slink out of the museum in the morning and find the Chicago entrance back to her home. She doesn't need me anymore to get around.

As for me, I've always wanted to see Edward Hopper's *Nighthawks*, his image of three lonely people in a diner. Tonight, I can commiserate.

It's a few rooms over, and I go inside and order a chocolate milkshake. The guy at the counter nods as he hands over the tall, frosty glass.

It's fantastic, and I feel as if I could stay here all night. No one talks to each other. The other three people just stare off with empty eyes at their lonely worlds.

I thought I would fit in here, but I don't. My heart is being ripped apart, but my world is not lonely. I have friends back home, enough to keep me from becoming an empty-eyed nighthawk. I have places to be that aren't this diner.

So I leave, and I walk to Monet's Japanese bridge, where Clio's already waiting. A guard sees me and calls after me in American English.

"What the hell are you doing here?"

"Getting a milkshake," I tell him, and keep going.

I don't bother hiding my British accent. It will make a better story when he reports it to the Chicago police.

"You want to be arrested, smart-aleck?"

No, I don't. I'd rather not be arrested and stuck on this side of the pond without a passport.

Surprise on my side, I spring into motion and run to the bridge painting, diving into it with Clio.

I don't make it all the way in. He grabs one booted foot. Clio pulls me farther into the Monet, and the guard yanks harder on my foot. With the toe of my other shoe, I push the boot off and slide into the painting, picturing a guard in Chicago bewildered by the worn black boot in his hand.

31

Clio and I stand at the front doors of the Musée d'Orsay. It's time for us to leave.

I pause as I grab the handle, remembering when she told me how easy it would be to free her. *You don't need a crazy car chase or knife fight to free me. Nothing violent, nothing dangerous. It's simple because art is grace. Art is class. You can free me by holding open the door and letting me out.*

I do the thing Clio didn't want me to do a few days ago. Because there is nothing for her on this side of the door. There is nothing to tie her to the museum. Not her frame and not me.

She crosses the threshold, and her feet touch outside ground for the first time in centuries. There is a woman beside me who wasn't there before.

Anyone can see her. She's no longer bound to the painting Renoir trapped her in. She's bound to being a Muse, and she can't wait to start up again.

I call Remy and ask him to let Thalia know the

missing Muse is coming home. "Meet her at La Belle Vie," he says, and I hang up, wishing I wanted to let her go, wishing maybe I felt like she does right now.

I would like to feel nothing; I want to be numb. But I feel everything. And worse, I feel it for someone who feels nothing for me.

We walk down the steps like two acquaintances, like two coworkers who did a job together. A job well done, but now we'll move on. To the next city, the next assignment. I walk her across the river and to the block with La Belle Vie.

I stop on the Rue de Rivoli, my heart aching, ripped to shreds as I get ready to free her in the best and worst possible way. I brace myself for this moment. For the serrated knife's edge of her farewell. "Goodbye, Clio."

"Goodbye," she says, her voice clipped and cheery. She doesn't even use my name.

"Do you remember what happened with us?" I ask tentatively because she seems like a robot, like she had her chip erased of all past memories.

Her grin is so friendly it could be an advertisement. "Of course I remember. We had a nice time together," she says, and smiles even bigger now, more brightly, but her eyes are empty. There's nothing there for me. "And now I get to go back to work."

Get to.

Not *have to.*

This is what she wants.

This is what she craves.

The work. Only the work. She only loves art.

"It's been so long," she continues, beaming, a new

thrill in her voice. "I can't wait to find out what's next, what new assignments are waiting for me. I've missed it so."

No, you didn't, I want to tell her. *You didn't miss it. You were tired of it. You wanted more. You wanted us. You wanted me. Dammit. You wanted me as much as I wanted you.*

I wish I could clasp her shoulders and impart this truth to her. I wish I could give her one-tenth of my love for her. Let it refill her. Fuel her. Renew her love in us.

And yet that's another impossibility.

Like all the ones we've faced.

On some level, I understand that her measured tone isn't personal. But that doesn't stop me from feeling, from wanting, from aching.

I ache for her.

For what we had inside *Starry Night*.

For everything we could have had outside of that Van Gogh.

But that is gone. Like drawn items disappearing with the snap of fingers.

Thalia steps out of La Belle Vie and beams, like a mother welcoming back a long-lost child. Clio rushes to her. She doesn't look at me, but I can't look away. I can't stop watching her.

I can't stop wanting her.

And I don't think I will ever stop seeing her everywhere I go.

32

Paris is quiet, and the sun peeks over the horizon like a small child looking out from under the covers before pitter-pattering out of bed. Pink streaks leak across the blue of night as I find my way home and crash in bed.

When I finally make it out of bed in the afternoon, my phone is brimming with texts. Adaline's are full of exclamation points and emojis. She shares the news coming in from the curators in all the museums.

Remy texts too, asking if I've seen my boot on the news (I haven't, but I pull up the BBC website on my computer), telling me he's going to have a party, and teasing me about seeing my Muse there. I answer the first and ignore the others. I haven't told anyone the personal cost of last night's triumph, and I don't know when or if I will.

I scroll through the news from museums across the world. If every memory wasn't excruciating, I would be tickled at the way the stories have grown and evolved, even overnight. The guards in Saint Petersburg. The

live bird in London. The "Cinderella Boot" in Chicago—
because it's like a fairy tale, the way the paintings have
all been restored. And why look for another answer
when the unknown makes for a better story?

It will be old news tomorrow and forgotten the day
after. All the noise of the rest of the world will drown
out the music of this minor miracle.

And I can't decide if that will be a relief or a tragedy.

* * *

The next week, I guide a group of tourists through our
galleries, including a brief stop at *Woman Wandering in
the Irises*. Hope rises in my chest when I see the painting
of Clio, as it does every time, every day, with every look.
But the canvas has been quiet at night. No one has come
alive, not even a painted version, like Emmanuelle or
Dr. Gachet. I keep waiting for the night when she might
break free, even if she's only a shadow of the Clio I once
knew. I'd take that. I'd take anything.

A girl with a Brown University T-shirt raises a hand
and begins speaking. "Isn't that the Renoir that was
missing for years?"

"Yes. Since 1885," I answer as clinically as I can.

"What happened to it? How does a painting just
vanish for so long, then reappear?"

"It's not so unusual, except that the artist is so
famous. Families hide their valuables during war or
disaster, and if nobody survives to remember where
they put them . . ." I give an open-handed shrug. There
you have it. Please, let's move on.

But another hand goes up. "Is it true that Monet and Renoir were in love with the woman in the painting?"

Another voice asks, "Does anyone know who she was, or what happened to her?"

"That's unknown," I say, going through my answer by rote. "She's not a model who appears in other works by the same artist. She could indeed be a woman whose family didn't want rumors affecting their social status. Or maybe she's someone trapped in a painting, who comes out at night when the museum is closed."

There are titters at my joke, and it feels so good to let out the truth.

"Or maybe she wasn't a woman, but a Muse under a curse, and she was set free to save the world's art," I say without a smile, without a knowing wink. No one says anything. What does it matter? No one will believe me.

"Then again," I say with a bland smile, "sometimes a painting is just a painting."

With that, I conclude my tour so that we can all escape from my melancholy.

I walk past Emmanuelle, then Dr. Gachet—imprints of who they once were long ago—and an idea comes to me. It's a crazy one, but I have to try. Maybe there is a version of Clio out there who still cares about me.

I'm done for the day, and it's only early afternoon, so I go to Gare Saint-Lazare station and buy a ticket. An hour later, the train rattles to a stop, and I disembark. I walk from the station to Monet's garden, a little less than an hour away by foot. The gardens are closing when I arrive, and the ticket taker tells me I will only have a few minutes.

"That's fine."

I have seen the gardens. For real and in paint. I'm not here today to catch the tail end of a tour or to snap photos of the kaleidoscope of colors. But the place Monet once called home is empirically gorgeous. Summer has stolen into Giverny, bringing with it the glory of reds, yellows, and oranges that blaze under the sun.

Some might say it's better than a painting.

They have never gone into *her* painting.

I walk through lush fields and past blankets of petals and stems. I make my way to the pond where a raft of water lilies floats lazily in the blue-green waters. The other visitors begin to file out as the bell signals closing time. I let them leave, and the sun dips farther. Long shadows fall across the pond, and the weeping willow brushes its branches against the earth.

I close my eyes, and I'm back in time.

I can hear her voice.

Recall her longing.

Her greatest wish.

I used to pretend there was a door at the end of this bridge. A plain, simple wooden door with an old-fashioned ring handle. Dark metal. You'd pull it open, and there. The other side. Now I've finally been on the other side.

I open my eyes and remove my notebook, sketching the door she described in painstaking detail. I take the last pinch of silver dust that I stashed away in London, and voilà. The door materializes. Clio always longed for escape when she was trapped. Maybe that Clio is here.

Maybe that Clio misses me. I reach for the handle and pull it open.

But there's nothing but a weeping willow on the other side.

I press a palm over my eyes. Stupid me. Stupid mind playing stupid tricks. She's gone, and all that's left is this emptiness, this loneliness, so terribly alive, in her place. No drawing will ever change that.

I flop down in the grass and lie there until the door disappears and an old man who tends the gardens tells me it's time to go.

I leave, still missing, still wanting.

Wanting this terrible ache to end.

33

Simon once again does his best-friend post-heartbreak duty: gets me out of the flat and distracts me with ridiculousness.

It's misery, but it's necessary.

I have to do something.

I have to find a way to get over her.

There is no other option.

We wander through the street vendors across from Notre Dame. Simon gestures grandly to the secondhand booksellers who peddle old books along with postcards of landmarks and matted prints of famous destinations.

"I say we apply for a bouquiniste license and set up shop."

"What will we be selling exactly? Did someone will you the contents of their attic?"

"The book vendor thing is just going to be a front for a ghost-removal shop."

I manage a small "Huh."

"Picture it," he continues. "Can you name anyone

else who has successfully exorcised a spirit, let alone the spirit of a great artist?"

"Can't say that I have."

"All we have to do is convince the tourists that Marilyn Monroe or Jim Morrison is inhabiting them, and we'll work our mojo again."

"We'll be rolling in euros," I say without much enthusiasm.

He pats me on the back. "Someday you'll be happy again, Garnier."

That feels as unlikely as a ghost inhabiting an artist.

As a painting coming alive.

Or really, as a woman in a painting staying in love with the guy who set her free.

Love like that only exists in stories.

I honor a commitment to another woman. The one at the Paris Opera Ballet.

The lights are low. The music swells. I feel more human than I have in days here in the opera house where the ballet company performs. Maybe because I'm away from the museum and its phantom people, like shadows on the wall. In here, art is alive for real, and it is flying.

Emilie is beautiful as she performs her solo in *The Sleeping Beauty*. No music tonight except what's coming from the orchestra pit. Emilie feels confident onstage, I can tell, no inspiration required.

When the ballet ends, I join the rest of the audience

in a standing ovation. As the dancers take their bows and curtsies, I lock eyes with Emilie, and my happiness for her is the first true happiness I've felt in days. It's vicarious and fleeting, but I'll take it.

Weaving through the balletgoers in their finery, I follow the directions Emilie gave me to the stage door. She emerges in jeans and a tank top, but her hair is still in a bun and she has full makeup on.

"You were magnificent," I say as I kiss each of her cheeks. "Do I know what I'm talking about or do I know what I'm talking about?"

"I think you're an oracle is what you are," she says with a laugh. "I can't wait to hear from you what I'll dance next."

"Hmm . . ." I pretend to listen. "You'll just have to audition for everything and get all the roles."

"*Quelle tragédie.*" She lays her hand on her forehead and pretends to swoon. "Doomed to dance in everything. Coffee?"

"Always coffee. Even when it's awful."

We walk to the café, order espressos, and talk about the ballet. She tells me how nervous she was before her solo, but how she left her fear backstage when she stepped under the lights.

"I could tell," I say, and Emilie smiles.

"I love talking to you like this. You really understand what it's like."

"I try."

"But it's more than trying. You just get it in a way that so few do, and so—" She stops when the waiter brings our drinks. After he leaves, she tells me, "I'm really glad you came. I know that Simon and Lucy had a lot of ideas about us . . ."

I'm forming as kind a letdown as possible when she assures me, "No, don't worry. It means the world to me that you came tonight as my friend and not because you want to date me."

Now I'm not sure what to say. Should I reassure her there's nothing undatable about her? Say "It's not you, it's me"? Or "I don't have a heart to offer because mine is lying shriveled up in Monet's garden"?

"Stop thinking so hard, Julien." She nudges me with her foot. "I could tell when we met there was someone else on your mind. And, of course, ballet is *always* on my mind, so I thought we'd be good as friends. And we are."

"We are." I toast her with my espresso cup and then make an impromptu suggestion. "My friend Remy is throwing an apron party. I hate the thought of going, but he won't take no for an answer. Simon and Lucy are going, and you should come too."

"An apron party? What is that?"

"Hell if I know, but I'd get an apron if I were you."

"You're not going to wear an apron, Julien?" she asks with a bit of mischief in her voice.

"He's making me go to the party. He can't make me wear an apron."

"Something tells me no one could make you go to a party. Maybe you actually want to go."

Maybe I do.

* * *

Remy wears a light-blue apron with red cherries. Sophie has gone meta and her apron has prints of mini aprons on it in orange, yellow, purple, and blue. Emilie sports leggings and a pink tulle apron, and Lucy is dressed to the nines in a black-and-white-striped skirt topped with a pink apron with black piping, like a sexy ice-cream-parlor girl. Simon can't keep his hands off her. He wears an apron with "Kiss the Chef" written on it in bold letters, and Lucy does as instructed.

"*Bonjour!* Felicitations to everyone but Julien," Remy declares as he invites us into his home.

"Why not Julien?" I protest, even though I know the answer.

"If you can't get into the spirit of the party, how can the party spirit get into you?" He pats my cheek and gestures grandly for everyone to follow him down the hall.

Monet's Japanese bridge painting is back on the wall. I force myself not to look at it. Seeing it makes my chest hurt. I force myself to look anywhere but at the door to the room that leads to the basement. The door that leads to her. To heartbreak.

Sophie brings around a tray of macarons—with combos of saffron and peach, caramel and pistachio, and even grapefruit-wasabi.

I pass. I don't need another reminder. Not when I'm only now starting to feel a smidge of *un-misery*.

"There is something wrong with someone who doesn't like macarons," Sophie says, narrowing her eyes.

"Just not in the mood." That feels true of just about everything these days.

"Suit yourself. But tomorrow you will wake up and think, 'I wish I had a macaron right now,' and it will be too late because I'm eating whatever is left over tonight."

She sashays to another group of partygoers as Remy drapes an arm over my shoulder. "Don't listen to her. Nobody ever died for lack of a macaron. Love, on the other hand . . ."

I tense, and he finally notices I'm not being coy about his matchmaking attempts. His confusion is obvious—not that he keeps his emotions close to the vest.

He turns to face me, one hand still on my shoulder, and lowers his voice. "Don't you want to see her again, Julien? You haven't come by at all. Have you just been going through La Belle Vie?"

I wince.

The pain in my heart is too much to hide. I turn to him, my jaw tight, my voice heavy, and tell him, hoping it will unburden me a little more. My God, I need it to. Do I ever need it to.

"She doesn't want to see me," I say heavily.

His jaw drops. "What? After all that? After all you did?"

"It's just one of those things about Muses," I say, adding a shrug, like that softens the blow to my soul.

It doesn't.

Remy isn't going to accept that as my final answer, so I explain briefly and emotionlessly what happened to us when Clio saved the art. "So, if you ever see me go near that trapdoor, handcuff me and keep me away. Please."

His eyes are sad. His lips turn down. "All right. But I won't let you stay away from our house. I would be a poor friend to let you cut yourself off from life because you are taking a break from love."

"I won't do that."

He gives me a sternly doubtful look.

I raise my hand. "I vow, I won't. How can I prove it?"

He studies me for another long moment, and then calls out, "Rafe, *mon chou*! Bring me the thing!"

I already regret this.

Rafe appears beside Remy, mouths *I'm sorry* to me, and holds out, hooked on his finger, an apron that looks like something a unicorn coughed up. There are pink and purple ruffles, silver ribbons, sparkling trim, and violet glitter.

So. Much. Glitter.

Remy holds it out like a monarch bestowing a medal, his expression imperious. I sigh and take my cue, bowing so that he can loop the apron around my neck. When I straighten, he takes my shoulders and kisses one cheek, then the other.

"Now, Sir Julien, I command you to lead off the dancing."

"Me?" I hardly notice Sophie tying the apron strings behind me.

"Someone has to go first. Music!" He claps twice and swans off through the gathered crowd of guests, then the unignorable beat of techno pop begins and people

move outside where there's room to dance in the courtyard, with the goat and the sheep.

Rafe kisses each of my cheeks too, claps my shoulder, and tells me, "You've made his night, you know."

Then he's off, and Sophie is pushing me to where
nobody has waited for me to start the dancing.

"I don't see any dancing, Twilight Sparkle," Simon
tells me, grinning like a madman.

Emilie grabs my hand and pulls me into an empty
space. "Come on. I know you can hear *that* music," she
says, pointing to one of the thumping speakers. She
pirouettes and moves gracefully into some clubby dance
moves that I can copy.

Music, art, dancing. Those have to be the balms for
me. They were for Clio.

Please, please let them be for me.

Lucy joins in, bringing Simon onto the impromptu
dance floor, and Sophie jumps around too. Remy pulls
Rafe out of the kitchen to dance with him, shaking his
hips.

I watch them all. Dancing the way they want,
listening to the music they like. I think of Gustave and
his subway art, of Max and his caricature classes, of my
friends and their random loves, like aprons and five-
legged calves and flash mobs on the curving corner of a
hilly street in Montmartre.

I don't know that Renoir would have liked this party.
But I do.

I'm pretty sure Clio—or at least the Clio I knew—
would have liked it too.

For several minutes, hell for maybe even a half-hour, I don't feel the ache.

I don't feel the misery.

I start to feel something else.

Hope.

Hope that I might make it through all this longing.

That I might find a way to come out on the other side of unrequited love.

Later, Remy disappears for a while. When he returns to the party, he pulls me aside, a small smile on his face. "Thalia wants to see you tomorrow morning. Can you meet her?"

I arch a dubious brow. "Why?"

He shrugs, saying he has no idea. "She just asked if you could be at the bridge between the two museums at nine. What should I tell her?"

I don't know if I like Thalia. I don't know if I want to see her, and I don't know what she could have to say to me.

But I still say yes.

It seems I can't let go of hope.

34

Thalia waits on the Louvre side of the river, one hand resting on the railing, the other on her waist. She wears slacks and a blouse, her red hair loose around her shoulders.

"Thank you for meeting me," she says.

"Well, it seemed rude to turn down the head of the Muses."

She manages a small smile, the kind that doesn't show any teeth. "I want to thank you for all you did for the paintings. Without your help, they'd have been lost, and I've been remiss in not extending my gratitude."

"What else could I do?"

"You could have let the art die."

"No," I say levelly, "I couldn't."

Thalia studies me for a moment, then nods. "So, you saved it, at great cost to yourself."

"Yeah." I watch the water, gray and murky, flowing under the bridge, wondering why I'm here. What I was hoping for. "Yeah."

Neither of us speaks for a minute, then Thalia breaks the silence. "You really loved her, didn't you?"

"Yes," I say with a huff. "Isn't it obvious?"

"How? How do you love her?"

"You asked before, and I told you already." I'm not going to flay myself to satisfy her curiosity.

Thalia nods, but then inches closer, her eyes imploring. "Would you mind, though, telling me one more time what it was like?"

It was my everything. It was all my days and nights, and as much as I desperately want to get over Clio, I am ruined for anyone else.

That is the reality. Because there is only—and will only ever be—her. "She made me feel like everything was possible, even when I knew it wasn't. I felt like the stars were ours."

Thalia nods, the corners of her lips turning up. "Thank you again." I shrug, and she says, "I have a gift for you, if you'll wait a moment." She pats my shoulder. "Stay right here."

I sigh, wondering what it could be and if I want anything from her.

Thalia's gone long enough for me to suspect she's not coming back. That she was pulled away to some orchestral emergency or poetic crisis. A violin somewhere is weeping away notes, a poem is drowning in the tears of its words.

Finally, she returns, and with her, coming toward me on the bridge, is Clio. She's wearing jeans and green flats, and she's so beautiful it makes my chest hurt, but I can't look away.

All that hope rises in me again. All my wishes rush to the surface.

I can't let go of them. I can only stand here waiting.

Hoping.

Craving.

Still loving.

"Hi," Clio says, a little grin curving her lips. Thalia has stayed back, giving us privacy.

"Hi." I try to keep my voice even.

She looks nervous, but hopeful too. I see a glimmer of it in her eyes, and don't know what to make of it.

"How are you?" she asks.

"Um, fine." My brows knit. There's a point to this, but I can't begin to guess what it might be. "You?"

She rocks on her feet, heel to toe, something she's never done before. Uncertainty is so unlike her. "I'm good."

Now what? I've wanted nothing more than to see her again, but here we are, and words fail me.

But it seems I don't need them, because it's Clio who has something to tell me.

"I went to see Thalia last night." She trails a finger along the bridge railing, looking at it instead of me. "We had a long talk."

Not what I expected, but I'll see how this plays out. "You did?"

She nods. "Yes. I was happy working again, but I was also troubled."

I'm swept up now, snared by an idea . . . a notion that this is rushing toward something I have to see. It may kill me . . .

But maybe not.

"Troubled by what?" I ask.

"Memories. I kept thinking about my time at the Musée d'Orsay."

"And?" I ask carefully, feeling like I'm on the cusp of something fragile.

Another nod. "I would replay them. Whenever I was working. Whenever I was helping artists to feel the love they needed, the memories all flooded back."

Oh God.

My muscles tighten. I am poised, ready to leap but not sure which way yet.

She meets my eyes now, closer to the unflinching woman I knew. "I kept thinking about our nights. About why I didn't go home as soon as I could."

"Tell me," I say.

Clio swallows, a little roughly. "The things we did are not things Muses usually do. My sisters all agreed. Going to the beach. Rowing boats. Dancing. Having picnics." Her lips curve into a not-so-bashful grin. "*Other things.*"

My fingertips tingle as if something precious is just out of grasp. "What sort of other things?"

"Kissing. Touching. Being together. *Wanting.* Those are not things Muses do," she says. "And every time I've worked, every time I've put love into art, I kept returning to those nights with you. And I started to feel things I've never known before."

"Like?" I ask, barely a whisper, but audible enough.

"Like . . . *missing.*"

That word. That one wonderful word.

"I *missed* you, and it was entirely new and kind of awful."

I wouldn't call the sound I make a laugh, but she peeks at me hopefully, then grows earnest again.

"I realized I'm not the same as before. I haven't been the same since I fell in love with you."

The last night at the museum, when we parted outside the doors, she was clinical and friendly. She didn't seem to feel anything at all. That Clio was worlds different from the woman in the painting.

"You remember all that?" I ask.

"I never forgot all that, but it was just . . . a fact." She tucks her hair behind her ear in such a human gesture my heart stutters. "But when I started working again, it was more than remembering. It was *feeling*. And the feelings didn't go away. They're part of who I am now."

I hold in a breath. I hold in all the breaths in the city. The potential in what she's saying hangs before me like a fragile snow globe I don't want to drop, don't want to break.

"And so, I went to Thalia to ask her for something."

I let myself hope.

I hope so much it hurts. But I'll take it. Because I think maybe, just maybe, it's the kind of hurt that leads to something magical on the other side.

35

Clio

The entire world feels new and brimming with possibility.

Excitement, anticipation, and hope all collide inside me in a mad frenzy, rushing to break free.

I want to tell Julien everything that happened last night.

Everything that happened before, starting with the power of memory, with how my heart and mind and soul went back to him, piece by piece, every time I inspired an artist.

All that love I channeled reminded me of all the love I had in the museum, in the paintings, in his arms.

He's waiting, and it's time to finish my tale and find out how it ends.

I glance back at Thalia, who's been waiting patiently and watching curiously. I motion for her to join us for this part, and when she does, nodding silently to Julien, I dive in.

"I went to Thalia and asked her to right a wrong."

She takes my arm, squeezes it affectionately. "She offered me a rare opportunity. Not everyone gets to fix a mistake."

I'm so proud of my sister Muse. Proud of her for saying yes.

Proud of her for knowing it was time to let me go.

I raise my hands, letting the sleeves of my shirt fall to my elbows. "No more bracelets."

His eyes widen as they land on my bare wrists then fly to my face. I'm still amazed myself.

And here's the most astounding, marvelous, incredible thing that I'm bursting to tell him: "I'm not a Muse anymore."

My God, it is wonderful to say.

It's wonderful to *be*.

"It was my choice," I say, laying my hand on my heart. "I expected I'd fall out of love with you, and I thought I had. But the memories of us kept the love alive. Suddenly, I wanted something I've never wanted in all my years—a life outside of what I knew. A world beyond a painting."

Julien seems to drink in what I'm saying, working it out, but not quite fully comprehending it yet. "Not a Muse anymore? Is that possible?"

I nod because I can't speak past the lump in my throat.

But I want to say the rest. This man gave up his whole heart for the world's art. He gave up love to restore beauty. He let go for the sake of something bigger than us.

"I asked Thalia to unmake me."

He frowns and looks at Thalia. "You did that?"

She clears her throat. "She's no longer eternal. No longer bound. No longer a muse of any kind."

I shrug, unable to make it simpler than this: "I'm just a woman. That is all."

That's what clicks for him. He believes in the impossible.

Like art coming alive.

Like a pencil drawing something into reality.

Like stepping into another world.

That's how I feel right now.

I want to inhale this world—drink it in, live in it, love in it, be in it.

"You're a woman outside the garden," Julien says in a hushed voice.

"I am no longer wandering in irises. I can wander anywhere. With my own two feet. I can't travel by painting anymore and it's wonderful to walk everywhere," I say the same way, full of awe and joy. I sigh gently, happily, then turn to Thalia. "I'll miss you too. But you'll take good care of the art, right?"

"It's on my to-do list forevermore." Thalia taps her heart then her own bracelets. She has two on each wrist now, hers and mine.

Julien glances between us, realization no doubt dawning and turning to shock and dismay. "You're not going to see each other again?"

I feel the same, but I've had a few more hours than

he has to process this. I knew it was part of my choice, but knowing you'll leave and saying goodbye are worlds apart.

Thalia shakes her head, and her voice breaks. "Not often. I'm quite busy and will be even busier now. But I've had more than a century to get used to not seeing Clio," she tells him with a gentle smile for me. "We made do without her then, and with one human muse on the scene now, and maybe more to come, we'll have help."

He nods crisply. "Right, of course. I'm on it."

She smiles her thanks at him, and then she asks me, "Then my work here is done?" But what she's really saying is farewell.

"It is." I clasp her in a tight embrace and then let her go on her way.

When she's gone, I'm left with Julien. I'm excited and nervous. As a Muse, I didn't have to worry about what happened next, because it was always the same. Here, I don't know what to expect. I don't know anything about how the world works without my shackles.

But I want to find out. My God, I can't wait to find out.

Julien takes my hand, brushing his thumb over my bare wrist. "How did it work? She took them off, just like that?"

"Just like that," I confirm, smiling with delight at his touch. With delight at being here with him. "Took them off and put them on her own wrists."

"So, all the paintings you inspired? They'll be okay?"

I nod. "Thalia will hold them up now. She's taken

over my duty, and now here I am. Look . . ." I flick my fingers—no silver dust comes out.

Only one thing could make me happier in this moment, and that's to tell him everything this means. I'm here to stay. No magic in the world can make me fall out of love with him again.

"Julien, will you have me back?" I reach for his hand and hold it between mine. "I want to be in your life because you are in my heart. I'm back for good because I'm in love with you."

"You are?" His face lights with happiness.

"I am. I feel it all. Everything I ever felt for you, only bigger and brighter." I trace a jagged line across his palm and whisper, "Sing in me, Muse, and through me tell the story. Of a new way back to you."

My heart is full to bursting, and Julien looks the same.

"Really? You really . . .?"

I take his other hand and tug him closer. "I feel like I'm dancing at the Moulin Rouge, like I'm on the beach in the South of France, like I'm floating under a starry night. I want to spend all my days with you."

My voice breaks as I'm overcome. I am overwhelmed with all I want becoming real. I am overjoyed that I'm here with him, on the other side, and he holds my face, brushes the hair from my cheek, and presses a soft kiss to my lips.

Oh, have I missed this and yet it's fresh and new.

It feels like a first kiss, and a promise.

It feels like all the starry nights and all the sunlit days I want to spend with him.

And then it turns deeper, longer, and we don't stop.

Because in our kiss, I can taste forever. A forever that's real, here in Paris together, Julien and me.

We break the kiss, and I'm laughing with happiness, and so is he. We kiss through our laughter, and when we pull apart again, I cup his cheeks and say, "I feel so much. But more than anything, I feel like a woman in love with a man."

And it feels like freedom. I'm free from the chains that bound me for centuries. Free from the only life I've ever known.

I'm free to forge a whole new one with this man. One full of love.

"And I'm still insanely in love with you," he says.

"Good. I was worried."

He scoffs like that's absurd. "Why would you worry about that?"

"Because once I started to feel love again, I felt how much I missed you. How painful it was to be parted. All I wanted was to make my way back to you." I squeeze him tight. "That's still all I want—just you, Julien."

"You have me," he says. "You don't have to question that at all."

He runs his thumbs along my naked wrists.

"You look so good without bracelets," he says, his eyes traveling lovingly over my face. "You look so good in the daylight."

I am so glad that anyone can see us now as we kiss on the bridge over the river outside the Louvre. Anyone can see us now, but no one pays attention, because this is Paris. We're just another pair of young lovers becoming another set of ornaments in this city.

We are not darting in and out of paintings after midnight. We do what anyone can do.

And today, we spend the morning kissing and strolling, but eventually, we have to speak of practical matters.

"So what do we do now?" Julien asks. "What do you want to do? Where are you going to live?"

"I don't know," I say with a laugh. "I haven't thought that far."

He raises a playful brow. "I have room. It's a little flat—"

"Yes!" The word bursts from me. I won't let that chance pass me by. "Yes. Yes. Yes. I want that."

"But I share the flat with my sister," he says, laughing.

"Oh." Had he not been asking what I thought?

"It's all right. It's a big flat, with our rooms on opposite sides. Adaline won't mind, but maybe you would."

"I don't care. It's with you." I feel weightless and buoyant, like the world is new and everything is possible. "Don't you see? You're the reason why I'm not a Muse anymore. I wanted to be with you. I want to be with you outside of the gardens. I want this city to be ours."

He slides his hands around my waist and pulls me close. "It will be. We'll walk around Paris, see everything. All the art—it's everywhere, and it's incredible. And you'll meet my friends." He gives a rueful laugh. "They'll certainly be dying to meet you."

It sounds amazing to me.

I loop my arms around his neck, and I can't stop smiling either. "I can't wait. And I think I might try my hand at painting. I have quite a good eye, and lots of ideas about what to make," I say, and slant a sly smile up at him. "The only thing missing is . . . a muse. Maybe you can fit me into your schedule?"

"Yes, I think I could work you in." He kisses my forehead, and when I close my eyes in happiness, he drops kisses onto my eyelids, my cheeks, my lips. "It's exclusive though. You can't have any other muse."

I shake my head, still smiling. "I don't want anyone but you."

That leads to more kissing, and after a while, we continue our walk. "Are you hungry?" Julien asks. "Because I could really go for a chocolate croissant. Funny thing—I know this great bakery, and I'd love to take you there."

"Take me there, Julien."

We amble along the river to the best bakery in Paris, together, outside the museum and free from the curse.

Free to be together.

Free to do what any other man and woman in this city might do.

Kiss.

And touch.

And laugh.

And love.

It's a wonderful world, this one. Full of art and love and food and friends and a new kind of magic.

The kind that love makes possible.

EPILOGUE

December 25—Four months later

Clio

"Christmas is my new favorite thing," I say between deep inhales of spicy-sweet steam curling up from the mug of mulled cider cradled in my hands. I'm bundled up in flannel pajamas, a thick sweater of Julien's, and fluffy wool socks, and tucked into the corner of the sofa for warmth.

"You say that about everything," Julien teases, mirroring me in the opposite corner.

"Not about wintertime," I reply. Perpetual summer in Monet's garden has thinned my blood.

"Me? I have only one favorite thing." He sips his cider, slanting a mischievous look at me from under his lashes. "My favorite thing never changes, because my favorite thing is you."

"Oh, Julien," I say, my heart melting, "that is the sweetest, cheesiest thing I've ever heard."

He wiggles his ice-cold foot into my bundle of blankets and finds bare skin, and I shriek, trying to wiggle away without spilling my drink.

"Incoming!" Adaline calls from the hall. "Should I avert my eyes?"

"No need," says Julien, but his grin promises we'll be scandalous later, and thinking about later warms me as much as the cider.

His sister ducks into the kitchen and comes out with her own drink.

It's rare that all three of us are home at the same time, between the hours Adaline puts in at the museum, the hours *Julien* puts in at the museum, plus his graduate classes and the occasional summons to troubleshoot a misbehaving painting, and the hours I put in at school.

I don't *go* to school.

I teach now.

Painting mostly. But drawing classes, too, at an art school in Montmartre.

I thought I'd become a painter, and while I do love creating, I find I love teaching even more. So much more that it feels like this was what I was always meant to do. I suppose in some ways that's true.

Perhaps in most ways.

Guiding others in their passion, helping them see the way through creation, is my new joy.

I'm, quite simply, happy as an art teacher.

Julien is happy too.

And together we squeeze so much life and love into every moment we're together. Also, there are practical matters to attend to. Things like protection, and we use it now, since I suspect I *can* conceive now that I'm human. But there will be time for babies down the road. Of that I'm sure.

For now, it's been good for me to discover who I am, beyond art, in this modern human world. I don't just mean learning to use the Metro or the time I exploded the microwave.

I'm learning what I love besides art and Julien.

I love meeting Remy and his husband, Rafe, in the park and playing with their new puppy, Rosa. Rafe brings me homemade pastries, and Remy occasionally brings regards from my sisters. They are happy for me and wish me well, even if they cannot fathom my choice. But having never experienced the kind of love I have with Julien, of course, they don't understand the despair of facing an eternity without it. Remy and Rafe get it – they have that love. Simon and Lucy understand too. They are wrapped up in each other.

Love…it makes us all human.

And so many of us love art, in so many forms.

Sophie and I are taking tap-dancing classes together. I had no idea what tap dancing was or that it would be so much fun, and for a while, that was my new favorite thing. The thing before that was the online video game Simon and Lucy taught me. (I play as a powerful healer, of course, indispensable on raids.)

Julien and I like to go to the ballet—on our first visit,

the lights came up at intermission and he found me teary-eyed and sniffling.

"What's wrong?" He'd put his arm around my shoulders, his thumb brushing soothing circles on my skin. "Does this make you miss being a Muse?"

I'd shaken my head in vehement denial.

"It's just so beautiful," I'd said, wiping tears from my cheeks.

I told his friend Emilie the same thing when we met her after the performance. Like many in Julien's circle, she seemed puzzled when we first met, as if trying to come up with why I looked familiar. Most accept at face value the story that Renoir's model for *Woman Wandering in the Irises* is my ancestor. Though I still catch Adaline studying me with speculation every now and then.

Whatever she's thinking, she's been welcoming almost since the day I walked into the flat with Julien on that summer afternoon four months ago.

First, she had to recover from the shock of Julien bringing a girlfriend home "out of thin air"—a phrase more appropriate than anyone knows.

"Join us, Adaline?" I ask now, and nod to the empty chair.

She raises her mug in a sort of toast and points toward her side of the flat. "Thank you, but I have a video date."

"On Christmas?" Julien asks, but his sister is already gone.

"Love knows no season," I tell him sagely.

His brows climb into his tousled hair. "Love? You think?"

"I don't just think. I know."

Adaline, as an expert and curator of such a large collection of Renoirs, consulted on an international forgery investigation, resulting in the capture of an infamous father-daughter forger duo who had come out of seclusion to flog what a London newspaper called "the most convincing Renoir forgeries that experts had ever seen."

When Oliver and Cass Middleton were arrested, Julien and Simon bought a round at our usual pub to celebrate. Julien suspected they'd taken what they'd learned from the spirit of Renoir and painted some new "lost" masterpieces.

The authorities theorized that they'd been inspired by the recent rediscovery of *Woman Wandering in the Irises*, and had overplayed their hand.

I'd toasted to them being jailed because Cass was the one who'd dealt my man all the bumps and bruises I had soothed that night under Van Gogh's starry sky.

And Adaline has been dating the Interpol agent in charge ever since.

Even as a Muse, I couldn't have inspired a result that had made so many people happy.

Funny that Renoir brought about so many good things by trying to keep good things from happening to humankind. He'd trapped me in the painting because he wanted to hoard inspiration and beauty—and love, in a way—for himself and those like him. He tried to stop an age of human enlightenment, and instead his actions brought Julien and I together to fall in love.

A love large enough to uphold a world full of art.

Wide enough to span the globe and bridge the gulf between everything eternal and everything mortal.

Strong enough to let me choose who and what I wanted to be.

Strong enough to bring me back to Julien.

Loving him has fundamentally changed me. We've changed each other.

Maybe our love will change the world, or maybe it will just change our small piece of it. I just know that it deserves to be nurtured and tended. That I want to see it reach its potential. That I will pour myself into making us thrive.

But I'm not a Muse anymore, and Julien, while beautiful to me, is not a painting.

And I'm so glad about both of those things.

Because when I pour my love into Julien . . . I get so much love in return.

And kisses. Lots and lots of kisses.

Like now. With his sister in the other room, I set down my mug, then his, and I loop my arms around his neck.

"Kiss me, my muse," I demand playfully.

"Anytime," he says, all too happy to oblige.

As he brushes his lips to mine, all thoughts of art and paintings fade away.

I am all woman, and I love this brave new life.

EPILOGUE

Julien

When the ballerinas first danced for me, I was shocked. When the cat leaped out of the painting, I was amazed.

When the good doctor repaired the woman I love, I was overjoyed.

And yet all of that wonder, all of that awe, pales in comparison to *this*.

To love.

To love staying, to love lasting, and to love changing you.

And to the everyday beauty in being with the person you adore.

I've traveled the world by painted bridge, I've escaped inside a cathedral, I've made love to this woman under Van Gogh's stars . . . and this right here feels like the truest magic—*staying*.

She is staying.

Every day, that amazes me.
And I love every day of it.

Be sure to sign up for my mailing list to be the first to know when swoony, sexy new romances are available or on sale!

AUTHOR'S NOTE

While some aspects of the history of art were altered for the purposes of this novel, many are rooted in fact. The following information is based on research into art and history.

• All the paintings cited in the story as hanging in the Musée d'Orsay do hang in the Musée d'Orsay, such as Van Gogh's *The Portrait of Dr. Gachet*, Manet's *Olympia*, Van Gogh's *Starry Night*, Toulouse-Lautrec's *Dance at the Moulin-Rouge*, Cézanne's *The Bay of Marseille Seen from L'Estaque*, Renoir's *The Swing*, as well as all the other Monets and Renoirs mentioned.

• All the paintings in the Musée d'Orsay, Louvre, Hermitage, Art Institute of Chicago, Metropolitan Museum of Art, Museum of Fine Arts in Boston, and National Gallery in London are actual paintings and are described accurately, and the dates and descriptions surrounding these paintings and their history are described accurately. There are two exceptions to this.

The first is the missing Renoir, known as *Woman Wandering in the Irises*. This painting was made up for the story. The second is the character of Emmanuelle. While she is based on a Degas painting that hangs in the Musée d'Orsay, her heritage and relationship to the dancer Emilie is made up.

• All the details Julien imparts on his tours as to the history surrounding certain paintings, the prices they have commanded at auctions, and the style and technique of certain paintings are accurate. This includes Julien's description of Renoir's hands near the end of the artist's life.

• Suzanne Valadon was the first female painter admitted into the École des Beaux-Arts. She and Renoir were contemporaries, and she appeared as a model in three of his paintings. Whether they agreed or not on the future of art is up for debate.

• The artist Rosa Bonheur dressed in men's clothes when she painted *The Horse Fair*. She also kept a pet goat on her balcony.

• During the Nazi era, Nazis looted countless pieces of art across Europe. Today, reputable museums and dealers are expected to research and know the provenance of European paintings that changed hands during this time to ensure that restitution of any once-looted ones has been made.

• Renoir reportedly likened female painters to five-legged calves in a quote attributed to him as "I consider women writers, lawyers, and politicians as monsters and nothing but five-legged calves. The woman artist is merely ridiculous . . ."

• As for paintings that come alive, well, that is for you to decide.

•Finally, museums are wonderful. We hope you delight in them as much as we do.

ALSO BY LAUREN BLAKELY

FULL PACKAGE, the #1 New York Times Bestselling romantic comedy!

BIG ROCK, the hit New York Times Bestselling standalone romantic comedy!

THE SEXY ONE, a New York Times Bestselling standalone romance!

THE KNOCKED UP PLAN, a multi-week USA Today and Amazon Charts Bestselling standalone romance!

MOST VALUABLE PLAYBOY, a sexy multi-week USA Today Bestselling sports romance! And its companion sports romance, MOST LIKELY TO SCORE!

WANDERLUST, a USA Today Bestselling contemporary romance!

COME AS YOU ARE, a Wall Street Journal and multi-week USA Today Bestselling contemporary romance!

PART-TIME LOVER, a multi-week USA Today Bestselling contemporary romance!

UNBREAK MY HEART, an emotional second chance USA Today Bestselling contemporary romance!

BEST LAID PLANS, a sexy friends-to-lovers USA Today

Bestselling romance!

The Heartbreakers! The USA Today and WSJ Bestselling rock star series of standalone!

P.S. IT'S ALWAYS BEEN YOU, a sweeping, second chance romance!

CONTACT

I love hearing from readers! You can find me on Twitter at LaurenBlakely3, Instagram at LaurenBlakelyBooks, Facebook at LaurenBlakelyBooks, or online at Lauren-Blakely.com. You can also email me at laurenblakelybooks@gmail.com

Printed in Great Britain
by Amazon